I0662501

DARK
PROTECTION

Dark Protection

Copyright © 2024 Willie Mae Jackson, MD, MA

All rights reserved. No part of this book may be reproduced (except for inclusion in reviews), disseminated or utilized in any form or by any means, electronic or mechanical, including photocopying, recording, or in any information storage and retrieval system, or the Internet/World Wide Web without written permission from the author or publisher.

Book design by:
Arbor Services, Inc.
www.arborservices.co/

Photography by Ayaka Sano
IG: @ayakasano.co

Printed in the United States of America

Dark Protection
Willie Mae Jackson, MD, MA

1. Title 2. Author 3. Thriller

Paperback ISBN: 13: 978-1-7354262-3-5

delves into this life and its challenging case with a close attention to medical and psychological realism. Under her hand, medical community and crime-solving departments dovetail and come to life in the form of a brilliant woman who has not a few secrets of her own to keep hidden. The dual efforts of problem-solving, navigating unfamiliar black magicians who come to target Dr. Montgomery, and contributing to the police's efforts come home to roost in a cat-and-mouse game in which the seasoned investigator becomes absorbed into a milieu even she barely can comprehend. Crime thriller readers who seek astute blends of medical mystery and psychological inspection will find the fast pace, changing scenarios, and realistic settings and characters in *Dark Protection* to be especially compelling and well-done. Libraries interested in a story that contrasts outer and inner demons will find *Dark Protection* a powerful winner, highly recommendable to patrons who enjoy medical mysteries and solid suspense stories well steeped in a sense of place, character, and purpose.

—Midwest Book Review

Fans of dark crime fiction are going to feast on every delectable word of *Dark Protection*, author Willie Mae Jackson's second outing following her best-selling *Make It Right*, both of which feature Donovan Montgomery, a forensic psychiatrist and profiler known for her unforgiving approach to avenging society's wrongs. This time around, Montgomery is paired with a police detective, a potential obstacle to her after-hours murderous activities. But as the body count increases in a series of gruesome, ritualistic killings, Detective Hadley proves to be more than useful as the pair take on ruthless drug cartels, kidnappers, and ruthless killers. As with the best crime novels, the attention to detail and engaging characters are what draw in the reader and help the story race along at a strong pace. That the author is a real-life forensic psychiatrist in the justice system lifts *Dark Protection* above its rivals. A highly recommended read for lovers of crime thrillers that are interlaced with unerring realism, off-beat romance, and front-page issues.

—Lex Jones, best-selling author of *The Other Side of the Mirror*

The players and locations in *Dark Protection* are so well drawn that you feel like you're standing right in the middle of the nonstop action—you can hear the gunshots, smell the air, sense the tension, see the spilled blood in the grimy Chicago backstreets. Jackson plots a vivid story of violent murders with intriguing twists and turns that keeps the reader glued to the page. And if that's not enough, there's kidnapping, human sacrifice, and a sociopathic heroine who is definitely not one to be messed with. As a big fan of gritty, urban crime thrillers, for me, *Dark Protection* is right up there with Paula L. Woods's *Inner City Blues*, Penny Mickelbury's *Keeping Secrets*, and Kyra Davis's *Sex, Murder, and a Double Latte*. I'll definitely be doubling back to read *Make it Right*, Jackson's first novel featuring the deliciously flawed Donovan Montgomery, and will be on the lookout for more upcoming thrillers in the series.

—Chris Roy, author of *Heroics and Cruelties* and
A Time for Violence: Stories with an Edge (with Andy Rausch,
Joe R. Lansdale, and Richard Chizmar)

Dark Protection is a thriller that ensnares the reader with an intricate plot and intense characters—particularly the enigmatic Donovan Montgomery, whose dual life as a forensic psychiatrist and vigilante is both chilling and thought-provoking. Willie Mae Jackson delivers a narrative with a little bit of everything—murders, mystery, twisted romance, and strange rituals—that makes it a worthwhile addition to the suspense genre.

—HP Newquist, four-time award-winning author of
BEHEMOTH and *Ten Years Gone*

An absolute must-read for lovers of Alyssa Cole, Barbara Neely, and Attica Locke. *Dark Protection*, by best-selling crime thriller author Willie Mae Jackson, thrusts top forensic psychiatrist Donovan Montgomery into the seething, homicidal underworld of the drug trade, a nightmare-place where she is delivers her own brand of murderous justice. Jackson's brilliant writing and sharp, authentic detail puts the reader in the thick of the action from the very first page, and keeps them there through to the satisfying climax. *Dark Protection* is in the league of Luke Jennings's *Killing Eve* and Samantha Downing's *My Lovely Wife*. If you're a fan of tough, realistic, urban procedural police thrillers—with just the right amount of romance and sex, make *Dark Protection* the next book on your reading list.

—Blake Rudman, Amazon best-selling author of
The Gentleman's Choice, Goodbye Stranger, and *Kutri*

Donovan Montgomery is part Kinsey Millhone, part Hannibal Lecter—and all brilliant. A malevolent, intricate tale of murder and madness.

—*USA Today* best-selling author David Niall Wilson
(*Deep Blue* and *This Is My Blood*)

Raves for *Dark Protection*

Donovan Montgomery, introduced in Willie Mae Jackson's *Make it Right*, returns in this twisty and exciting thriller that blends the streetwise, the political, and a surprising touch of the bizarre. Known to the world as the Chicago PD's "ace forensic psychiatrist and profiler," Montgomery also serves as a vigilante "avenger" under the cover of night. On top of that, she's interviewing some of Chicago's influential political figures, including Roy Barns, a gubernatorial candidate, for a book on the pros and cons of drug legalization. When Barns's goddaughter is found dead in his front lawn in what appears to be a ritualistic killing, Montgomery is called in to provide her expertise on the case. But Montgomery, who's not much of a team player, is less than pleased when the police chief tasks her with partnering up with Detective Beau Hadley, a new transplant from Wyoming. With her own killer instincts and special methods for doling out justice, Montgomery is a multidimensional character that is sharp-witted, book and street smart with her own deadly inclinations when handling the "bad guys." In this action-packed thriller, Jackson intricately weaves a gritty suspenseful tale involving the cartel, a morally gray protagonist, and a string of murders that all tie back to the worship of Santa Muerte (Saint Death), also known as the "Lady of the Shadows." Tension builds as Montgomery walks the fine line of keeping all of the complexities of her own life from bleeding together, from her long-distance romance to her vigilante double life, all as people around her become targets. *Dark Protection* is a gripping thriller with shocking plot twists readers will not see coming. With elements of mystery, vengeance, and soft moments of romance, fans of fast-paced suspense will be captivated by this engrossing and highly engaging novel. Realistic in its detailing of police work, politics, and the drug business, this is a tough-minded tale with visceral action, crisp dialogue, and the feel of the streets. **Takeaway:** Hard-edge street-level thriller whose hero makes her own rules of justice. **Comparable Titles:** Jeff Lindsay's *Darkly Dreaming Dexter*, Caroline Kepnes's *You*.

—Publishers Weekly–BookLife Review

Dark Protection is a gripping tale that leaves you engaged and on the edge of your seat, not letting up until the very last page. Full of gory depictions, well-researched details, intense emotions, breath-hitching suspense, and pages of drama—this is a read you won't want to miss.

—C. D. Gorri, USA Today best-selling author of
The Dragon Guard series and The Macconwood Pack Series

Forensic investigator and profiler Donovan Montgomery is used to bodies and questions, but in *Dark Protection*, her normal modus operandi and duties are thrown into doubt by a supernatural overlay of possibilities. These drive her from her familiar forensic environment to the unfamiliar streets of Chicago's psychic community. Donovan is an inherent loner, but her job as Chicago's top forensic psychiatrist forces her into all kinds of interactions that threaten her secret ... she is a killer. Explicit sexual scenes pepper the story, but reinforce Donovan's relationship choices, passion, and unusual ways of seeing her world. Dr. Montgomery also struggles with OCD and keeping even her lover Tristan at arm's length. Her passion for forensic psychiatry allows her a degree of distance which is challenged by her latest case. Willie Mae Jackson

DARK PROTECTION

WILLIE MAE JACKSON, MD, MA

This book is dedicated to my dearest Tayari. Thank you for the everlasting connection and inspiration; I am infinitely filled. To my village, thank you for your ongoing love and support. I am forever grateful. To people all over the world, continue to be curious and move in faith. You're worth it.

Prologue

He wiped clean the bloody machete in his hand. The dank room smelled of rotting flesh and carne asada. A paper tree air freshener swung, impotent, from an exposed bulb. Still mesmerized by the ceremony he'd just performed, he glanced around the small home office he had carefully crafted five years prior when he moved into the abandoned Englewood house. It pleased him.

Two upholstered chairs, pushed against one wall, immortalized other happy, holy occasions for him. Both were stained, one showing its springs through the thin material. The plastic table between them held a nearly empty plate of food from his favorite taqueria with the current issue of *Smut Butt* tucked beneath it. An old desk held some of his most treasured possessions: a silver-plated skull with long horns and jutting tongue; a boom box and stack of CDs from El Comando, Toxodeth, and Bob Seger; a goat-shaped paperweight; and a mug stuffed with pens and pencils, "World's Best Dad" printed across one side.

Behind the desk hung a shelf housing mason jars. Plastic flowers thick with dust were displayed around them. Some were empty. Some contained human hearts. His eyes scanned the jars then dreamily lit on an old oak sideboard on the opposite side of the room. It was an ornate piece with three drawers down the middle and a cupboard door to either side, roses carved into each. It served as a throne for the three-foot-tall statue of a skeleton whose empty sockets oversaw his ritual work. Disproportionately large for the makeshift altar, the female figure held a scythe in one hand and globe in the other. A black cloak draped loosely over her exposed bones, its hood framing her smiling, skinless face. A plaster owl stood sentinel at her feet. At each end of the crowded sideboard, colorful prayer candles burned, each depicting a different saint. These were surrounded by money, cigarettes, and mini bottles of Cuervo Gold. Some were empty, some were not.

Sweat ran like tears from the man's forehead and cheeks. A drop hit the carnage caked on the eighteen-inch blade still clutched in his fist. Shaking himself from this reverie, he placed both rag and machete on the edge of the desk and unsnapped the blood-splattered rain poncho covering his tracksuit. He tossed it onto one of the chairs.

Someone knocked. The man's eyes slowly closed in anticipation. He scratched his testicles then crossed himself, taking in a deep breath and holding it for a moment. "Enter," he finally said.

A young Hispanic man cautiously opened the door and stepped into the office holding a tray. It held a pitcher filled with blood and a Styrofoam plate holding a heart. The man in the tracksuit nodded for him to place the tray on the desk. As the young man moved to do so, he fumbled. Though his anxiety was apparent, he remained stoic. The man in the tracksuit chuckled. The young man deposited the tray and paused, waiting for any further instructions. There were none. Backing out, he glanced from the man to the statue before closing the door.

Now alone, the man in the tracksuit removed a chalice from the sideboard and filled it with blood from the pitcher before setting it on the altar. He then picked up the heart and placed it at the statue's feet. Licking his fingers, he stepped back and solemnly addressed the skeleton. "Feast till you're full, Skinny. You have my back; I have yours."

Chapter One

He could see the sheet-covered body just beyond the yellow tape that cordoned off the entire front yard of the large two-story house. Approaching the crime scene on Prairie Avenue, Cook County Lead Medical Examiner Alfredo Ramos observed the crumpled form next to the trash bin by the curb at the end of the driveway while trying to park his car. Trash day impacted parking on even this quiet upscale street. Four police cars restricted any remaining space near the house. He passed, turned into a driveway, and doubled back, ending up a few doors away.

Detective Beau Hadley, a new criminal investigator for the Chicago Police Department, had called on the doctor at four thirty that morning. In the call, the detective shared everything he knew. The remains of a young woman had been found naked, her heart crudely cut from her chest, her wrists slit, and blood drained. He went on to say that, for the moment, no media had arrived. If the doctor could get there fast, he might be able to assess the situation "before any circus tents are pitched." A coroner's van had been dispatched, and the detective was on his way.

Alfredo Ramos had shaken off sleep, pulled on pants, and found the address in record time. His first impression was that things were under control; the deep yard that separated the house from the curb fluttered with various law enforcement personnel.

As he got out of his car, Alfredo watched a crime scene investigator conclude her photographs and return her camera to the case hanging from her shoulder. Despite the pre-dawn hour, an older couple and a young man on a bike had stopped to assess what was taking place. The couple and bicyclist were standing as close to the crime tape as the police would allow. One officer had engaged them in conversation while another patrolled the sidewalk to warn off any additional onlookers. A coroner's van pulled in silently behind a cop car in the driveway.

A man kneeling by the body stood and locked eyes with Alfredo then moved to greet him. Pulling off surgical gloves, he approached, extending his hand. "Doctor Ramos?"

Alfredo shook it. "Detective Hadley?" The two exchanged nods in silent greeting.

As they turned toward the bloody sheet, both extracted fresh gloves, sliding them on as they talked.

"It's very nice to meet you, sir," said Detective Hadley.

He was a young guy—maybe early thirties at the outside—with an easy smile and All-American Boy good looks. He had a slight accent that Alfredo thought might come by way of Texas.

"I've noticed that when I mention your name," Hadley went on, "it seems to inspire an outpouring of praise and affection. Thanks for getting out here so fast. I appreciate it. I surely do. Just got here myself a few minutes ago." His expression lightened as a broad smile stretched across his face. "You know, I've been an officer for just about five years, but this is my first case as a detective. Hell, this is my first case in Chicago."

"What a welcoming committee this makes," Alfredo said.

The two men stood over the body. "Yeah, I never saw anything like this in Wyoming, I can tell you that right now. Nasty."

Ah, not Texas. Wyoming.

Alfredo gave the newest member of the Chicago force a second appraisal. A newbie, was he? Hell, he made the doctor, who had decades on him, feel suddenly old. His eyes were so blue and hair so blond that he appeared to glow, even in the morning shadows. The kid seemed genuine and refreshingly humble, but Alfredo saw something else in those Wyoming-sky blue eyes—an intellect, the kind that reads without a word being spoken.

"Violent death always is," Alfredo responded.

The doctor knelt. The detective followed suit. A young uniformed officer approached and squatted between the two men. Detective Hadley provided introductions: "Doctor Ramos, this is Officer Spencer. Spencer, this is our chief medical examiner, Doctor Alfredo Ramos. Officer Spencer and his partner were the first to arrive in response to the nine-one-one call."

"Who called it in?" Alfredo asked. He surveyed the young officer—his acne, the patchy mustache that did not quite cover his upper lip. He appeared to be several years younger than the detective.

They're sending us babies, Alfredo thought.

"Selena Chavez, the housekeeper," said Spencer. He turned his head toward an old woman on the home's substantial porch.

Alfredo followed his gaze. The woman's fingers were covering her mouth and an officer stood with her, one hand cupped around the old woman's elbow to hold her steady.

Alfredo grunted and nodded before pulling back the sheet, exposing the naked corpse down to its abdomen. He heard Spencer clear his throat.

The doctor was no rookie, but even he was taken back by the damage done to this poor girl's body. He made every effort not to wear his reaction on his face. He, no less than the two younger men, was trying to perform his duties as if this were just another crime scene. But the brutality of the murder surpassed anything the doctor had seen in his twenty-six years as a medical examiner.

He glanced at the other men. The young officer had turned his head from the mutilated torso to stare down into the woman's open eyes as if someone was daring him to. Alfredo suspected the kid would be dreaming about those eyes tonight. He noted that Hadley's head was tilted toward the body, but his eyes were lowered.

Alfredo studied the corpse, taking in the paste-gray pallor that made the gallery of tattoos on her arms and torso stand out in garish and grim relief. He studied the slits in both wrists, the blue and yellow bruises below those slits and on her neck, the imprints of her fingernails in her palms, her wide-open eyes, mouth, and empty cavity where her heart had been.

Officer Spencer cleared his throat again. "So, Detective, like I was telling you when the doctor pulled up, we were able to confirm what Mrs. Chavez told Martha … Officer Calderon. The house is owned by Congressman Roy Barns, forty-seven. Well, he's a former congressman, anyway."

"Same Roy Barns who's running for governor?" That piqued Alfredo's curiosity.

"Yes, sir. Same guy." The officer's facial expression slipped slightly. "It's so weird, I just saw him on the news."

The detective confirmed that he, too, had seen him on TV the night before. "Wow. Right. He was at a rally in … in …"

"In Milwaukee, sir. He spoke at a fundraiser. Martha … sorry, Officer Calderon asked the housekeeper about it. Her Spanish is better than Selena Chavez's English, so she was able to find out a few things. Mrs. Chavez said her boss attended the rally with a guest—a William Vandenberg. They dined out together after the rally with some of his campaign staff, then spent the night in Milwaukee. He's expected home this morning."

Hadley nodded. "Yeah, I saw him recently on a *60 Minutes* kind of show. He was talking about legalizing drugs like they're doing on the left coast."

"I've heard about that. I don't know. Sounds crazy to me. Anyway, that's what he was talking about at the rally."

"So, maybe depositing this young lady here was somebody's way of telling Mr. Barns that they disagree with his politics. Surveillance cameras?"

"No, sir, not on the street."

"Mrs. Chavez lives here?"

"Yes, sir. There's a little mother-in-law unit in the back. Says she's been here for about seventeen years, moved in shortly after Barns became a congressman. His twin boys were still in elementary school at the time and his wife needed some extra help, so they hired her. She died about seven years ago—Mrs. Barns, I mean. Mrs. Chavez stayed on to help out with the house."

"Where are the twins?"

"College abroad."

"Do we know why Mrs. Chavez was up so early this morning?"

"Yes, sir. I guess she always gets up around four or four thirty."

The detective flashed the officer a quizzical look.

"My gram does too, sir. She and Selena Chavez are about the same age."

Hadley shrugged.

"You know, she even looks a little like my gram," Spencer added.

All three men turned toward the housekeeper and the police officer, who now had embraced the woman and was patting her back. Alfredo saw more this time: the burgundy polyester pants, the cotton scarf tied around the curlers in her hair, thick ankles, white orthopedic shoes. She resembled everyone's grandmother, even his.

"So, that's what we've got, sir."

Hadley smiled at the younger man. "Thank you, Officer Spencer. Great work. And go tell Martha, I mean Officer Calderon, that she's my hero. Awesome job."

Still a bit befuddled, the young officer rose and stepped away.

"So, what are your thoughts, Doctor?" the detective asked, peering down at the victim's exposed ribs and organs.

Alfredo leaned back from the body to consider his words. "Not like anything I've ever seen," he said at length.

"Ritual killing, you think?"

"Possible. She was restrained. Her blood has been drained. I need to get her to the lab, but it certainly looks that way."

"Sexual assault?"

"I'll let you know. Could be that her clothes were removed to make it easier to drain the blood and open the chest. Exsanguination doesn't happen by accident, and clothing would only get in the way of collecting the blood. Taken together, a missing heart *and* missing blood does tend to suggest a ritual of some sort."

"And for unknown reasons, the murderer dropped her here." The detective rotated his head; his vertebrae realigned with a soft crack. "Okay. Murder weapon?"

"Something small opened her wrists. Could have been anything from a surgical scalpel to a razor blade or box cutter. A wide blade opened her chest. Rough cuts, no precision. A large chef's knife perhaps, or an agricultural tool of some sort. We'll run a CT scan, maybe some other imaging methods. That'll tell us more. And if we get lucky, the blade or blades will have left something behind for us."

"Doctor," Hadley murmured, leaning toward him, "was … was she alive when this happened?"

Alfredo could see that the new detective was eager to hear him say that she was not. Before answering, Doctor Ramos brushed his palm over the victim's face to close her eyes.

"Usually with any kind of stabbing you can see at least some subcutaneous fat around the edges of the wound. That is if the victim's blood is flowing at the time of the assault. I don't see any here, Detective. The wounds do not appear to be antemortem, but I can't say for sure. It's unlikely the heart was removed prior to the blood being drained simply because it would make collecting the blood more difficult without a working heart. Nothing to force it out of the veins, you see. We'll run a battery of tests, of course. Toxicology will let us know if she was drugged first."

Beau Hadley nodded vigorously. "Well then, all we know for sure right now is that it didn't happen here. No sir, this young gal was murdered somewhere else and brought to this house—this house specifically." He turned toward the Barns home.

The sun peeked over the horizon as a few more lookie-loos arrived to strain against the yellow tape. The coroner's assistants from the van had a gurney ready to transport the dead woman as soon as Alfredo okayed it. He locked eyes with the housekeeper on the porch. Her arms dropped to her sides, deflated.

Rising, he told the detective, "I'm so sorry she had to find this."

Detective Hadley reached up and gently pulled the doctor back down next to the corpse. The doctor was surprised but went with it.

"Mrs. Chavez seems to be doing some better now, but she was beside herself, Doctor. She really was. Saw something next to the trash bin and came out to see what it was. When she saw the blood on the sheet, she thought someone had left a dead dog there, something like that. Whatever it was, she knew it was no good. So she called nine-one-one."

"She didn't pull back the sheet?"

"No. No, she didn't. But I guess she was standing next to Spencer and his partner when they did. You can imagine."

"Yes. Yes, I can."

"But when I got here and removed the sheet, that's when she saw this."

The detective carefully uncovered the corpse's feet. A tiny plastic statue of a brown-robed skeleton holding a scythe in one hand and globe in the other had been tucked next to the body against an ankle. Alfredo's eyebrows lifted.

"I took some pictures," said Hadley. "So did the crime scene investigator. Seems Mrs. Chavez knows what this is. It's a saint who's supposed to help people pass from the earth to heaven from what I can gather. Ugly little thing. The lady's English isn't stellar, but she worked hard to express to me the importance of leaving it right where it is. She calmed down a little when I put it back. No harm, I figured. Besides, I wanted you to see it before you moved her." He nodded at the dead woman.

"All right if I take closer look, Detective?"

Hadley picked up the four-inch statue and handed it to Alfredo, one gloved hand to another. Like Selena Chavez, Dr. Alfredo Ramos recognized the figure.

Up on the front porch, Mrs. Chavez seemed to realize what they were doing and pulled away from Officer Calderon to hurry toward them. As she approached, Hadley drew the damp sheet over the dead girl, then both men got to their feet and faced the housekeeper.

"You are Mexican, *señor*?" she asked Doctor Ramos.

"*Sí, señora, de la Ciudad de México. Lamento mucho que te haya recibido tal horror esta mañana.*"

The woman crossed herself and shook her head. In her native tongue, she railed passionately about the horror of it. Why would someone do something like this? Why would they leave the poor girl there—with the trash? A dozen other perfectly logical questions flew from her quivering lips, not one answerable.

Alfredo bowed his head compassionately and let her vent for a moment. He glanced at Hadley, who was surveying the growing crowd.

"Doctor Ramos," said the detective, "you and I both know that a bunch of news crews are gonna be rolling up this street in about a minute. Maybe we should wrap this up."

Alfredo understood that to be an accurate assessment and wondered why it hadn't happened already. He handed the statuette back to Hadley, mouthing the words, "Evidence bag," then, snapping off both gloves, took the housekeeper's hands in his.

"I know, señora. Sometimes this world is a cruel, pitiless place. But other times, it is quite beautiful. Try to remember that. Be well, señora. Detective Hadley will be in touch."

With Ramos's nodded approval, the paramedics bagged the corpse, sheet and all, but as the doctor stepped away, Mrs. Chavez grabbed his jacket sleeve, and in broken English said, "You know Santa Muerte. I know you do. Today she wears brown. That means she wants to communicate with the spirits. I think that maybe somebody cared for this poor child, for her soul, to place la Señora de las Sombras with her, and that they want for her peaceful passage to the other side."

Before Alfredo could respond, the housekeeper reached up and laid her puffy hands against his cheeks. "You know why the television people are not yet here. You know why all of the neighbors are not yet pushing past *la policia*. Santa Muerte is protecting this child. This child has been chosen. Please, please, *medico*, put her back. Only Señora de las Sombras can protect this girl from whatever devils have done this. Please!"

Detective Beau Hadley, having heard this exchange, nodded approval to the doctor and handed back the statuette. Alfredo asked the paramedics to pause in their grisly task so he could unzip the bag and pull back the sheet. He removed the statue from the evidence bag and tucked it beneath the young woman's ankle.

The housekeeper began to cry. "*Dios te bendiga, medico. Dios te bendiga. Que la Santa Muerte y todos los santos cuiden de ti y de los tuyos*. God bless you."

The paramedics lifted the gurney into the van. Ramos returned to his car. Before he got in, three news trucks rolled past him. He watched as neighbors suddenly appeared at their front doors, some shuffling toward the house where the police cars were parked.

Like zombies, he thought. *And as if on cue. They waited until we were done here, and now they come. Weird.*

He thought about what Mrs. Chavez had said, that Santa Muerte was playing a hand in the investigation. Then he turned on the radio and aimed for the nearest Starbucks.

Chapter Two

Donovan Montgomery opened her eyes. Dawn filtered through the shade and across the bed, casting seductive shadows. The man lying beside her was still asleep. She smiled. God, but he was handsome; his full lips were kissing distance from hers, the morning sunlight burnishing the dark mahogany skin with a flush of ruddy gold. She felt the urge to reach out and caress his shoulder so that he'd open his eyes. When they were together, she reveled in the way he looked at her—as if nothing else was worth seeing. As if she were the focus of his entire being.

Merely imagining that produced a flame deep in her belly and a spreading warmth in her limbs. She reached for him, then caught herself.

Damn it. Montgomery. You know better than this.

Or at least she should.

The world knew her as the Chicago PD's ace forensic psychiatrist and profiler. Millions had watched her testify in court for a number of high-profile murder trials. They'd heard her interviewed on the evening news, on National Public Radio, on a variety of podcasts. Both of her books on criminal profiling were bestsellers. She was photogenic and personable—a brilliant Black woman with movie star looks and a mind as sharp as a surgeon's scalpel. The media, like her readers, could not get enough of her.

But Dr. Donovan Montgomery knew what the media did not. She was a killer.

Being a successful killer (meaning one who did not get caught) required discipline, attention to detail, and remaining detached. That man lying there, with his carefully curried hair and beard, into which he allowed the most tasteful of silver accents to appear, was a challenge in that area. Though she saw him so rarely, he yet had the power to draw her in. She'd told herself repeatedly that his scarcity provided interest while fending off attachment. Attachment to Tristan Liaquat would make her vulnerable. Vulnerable was not in her DNA.

Her gaze drifted from Tristan's face down the full length of his body, stretched languidly on the crisp fitted sheet. The top sheet, crumpled in cloud-like puffs at the foot of the bed, created a perfect backdrop for the gift he had given her last night—a Hermès Kelly bag nestled in the pale gray folds. The purse, like its giver, was a work of art. A ray of morning sun illuminated the shiny black crocodile leather, making it gleam as if sprinkled with fairy dust.

Right, she thought, *that's why I'm feeling particularly warm and fuzzy this morning. It's all good.*

Tristan took a deep breath and rolled over onto his back, exposing himself to the light filtering in from the bedroom window. Donovan could not have resisted that temptation if she'd wanted to. She put out her hand and traced the length of his penis from root to tip, watching in awe as it woke to her touch, expanding, lengthening. She gave it another stroke and it leapt to its full potential, thick and hard, the roseate, flared tip kissing his navel. Heat licked through Donovan's vagina as if anticipating the moment of penetration; she arched her back involuntarily.

"Well, good morning," he said.

Just the sound of his voice excited her into the mistake of peering up into his eyes. She fell headlong into that *look*—the one that made her want to stay frozen in this moment forever … and run like hell as far from Tristan Liaquat as she could.

Did he know this about her? She thought she had one of the best poker faces on the planet, yet always felt that Tris heard and saw every thought that flitted through her head … and felt every sexual impulse that darted through her body.

As if to underscore that notion, he smiled, rolled over to face her, then reached out and pulled her naked body against his. His erection flexed and pulsed against her belly, feeding her rising heat and making her desperate for him to roll her over and bury himself inside her.

She would show none of this.

"Morning," she responded, her voice husky. She wriggled against his cock, cooly coy, she thought. She was ready to beg for it, but she wanted *him* to beg, to struggle against desire as she did.

His hand glided from her waist down over her buttocks, and she knew why she'd never once been able to feign cool with him. As ever, she wanted to spread her legs and demand that he fill the void between them. She had always been weak to his advances, an atypical, Pavlovian response that no other man had ever inspired in her. Still, she stubbornly tried to maintain control; she *needed* to maintain control.

"Let's play a game," she murmured. "Let's see how long we can lie here without—"

He cupped one large palm around her right breast, then dipped his head, taking the pert nipple into his mouth and gently suckling. She moaned, feeling as if lightning had invaded her blood. This prompted him to suck harder, then harder yet, causing the lightning to rage until it was almost pain. She came with her whole body, arching her back again, struggling to turn over in his embrace, still desperate for the killing thrust.

He lifted his head, said, "That was new," and took her left nipple into his mouth, running his tongue around it, teasing it, then, as she growled in a mixture of pleasure and frustration, he gave the breast a sudden hard pull and rolled her over onto her back.

She spread her legs reflexively, hungrily, and he thrust his penis deep into her. She roared as she came again, feeling the orgasm all the way to her core. Tristan climaxed seconds later. The bucking and pulsing of his cock (she swore she could feel every curve of the head, every vein and nuance of the shaft) sent her into a third orgasm, and she clamped down on him hard, then locked her legs around him as they rode it out together.

"You win," he purred in her ear.

Did I? Did she win when her carefully constructed ramparts crumbled like papier-mâché before this man?

While Donovan dashed to the bathroom to clean up, Tristan called room service to have coffee sent to his suite. She slid back into bed, propping herself against the quilted leather headboard, and wove her fingers between his.

He gazed at her as if seeing her for the first time. "Damn, girl, you are the most perfect, gorgeous thing I have ever seen."

"You've been telling me that for more than ten years now."

"Yes, I have. And it gets truer every time."

His expression shifted from wistful to thoughtful. The shift was slight, but Donovan knew this man and knew what was coming next.

"Listen, Donovan, you know I'm flying out tonight for LA, staying as long as the firm needs me there, then going straight home to Georgia. I don't know when I'm gonna get back."

"I know. You told me last night at Hugo's. I'm sure whoever you've got in Atlanta will be happy to see you."

He glanced down at their clasped hands. "You know damn well I don't have anyone in Atlanta. Hookups, sometimes, but no *one*. I live for Chicago, baby. I wish we could be together more and longer. All the time."

"Tristan ..." She sighed. "Hey, at least we had time, this time, for dinner and a sleepover. That's pretty good for us. Beats a quickie on my hearth rug."

There was a knock at the door. Tristan got up and started to grab the sheet that cradled the Hermès bag.

Donovan shook her head. "Not that one, luv. That's for my new friend. Look how happy she is swaddled up like that."

He grinned, grabbed a pillow instead, and went to answer the door. "The Waldorf is known for many things," he said, "discretion among them. This will do. They've seen worse."

She gazed at the six-foot-two-inch stud walking toward the door, then at the Hermès bag. "Well, they certainly haven't seen better," she told the purse. If the room service person had an opinion about Tristan's state of undress, they didn't voice it aloud.

Donning hotel robes with coffee in hand, Donovan Montgomery and Tristan Liaquat moved their private party to the front room of his suite. They cuddled on the couch across from the fireplace where much of their post-dinner evening had taken place. A stunning bouquet of lilies graced the small glass coffee table, as did an ice bucket, empty bottle of Dom Pérignon, and two crystal flutes.

Donovan could hear her cell phone vibrating inside her clutch. Tris asked her to ignore it. She could not. Reluctantly pulling away and retrieving her cell, she saw that the caller was Chief of Police Evangeline Newsome.

"Chief, good morning. What can I do for you?"

"Doctor, I'm sorry to call so early, but we have a situation here, and I'd like to talk to you about it ASAP. Young woman, naked, heart cut out of her chest, both wrists slit and blood drained. A housekeeper found her wrapped in a sheet at the curb of a home in Bronzeville."

Phone to her ear, Donovan stepped out onto the terrace. "Do we know who she is?"

"Not yet. And this is going to get— Listen, I'm gonna need you in on this one. But, unbelievably, I've got another fire to put out right now. It'd be so effing great if I could just focus exclusively on a naked, heartless, bloodless, anonymous body, but apparently … Donovan, just swing by this morning before you go into the office, okay?"

"Yes, of course. I'll be there."

Donovan remained on the terrace for a moment, considering what she had just heard. Tristan stepped out to join her. He slid his arms around her shoulders from behind. "Everything okay?"

She was not going to give him any specifics. That was their deal: She never talked about her forensic work with the Chicago Police Department, and he did not discuss the negotiation of intellectual property rights for corporate conglomerates around the world. She had always liked this arrangement. Though his high-powered position afforded him a lifestyle that he, and occasionally she, fully enjoyed, the ins and outs of it were a bit too dry for her taste.

Donovan put the phone in the pocket of her bathrobe and turned to face him, sliding her arms around his waist. "I'm afraid duty calls. They need me at the station."

He lowered his hands to squeeze her ass. "You want to take a shower first? You'll want to be fresh."

She laughed and pulled away. "That's inviting for more than one reason, but I'm calculating the distance between the Waldorf, home, my office, and the police station, and I think the station is closest, so … precinct first, then home and a shower. I'm thinking this might be a long day."

"Okay," he said with noticeable disappointment. "Do your thing, Doctor Montgomery." He stepped back into the bedroom and disappeared into the bathroom. Donovan felt something like disappointment too.

She heard the shower turn on and felt a pang of regret, but knew she'd made the right choice. There was only one way to remain detached from Tristan Liaquat, and that was to simply do it.

Close that door, open the next.

She was already intrigued by the murder and eager to hear whatever the chief had to share. Taking a deep breath, she stepped into the front room and began to reassemble herself in the evening wear from the night before, all cast casually across a love seat near the fireplace. In the not-so-distant past, she would have never been able to leave clothes casually discarded *anywhere*. Her obsessive-compulsive tendencies would not have allowed it. But she had worked hard on overcoming the manifestations of OCD that were useless or worse.

Go, me. Montgomery one, OCD zero.

Her memory shot back to what she was doing when the clothes came off and wondered how she'd managed not to leave a trail of evening wear and lingerie all the way from the front door to the hearth.

As she shimmied into the black satin bustier and crimson floor-length gown that were perfectly appropriate for a night on the town, she realized they would make a completely different impression at the police station. Well, she'd be quick about it. Maybe no one would notice.

She hurried to strap on the Louboutins resting on the carpet, returned her delicate garnet and pearl earrings to her ears, then checked her reflection in the glass of an art print. From where she stood, she could see the bed, the crumpled sheet, and her new best friend, the shiny black crocodile Hermès Kelly bag. She returned to the bedroom, snatched up the Hermès purse, and placed her small beaded clutch inside.

What am I gonna do with that man?

That was not a rhetorical question. She really did need to decide where this relationship—no, it didn't help to call it that—this liaison was going.

Tristan appeared from the bathroom, glistening from his shower and towel drying his hair. "You look amazing," he told her.

She ignored the fact that his lean, brown body shimmered as if covered in diamonds, and gave him a quick kiss and a smile. "It's eight a.m., Tris, and I look ridiculous. But thank you."

He met her eyes, and the two stood like that for a frozen moment. Then, she darted in to give him another quick kiss, but he brought his hands to her face, and what she had intended as a short, sweet goodbye became a long, tender affirmation of something Donovan Montgomery did not want affirmed.

She stepped back, smiled, and said, "Thank you for this gift, Tristan, and dinner, and … a most extraordinary night and morning."

When she turned to go, he caught her hand and arrested her movement toward the door. "We've been doing this for a long time, luv. Maybe it's time for us to discuss bumping our relationship to another level."

A prickle of sudden hyperawareness made the hair on the back of Donovan's neck rise. "Huh. You gonna move to Chicago, or am I gonna trot all over the globe with you?"

He grinned and shook his head. "I don't know. I don't know. How about we make a pact to discuss it …"

"… next time you have a layover in Chicago," they finished in unison.

She gave him a noncommittal smile, scooped her taffeta coat from the love seat, and made it all the way to the door of the suite before he said, "I'm serious, Donovan. We should talk about us."

She glanced back at him. His expression was serious. "Tristan, next time you find yourself in Chicago—whenever you find yourself in Chicago—you know where I am … and you have a key."

As she pulled the door closed behind her, she thought she heard him murmur, "What I want is *the* key."

In the hotel's circular courtyard, Donovan handed a valet the ticket for her car. Tristan had offered to send a car for her the night before, but she had insisted on driving to the Waldorf. She always preferred to have her car. Her life was complicated, and she never knew when she might need to uncomplicate it. Whether she needed sanctuary, a thinking cap, or simply to make a quick getaway, her car provided it. And on that morning, it served as all three.

The parking attendant got out of Donovan's white Prius and held the door. He exchanged her key fob and a smile for a twenty-dollar bill, and she was on her way. Pulling out onto East Walton, she retired all thoughts about the night before and turned her attention to the next chapter of her day.

Chief Evangeline Newsome had always done right by Donovan. She trusted her, gave her space, listened. Donovan liked that about her. As another Black woman in a position of authority, the chief's earthiness was a plus, as far as the doctor was concerned. She played no games. She spoke her mind.

Donovan had never heard her quite so rattled.

Regardless of her eagerness to assess the situation in person, she knew she had at best twenty minutes in front of her before that would be possible, as the roads were already clogged with morning traffic.

She thought about what it would be like to cut someone's heart from their chest. She supposed that it would be more difficult than one might imagine. She had never done it. Of all the criminals whose lives she had taken, of all the ways in which she had set right what the courts or attorneys or police had botched, none of those killers had cut out a human heart, so neither had she.

Who would do that? she asked herself. *And why?*

She found herself fighting a strong, hot urge to go back to Tristan's suite at the Waldorf and take him by storm.

Chapter Three

Donovan pulled up in front of the five-story precinct on Michigan Avenue and parked. As she entered the building, two officers—a man and a woman—chatting near the Records Department spotted her.

"Doctor Montgomery!" the male officer called out, smiling broadly. "Where'd you find a fancy dress ball at this hour of the morning?"

"Morning, ma'am," the other chimed in, casting her companion a quelling glance.

The security guards there were clearly bemused by her over-the-top wardrobe and movie star entrance. They'd have to be content to imagine what it implied. She replied with a wave and wry smile and got through the metal detector as efficiently as possible. Avoiding eye contact, she made her way past the long check-in counter and through the room housing cubicle after cubicle assigned to Chicago's finest. She felt many eyes on her, but no commentary. Finally reaching Chief Newsome's office, the doctor felt as though she had successfully negotiated an obstacle course.

Evangeline Newsome was behind her industrial metal desk scribbling feverishly on a report form when Donovan stepped in and closed the office door. The chief saw her, took in the picture Donovan presented, and dropped her pen.

"Jesus Christ. Do you roll out of bed looking like that?"

"Not usually," Donovan answered, momentarily distracted by a fluorescent light flickering overhead. "But, then, it wasn't my bed."

The chief nodded. "Have a seat, Doctor."

Donovan placed the Hermès on one green leatherette chair and sat on the other, making sure to tuck aside the black taffeta billowing around her ankles. "Chief, you sounded particularly harried on the phone. You okay?"

The large woman across the desk leaned forward, folding her hands in front of her. "Well, along with the regular helping of murder and mayhem I start my days with, my husband forgot to take out the garbage before he left, so the family gets to live with that for another seven days. Meanwhile, this damn blinking light is either gonna drive me mad or bring on an epileptic seizure—and I don't particularly care which."

"You don't have epilepsy, Evangeline."

"Yet. Oh, and my car's in the shop, so I had to take the El." She leaned in farther. "I had to take the God. Damn. El. So, no, not really 'okay.' Not in the commonly accepted sense."

She leaned back against the chair and ran her eyes down the length of Donovan's ensemble. "Odds are good you're doing somewhat better than I am this morning."

The doctor grinned, nodded affirmatively, and crossed her legs. "Oh, there's no doubt about that. Thanks for your candor."

"That's on you, Miss Thing. You asked," the chief said, glancing back down at the open file on her desk. "You interviewed Roy Barns recently for the book you're writing on the pros and cons of legalizing drugs, right?"

"Yes," Donovan answered, the grin slipping from her lips as her eyes focused hard on the woman behind the desk. "Yes, a few days ago. He's the most vocal proponent. And, in that he's running for governor, I thought he'd be a logical place to start the interviews. I want to sit down with one or more of the cartel kingpins as well. Get their opinion."

"I've read about it," Chief Newsome said. "Seems counterintuitive to me."

"There's a rationale that legalizing drugs would reduce the violence and drug deaths impacting Chicago—the African American community most especially. Given that recreational drugs would be taxed like any other commodity, there'd be more money that could then be directed toward treatment, in addition to what was saved on policing, court cases, and incarceration." Donovan waited for a moment before adding, "Forgive me, Evie, but you didn't call me in here to talk about this. I'm thinking you called me here to talk about the girl whose heart was cut out of her chest."

"Yeah. Yes, I did." Newsome nodded, meeting the doctor's gaze. "Donovan ... the body was deposited at Mr. Barns's home over on Prairie. It was discovered at his curb right next to his trash bin ... by his housekeeper. She was concerned about whatever was wrapped in the bloody sheet and called 911."

Donovan processed the information as methodically as she always did, but was taken back by the congressman's reappearance in her life. "That's wild. I was just there."

"You interviewed him at his home?"

"Yeah. The press has been at his heels recently, which he's absolutely encouraged, but he wanted us to have some privacy for the interview. He was very gracious. And I met his housekeeper. Nice lady. So she found the body, then."

"Yep. I think an officer is still with Mrs. Chavez. Barns isn't home yet."

"Where is he?"

"He spoke at a rally last night at the"—she read from a sheet of paper in the file still open on her desk—"the Henry Maier Festival Park in Milwaukee."

Donovan raised her eyebrows. "Outdoors. At night. On the lake. At this time of year?"

"In the South Pavilion." She closed the file. "He spoke on the drug issue among other things, went to a fundraiser afterward, and spent the night. He's been contacted."

"Okay. And on the phone, you referred to the vic as bloodless. You mean her blood had been drained? Literally?"

"Right. Both wrists slit. The ME says this suggests a ritual of some sort. And this is where you come in, Doctor Montgomery. I've got a strong feeling that her murder had something to do with the aspiring governor's drug platform. At least it's the most obvious connection. Why else would the body be deposited at his house? Just random chance?" She shook her head. "Nah. He's been so vocal recently about the virtues of legalizing the kind of drugs most people could have never dreamed might be made available—meth, cocaine, heroin—while at the same time demonizing the cartels. The man's everywhere—TV, radio, all the socials. Difficult for me to believe that there isn't some connection."

"Okay, so you want me to profile the killer or killers."

"Mm-hmm. Help me figure out what kind of person would go to those lengths to make a point. Maybe that'll help me figure out what point that might be. I want you to go meet our girl while she's still on Alfredo's slab. I've told him to expect you."

Donovan got up. "That sure of me, were you?"

"There's something else. You're not gonna like it. A Detective Beau Hadley's been assigned to the case. He's aware of your background in forensics and profiling, and specifically asked for your input. He'll be in touch."

"Evie, you know I don't collaborate."

"I know you don't, but I already told him you'd help him out."

Donovan raised an eyebrow. "I'd help *him* out."

"Look, the guy just transferred here from Wyoming. Academy creds are impressive, so is his work ethic, but he's new to homicide. This is his first case."

Donovan didn't try to hide her exaggerated eye roll as she moved to the office door and turned the knob. "Welcome to Chicago, cowboy." She didn't miss the twitch of Newsome's lips as she tried not to smile.

"By the way," the chief said as Donovan started to open the door, "about that book you're working on—I thought you'd be interested to know that an Empresarios lieutenant is being held at MCC, a Ruben Ortiz. They made him for trafficking, but turns out he has a brother in on charges of killing those two cops in Chinatown last week, and Ruben wants to cut a deal. Says he knows who the cop killer really is. He'll give him up in exchange for his brother's release. He's been informed that he's gonna have to cough up more than that. Now he wants WITSEC. His attorney's already working on it with the Feds. They're deciding whether to hold him till trial or allow him into the witness protection program. If you want, I'll clear it so you two can have a chat."

"You bet I want," Donovan assured her, then exited her office with a swish of taffeta.

Chapter Four

Out in the precinct bullpen, Donovan stopped. In a visitor's chair in one of the cubicles across the room sat a thin, dignified, middle-aged Black man with graying temples and black-framed glasses. His dark blue suit jacket hung open over a white shirt and thin tan-and-blue striped tie; the collar was unbuttoned and the tie knot loosened.

She would have recognized Congressman Roy Barns even if she hadn't recently interviewed him; as Chief Newsome had pointed out, he had been all over the media in the past weeks. Donovan knew that he was about to become even more recognizable. He'd be a household name in Chicago, only this time for the darkest of reasons. The media would devour the grisly murder on Prairie Avenue and feast on everyone and everything surrounding it.

Barns was seated across from a desk cop, Officer Gary Stevenson, and next to a man she did not recognize—Caucasian, similar in age to Barns but sturdily built. His hair might be blond or a mixture of blond and silver; it was hard to tell at this distance. She watched for a moment as the officer asked questions of Roy Barns and typed answers, then stepped back into Newsome's office and quietly closed the door.

"What is it?" the chief asked.

"Chief ... did you wear a coat this morning?"

"Well, not my opera coat, but yeah. It's Chicago. Why are you asking me this?"

Donovan motioned toward the hat rack in the corner. On it hung one long cardigan and a mid-calf length green puffer coat. "That it?"

Chief Newsome, who had already retrieved her pen and gone back to the file in front of her, put down the writing instrument and again folded her hands on the desk. "Yes."

"I need to borrow it."

Chief Newsome leaned back and crossed her arms. "You got in here dressed like that. Why the costume change?"

"Barns is here. He's with Stevenson. I want to talk to him. I don't want him to be distracted by my ... costume."

Newsome frowned. "Distracted by your costume?"

Donovan gestured at her gown. "Evie, I look like a damned Barbie doll."

Newsome picked up her pen and went back to work. "Fine. Do what you need to do, but keep it brief. Poor soul. Must be pretty shaken."

Donovan exchanged the taffeta wrap for the voluminous green puffer. The vivid red of her gown's skirt cascaded below the hem of the coat, making her resemble a caricature of a Christmas tree. She gathered the skirt and tucked it around her waist. The signature red soles of her Louboutins clashed just as much as the gown had, but men, she'd come to know, rarely noticed shoes outside of the bedroom. Zipping up the coat, she grabbed the Hermès and once again opened the door.

"Hey, Don," the chief added without looking up, "I want it back tomorrow. No encores."

I really like that woman.

"Sure thing, Chief." Donovan adjusted the coat collar, then made her way through the cubicles to Stevenson's desk.

The former congressman saw the doctor as she approached. Recognizing her, he rose. The man sitting next to him turned to see what had caught his eye. As Donovan neared the desk, the second man rose as well.

"Doctor Montgomery," Barns said, extending his hand. "I'm surprised to see you here."

She could read the confusion in his tired eyes, the disoriented sadness that she had seen in so many others when given the life-altering news that someone they knew or loved had been murdered. She had yet to find out if he knew the victim, but whether he did or not, finding out that a mutilated corpse had been deposited next to his trash bin provoked an identical reaction.

"Congressman, hello. Chief Newsome has asked me to step in on the case, see if I can help profile the killer or killers. I'm so sorry. This must be such a shock."

He held her hand tightly with both of his, one atop the other. Donovan identified the gesture as a "politician's handshake," one meant to imply warmth and sincerity with constituents. But on this occasion, she read it as something closer to a silent plea for help. She could feel him trembling. His palms were moist.

Officer Stevenson nodded in Donovan's direction. "Morning, Doctor. Detective Hadley got hold of Mr. Barns and asked him to come by the station before going home, fill out some paperwork. The detective is on his way here now. He wants to drive Mr. Barns to the medical examiner's office, see if he can ID the body. Still a Jane Doe at this point."

Donovan had yet to meet the new detective, but she understood why he wanted to be with Roy Barns when he saw the remains. That way he could assess the politician's reaction, his demeanor, and take note of what questions he asked or chose not to ask.

Officer Stevenson's phone rang. He took the call. "Excuse me for a minute. I've got to deal with this," he said, fishing out a keyring from a drawer. "I'll be right back." The officer left the three standing at his desk.

Realizing his companion had not been introduced, Barns pulled away from the doctor and placed a hand on the man's shoulder. "Forgive me, Doctor Montgomery. This is William Vandenberg. Bill, this is Doctor Donovan Montgomery. She and I met a few days ago. The doctor is writing a book on the pros and cons of legalizing narcotics. She wanted to talk to me about that."

Vandenberg tried to smile, extending his hand. "Doctor."

Up close, Donovan could tell that Bill Vandenberg's hair was still mostly blond. His handsome face was boyish. He, too, wore a suit but no tie. Donovan took his large hand in hers. He was not trembling. His palm was dry.

"Bill went with me to the rally and fundraiser," Barns said. "He operates a half-dozen rehab clinics across the country and wants to expand the chain to Chicago. God knows we need the help. He's not only my closest friend, he's also been my biggest supporter. In fact, he's the one who convinced me to throw my hat in the ring."

Vandenberg gave a fleeting smile. "Illinois doesn't have anyone who could do a better job as governor. That's for sure. Nice to meet you, Doctor Montgomery. I only wish it were under different circumstances. This … This is … unbelievable."

She watched the body language between the two men. Both were focused on her, but Barns kept one hand on Vandenberg's shoulder, and Vandenberg kept one on the congressman's back. These were close friends, and she assessed that William Vandenberg was braced and ready to catch Roy Barns before he hit the ground, were he to require it.

The congressman removed his hand from his friend's shoulder and stuck both in his pants pockets. "Doctor, do they think there was some reason the young woman was left there? At my house, I mean? Could this be some random act of violence?"

"It's too soon to know those things, Mr. Barns. I'm sorry. We're going to sort everything out as quickly as possible. I promise you that. As Officer Stevenson said, Detective Hadley is on his way here now. Once you've been to the medical examiner's office, we'll at least know if you recognize the woman."

He whispered, "Dear God," under his breath. Donovan knew this face too. He was praying that he did not know the girl.

She then turned to the other man. "Rehab centers. The congressman's platform and your business work well together. Legalizing drugs would inspire a demand for more rehab centers for sure. A necessary component—and profitable."

The man smiled, but his eyes clouded. "I have a very personal interest. My daughter's been in and out of the Gateway facility on

Jackson more than once. It's taken us three tries, but I think she's finally got it licked."

Officer Stevenson stepped back behind his desk, throwing the keys in the drawer. "Sorry about that. I think we're done with the paperwork, sir. But if you'd like to wait here for Detective Hadley, you're welcome to."

Donovan again shook Vandenberg's hand. "I'm sorry that your daughter's had such a rough time, but it's wonderful that she's still determined to win."

"Thank you. Yes, her mother and I are ... We're in it to win it. She'll beat this thing. I know she will."

"And Congressman Barns—"

"Call me Roy."

"Roy, this is the strangest turn of events, meeting you for the first time then seeing you here about ... this. Please take care of yourself and Mrs. Chavez. You've got the number of my private practice. You call if you want an appointment, okay?"

He thanked her. Donovan meant what she said. She would see him whenever he wanted to talk. Because whatever he had to talk about was getting more interesting to her by the minute.

Chapter Five

Donovan excused herself, eager to get to the girl on Alfredo's table. On the drive from the precinct to her townhouse, she considered everything that the chief had told her about the murder, then sorted through her personal assessment of Roy Barns. Gentle yet dynamic, polished yet accessible—these facets of character and his quiet gravitas made him an easy man to like. He inspired trust. But based on her experience, those very qualities had masked some of the most nefarious criminals and ghoulish deviants she had encountered. As for Vandenberg, he was too connected to the former congressman for her to dismiss. Though logistics cleared both as suspects, either one might be connected to the murder.

Whoever Barns truly was, she had no doubt that the combination of his charming professorial looks, coupled with the politically awkward discovery next to his trash bin would allow the media to own the man, each outlet wringing out every drop of titillating bloodlust masked as compassion, and they would not turn away from the story until he served no further purpose. The gubernatorial candidate would be their slave and their darling until the murder was solved. If there was anybody in Chicago who hadn't heard or read about Roy Barns before this, they would now.

Turning off 94 onto Foster Avenue and into the quaint familiarity of Lincoln Square, Donovan was soon at her townhouse. She was showered, freshly made up, and back in the Prius in less than twenty minutes, dressed in a camel-colored moleskin pantsuit and red blouse, which accented the deep chocolate of her skin. It would take another twenty minutes to get to Alfredo's office if the traffic lights worked in her favor.

Pulling into the parking lot of the Robert J. Stein Institute of Forensic Medicine, she parked, got out, and retrieved an empty casserole dish from the back seat before making her way across the large warm gray concrete slabs leading to the entrance.

Greeted by warm hellos and friendly nods, Donovan paused to talk to the morgue attendant at the desk.

"Doctor Montgomery! Hi! Doctor Ramos is expecting you. How have you been? We haven't seen you in a while."

"Hello, Jasmine. It has been awhile. But then every day I'm not needed here is a good one, right? No offense."

"None taken." The woman smiled and nodded toward the rear of the building. "He's in the autopsy suite."

Donovan thanked the attendant and made her way back toward the morgue. The medical examiner's staff were kind and professional, and all but the newest of them knew Donovan. She'd spent many hours here. The Cook County Circuit Court and a long list of private attorneys had solicited her services on myriad criminal cases, her prowess at psychological autopsies making her an invaluable asset.

As far as she knew, Donovan was the only professional allowed to walk unescorted to an occupied autopsy suite. That had less to do with her work and more to do with Chief Medical Examiner Alfredo

Ramos. Were she to have a godfather and mentor, it would be him. That friendship, and the trust it represented, afforded her privilege denied even the highest-ranking city official. She could, and did, walk in on his autopsies whenever she had business to discuss, or needed advice on which dress to wear to court, or wanted his input on a new restaurant that intrigued her but had not gotten stellar reviews. Alfredo Ramos and his partner, Mark, were dedicated "foodies."

As she opened the door to the suite, Alfredo barked, "Halt!" She did. He tapped the foot control of the voice recorder into which he saved his pathology notes, and without looking up, addressed his visitor. "*Hola, cariño*. I'm going to need you in full beekeeper regalia, please. We don't know what we've got here. It's all right there next to the door."

In biohazard gear from head to toe, Alfredo's focus and gloved hands remained deep in the victim's midsection.

Donovan knew the drill. She placed the casserole dish and Hermès bag on the steel counter inside the door and picked up the long-sleeved, fluid-resistant jumpsuit. She slid it on over her pantsuit, then donned the face shield and double latex gloves laid out for her.

"Your husband's cobbler was ridiculous," she told Alfredo as she settled the mask over her face. "I ate every morsel Mark sent home with me last week. I'll leave the dish here. Try not to forget it."

"Yes, he's a regular Martha Stewart. I only let him bake for esteemed company such as yourself. Otherwise, we would both be enormous. Is that what I think it is?" He referred to the purse next to the dish.

"Yes, it is. Nice, huh?"

"Nice? More like museum-worthy. How long have you been on the waiting list for that?"

"It was a gift."

He chuckled. "Of course it was. Tristan's in town?"

"Not now. Flying to LA as we speak." Donovan gave the gloves a last tug. "Okay, Doctor. I'm ready."

She stood with her arms at her sides and waited. Alfredo straightened up, placing the speculum he had been using on an aluminum tray, and assessed his friend's HAZMAT attire as he snapped off soiled gloves, tossed them in a nearby metal trash can, and washed his hands. Grabbing a fresh pair from a box and working them over his fingers, he nodded approvingly.

"Still pretty. You're the only human being I know that makes a HAZMAT suit look like it belongs in a fashion magazine."

She approached the table. "You too, Doctor Ramos. Very pretty. What do we know so far?"

They stared down at the young woman splayed open atop the cold metal slab. Her bloodless body had turned a ghostly shade of gray, the flesh around the deep cuts on both wrists was swollen like two gaping mouths, and her rib cage, which Ramos had cracked open for examination, revealed the cavity where her heart had been.

"That it wasn't suicide."

Donovan winced. "Anything else? I understand her clothes had been removed. Was there a sexual assault?"

"No, there wasn't. It would be easier to collect blood without the clothing. I think that's what that was about. Maybe she bled out in a tub. Something like that. Or maybe that's part of a ritual. Hard to tell with only one data point. Though I pray to God we won't get more."

"Was she dead prior to the blood-letting and ... extraction?"

"Unlikely. Once the heart stops pumping, exsanguination is difficult at best."

"I notice there's bruising around her neck and wrists and self-inflicted wounds in her palms from her fingernails. That certainly suggests that she was restrained, that she struggled."

Alfredo met Donovan's eyes. "I suspect that her struggles took place ... early in the process. Judging by the wounds, they slit her wrists, let her bleed out, then removed her heart, once it had stopped."

Donovan nodded. "Small mercy."

"Very small. So, you asked what we've got—we've got a young woman, early twenties, Caucasian, five foot five, 118 pounds. That's what we've got. Tox results aren't back yet. So far, no ID. The ultraviolet revealed nothing of note, no little deposits that would indicate anything other than the obvious. I'll run tests of her hair and nails, bloodwork and saliva sample, etcetera. Until then, we have little information."

"A ritual killing," Donovan said. "You with me on that?"

"Absolutely. But to what end? What was the sacrificing of this young woman supposed to accomplish?"

Donovan ran a gloved finger across the track marks freckling the inside of the dead girl's arm. "She had a habit."

"*Had* being the operative word. Look at these." Alfredo exposed the victim's legs, revealing dozens of tiny needle marks covering the inside of both thighs. "They appear to be scarred over—I've yet to find any fresh ones. I could be wrong, but it does suggest that her addiction was in the past. The tox report will tell."

Donovan touched the flesh folded back from the victim's chest. She carefully took the skin flap in her hand and folded it back over the open cavity. She picked up the skin on the other side and did the same in an attempt to reconstruct the incision.

"Looks like she was cut open with a flat blade, but it was done so crudely. Frantic slashes. Crime of passion? A ritual killing but a crime of passion?" She shook her head.

"Maybe the killer or killers were in some sort of ... of religious fervor. An unholy passion," added Alfredo.

"Mm-hmm. And in that she was obviously deposited so as to be found, we can be confident that someone is sending a message."

Alfredo raised an eyebrow. "Indeed. But what is the message ... and who is it for?"

Donovan focused on the girl's many tattoos, touching one and then another. "You know who lives in that house where they found her, of course."

"Gubernatorial candidate and ex-congressman Roy Barns."

"Odds are good that message was for him or someone connected to him."

"Well, connecting the dots is why you make the big bucks, *mija*. Anyway, I'm glad Newsome brought you in on this one. I'm sure you'll get to the bottom of it—one way or another."

The subtle insinuation surprised her. Glancing sideways, Donovan observed no emotion in Alfredo's eyes. There was neither judgment nor approval as he continued to stare down at the corpse. She knew that getting to that place had been a struggle for him, a process, and she respected his learned ability to trust her.

Though it had never been discussed, Donovan was aware that the brilliant doctor had long since deduced her deadly extracurricular activities. There had been too many coincidental deaths of those malevolent characters who had slithered through the cracks of justice. To the public eye, her hands were clean. Doctor Alfredo Ramos's choice to turn a blind eye allowed her to keep it that way. And for that, he held a unique place in her psyche. She considered it something akin to love.

"Thanks, *papi*. I'll make you proud." She bent to examine the series of artful tattoos that wended their way down both arms, ending just above the swollen wounds at the victim's wrists. "This poor girl had some beautiful ink. The scarring next to this one makes me think she had something removed, or was in the process of having it removed."

Alfredo leaned in and brought Donovan's attention to one particular bit of art on the girl's bicep. It depicted a skeleton shrouded in red, holding a skull in one hand and scythe in the other. "See this?" he asked, "That's Santa Muerte, Saint Death. She's not sanctioned by the Church. She's a *faux* saint, a folk saint. But millions of people follow her, not only in Mexico but around the world. She's quite popular in the US. For some members of the Mexican cartels, Santa Muerte is said to be the most powerful of the 'narco-saints.' They believe that she offers them protection from the law, that they can get away with anything—murder, trafficking—and she'll keep them safe. They say that El Capricho has been able to remain in hiding as long as he has because she's protecting him."

Donovan stood up from the body and straightened her spine, turning to face Alfredo directly. He mirrored the movement. They stood face-to-face for a moment, during which Donovan read her old friend. She knew him well enough to be certain there was more to this story.

When he didn't speak, she asked, "Tell me more?"

He canted his head to one side, his gaze going over her shoulder. Talking about this made him uncomfortable. "They make offerings to her. Sometimes human sacrifice plays a part in that. She's believed by some to be the premier guardian of the underworld."

"Huh. Kyped Hades's job, did she?" Donovan turned and walked across the room to where she'd left her purse and began to remove the protective gear, gloves last, tossing all in a bin designed for biological refuse. Alfredo followed her and removed his gear as well.

"People get all sorts of tattoos, Alfie," Donovan told him. "Why did you give me the Wikipedia explanation on that one?"

"Hey, when do I get to tell you about something you don't already know? And there's this." He exhumed a palm-sized plastic statue in an evidence bag from the pocket of his pants. Donovan's lips parted.

"It was wrapped in the sheet with the body when they found her." He held the statue between his index finger and thumb, turning it slowly so Donovan could see its entirety.

"You notice that the tattoo shows a skeleton draped in red. This one's in brown. Santa Muerte is depicted in several colors, all said to conjure different protections. And you're right—I'm sure a multitude of young women sport such a tattoo. It's easy to imagine that many show the figure in red, as that represents love, passion, and the like."

"And brown?"

"Well, like everything else with this *faux* saint, that depends on who you ask. But commonly brown means dirt, which represents the grave and all aspects of communications with the dead. Barns's housekeeper was determined that I keep the statue with the body to protect her soul as she made her way to the other side. I stuck it back in the sheet to calm the poor woman down, but I wanted you to see it. If Newsome thinks this is drug-related, it might be noteworthy."

Donovan studied tension in her friend's face. "Alfredo, what do you think?"

He placed the figurine on the metal countertop next to the Hermès bag and crossed his arms. "My grandmother was a devotee of this folk saint. Of course, she also believed in virgin birth and that Elvis faked his death and was living in Idaho. Don't ask. That said, as I recall, a brown-robed Muerte isn't always a great thing. White equals good, red equals love, and so on. But brown … it represents more of a gateway, a portal to the other side. Not necessarily a benevolent spirit. I think Mrs. Chavez was trying to put a rosy cast on an ambiguous symbol."

"One that was obviously left there with purpose. What do you make of it showing up with the body?"

"I'm not sure. Maybe nothing. But it showing up with a body that bears *that* tattoo. It's … an interesting detail. It argues strongly for the ritualist aspect of the murder." He shrugged, kissed Donovan's forehead, then turned to pick up a clipboard from the counter. Removing a pen from his shirt pocket, he began to write.

Donovan took that to mean they were done for the moment and picked up her purse. "Don't forget the casserole dish," she said.

"Eh, I probably will. Take the saint."

"What?"

He gestured to the plastic statue. "Take it. You may find it of more use than the local detectives."

After a moment of hesitation, Donovan picked it up and stuck it in the pocket of her blazer. Was it weird that the thing gave her the creeps?

The things that get under our skin …

As she left the building, Donovan saw a tall young man walking toward it. He was of average build, button-down shirt under a fleece-lined jacket, and sporting a Stetson hat and, yes, cowboy boots. She instinctively knew that this walking cliché was the detective Newsome forewarned her about. Passing him on the way out was unfortunate timing, as far as she was concerned.

"Doctor Montgomery!" he called out, bounding over to her. "How lucky am I? I knew we'd be meeting up soon, but …" Before she could devise an alternative exit strategy, she found herself in the grip of a firm, warm handshake with the man. "Where are my manners? I'm Beau Hadley, Detective Beau Hadley. I've been assigned to the case of the girl found—"

"On Prairie Avenue. Yes, Chief Newsome told me. Nice to meet you, Detective. Doctor Ramos has just completed the autopsy. I understood Congressman Barns would be with you, that you are hoping to see if he can help ID the victim."

"Yes, ma'am. He'll be here any minute. His friend, Bill—"

"Vandenberg."

"Right. He's driving him over so he can take him home after. They just got back from—"

"Milwaukee."

"That's right." He smiled, bright and white, and pushed back the brim of his hat, revealing a mop of golden blond hair. "You do seem to be pretty well up to speed on things, yes indeed. You know, Doctor Montgomery, I am a big fan of yours. Now, that's probably not the most professional thing I could say right here, maybe not even that appropriate given the circumstances, but … holy cow." He planted his hands in his pockets and shook his head. "I am a fan. Read everything you've ever written. Not just the books. Articles, too. Everything. Your profiling skills are, well, they're more than impressive."

Holy cow, indeedy.

She glanced lovingly over at her car where it sat in the visitor's parking lot, wishing she were in the driver's seat with the door closed. "You're very kind, Detective, but—"

"Beau. Call me Beau. I'll bet you've got a million things to do. I'll let you go. Really great to meet you, ma'am. An honor." He actually tipped his hat.

Donovan smiled and took a step toward the parking lot.

"Oh, Doctor Montgomery, just …"

Donovan stopped and turned back toward her fan. He was standing there with one index finger raised in the universal "one more thing" pose.

"Chief Newsome did tell you that we'll be working together on this, didn't she?"

Will we?

"Not exactly—"

"I know that's not how things usually go, you being a forensic psychiatrist and all. But I'm a newbie." Again, he flashed a toothy, self-effacing smile. "I'm gonna need your guidance on this one. I surely am."

"Yes, well—"

"Thank you so much, Doctor. That young woman in there thanks you too. I'm sure of it."

Donovan could see no alternative but to say, "You're welcome. I'm afraid I do have to get going, though. Nice to meet you, Detective Hadley."

She'd taken two long strides toward the Prius before he called out again. "Beau! Call me Beau. Listen ..." He took two longer strides and caught up with her as she reached her car. "You were just in there. You've talked to Doctor Ramos. What do you think? What's your take on this thing so far?"

Donovan stared at the young man. Something in his eyes let her know she was not dealing with the unpolished, starstruck fool he presented himself to be. There was something much deeper going on behind the effusive country charm, something shrewd and highly intelligent. He knew as well as she did that they were playing chess, not checkers.

Don't even try to make me underestimate you, cowboy. I will not oblige.

"You have my number?" she asked.

"Yes, ma'am. Yes I do."

"We'll talk. Now, go solve some crimes, Detective." She winked, unlocked the car door, and climbed inside. He bent to look in the driver's window.

"Will do, Doctor Montgomery. You can count on it."

Chapter Six

Merging onto I-94, Donovan brought down the driver-side window of her Prius and turned up the radio, happy to have escaped Detective Hadley's attention, at least for the moment. "Slow Down" by VanJess filled the interior of the car. She smiled. Taking Exit 47A, she turned onto Western Avenue toward Lincoln Square. She had maintained her private practice in Lincoln Square for well over a decade. It suited her, the old-school charm and high-end glamour, and conveniently positioned her only minutes from her townhome on Winnemac.

She passed the mundane clutter of banks, dry cleaners, and the like, taking in the nineteenth-century vibe of brick and cobblestone, streetlamps that bracketed on-trend eateries, art galleries, and an eclectic array of shops interspersed with fountains and planters.

At a stoplight, she observed a crowd gathered around the seven-foot, six-inch statue of a beardless Abraham Lincoln next to the Walgreens on Lawrence. Their banners and T-shirts let her know that this pop-up party was in honor of the Cubs' victory over the Pittsburgh Pirates the day before. It had been a home game played at Wrigley Field.

"Go, Cubs," she said aloud.

In that moment, the heartless, bloodless corpse that had dominated her thoughts was nowhere to be found. The light turned green. She drove past the sage green archway that marked Lincoln Square and parked in front of Geraldine's, drinking in the smells of baked goods and coffee, and entered the adjacent building. She took the stairs to her third-floor suite, the same suite she had occupied for her entire tenure as a psychiatrist.

Angel Torres, who handled appointments, correspondence, and everything else from scheduling car repairs to dealing with the press, was on the phone when Donovan entered the stylish waiting room. The two had grown up together, and as far back as Donovan could remember, everybody had liked Angel. She was a positive "yes, we can" sort of woman, but even when she said no, people tended not to take it badly. That was a talent that Donovan did not possess, and it made her life easier. Having someone working for her whom she actually trusted was invaluable.

Angel cupped her hand over the receiver as Donovan approached, mouthing, "It's your editor."

Donovan rolled her eyes in response. She removed the small statue from her blazer and swung the Hermès bag over the same arm. As she reached the door adjacent to Angel's desk, which led to the inner office, Angel gently grabbed her arm to halt her.

"She just came in, JoAnne," she told the caller. "She'll be with you in a sec." Putting the call on hold, Angel let go. "You gonna tell me where you got that?"

"The plastic skeleton or the purse?"

"Give me some credit. Vintage Hermès Kelly? That's from Tristan. Am I right?"

Donovan blinked slowly and gave Angel a down-the-nose look.

"I mean, who else? And you will be telling me about that later. But Santa Muerte? What's up with that?"

Impressed and surprised that Angel so readily knew about the figure, she grinned, reaching for the doorknob. "We'll talk. I need to take Jo's call or she'll be dogging me all day."

Before entering her office, she glanced in the direction of the sterling silver coffee urn and serving set perpetually ready for visitors and patients. The smell of fresh coffee filled the room. "Ange, buy me another thirty seconds before you transfer her, okay?"

Angel scrunched her brow. Smiling, Donovan walked toward the elegant table housing the coffee and assortment of teas, listening to her secretary and childhood friend make small talk with the bristly editor.

"Hey, JoAnne, how come that big publishing house doesn't want to write a book about me? Yeah, we could call it something like 'Angel Torres: Raven-Haired Latina from Albany Park.' What do you think?"

Donovan took a sip of coffee as she sailed past Angel's desk and into her office.

Angel snorted. "No, I'm not serious … Yes, she did ask me to stall … Yes, she has the coffee now. But, you know, it's not a bad idea. Okay, I'm putting you through … You too. Bye."

Settling in at her desk, Donovan took the grim little statue out of the evidence bag, set it next to the intercom, and pushed a button, putting her editor on speaker. "Hi, JoAnne. Sorry I haven't gotten back to you."

"Is your cell working?"

"Yes, it is. Again, my apologies. I've been on a forensics case. What can I do for you?"

"I've called you three times."

"I know you have. What were you going to tell me in those calls, Jo?"

She recognized the slow exhale audible from the other end of the phone: cigarette smoke and agitation. JoAnne Champion had edited both of the doctor's books, both bestsellers. Donovan knew the woman to be short-tempered and long-winded but very good at her job. A marriage of convenience, Donovan always listened to JoAnne, and sometimes even heeded her advice.

Because of the timely topic, her publishing house had already leaked information to the press about the next book, *The War on Legalizing Drugs: Impact on American Addiction*, and her editor was already feeling the pressure, though the manuscript was still being written.

After a lengthy exhale, she asked if Donovan had gotten her interview with Roy Barns, as she had just heard about the murder. Donovan told her that she had.

"Good. Jeez, what a thing. Heart cut out? Who does that? Poor kid. Though this will probably work in our favor. If Publicity makes it known that you spoke to Roy Barns—like, the day before it happened—"

"What can I do for you, Jo? I'm expecting a patient in a few minutes."

"Right. Listen, I read the first few pages and, of course, I'm loving it. But I wanted to just put a little bug in your ear about the tone."

Donovan, who had been leafing through the file on the new patient she was about to see, stopped and gave JoAnne her full attention. "The tone?"

"Yeah, you know, I'm just wondering if we can massage it a little to make it more … accessible. You know? Maybe some anecdotes. Let the reader know that you're one of them. Keep it from getting too dry and clinical. What do you think?"

The doctor stared at the phone as if seeing the woman directly. "I'm compiling interviews and data right now. This isn't a book about me."

"Oh, I know that, honey. And the topic is so effing timely. It's just perfect. Really. So many people fighting addiction, cartels trying to push that trash into every school kid's backpack. It's just ... Well, you're a very big name, Donovan. People want to know more about you. You don't have to get too personal. Just warm it up a bit. Maybe we can bring in some points that make this a personal quest for solutions. Donovan Montgomery has had experience with this stuff herself kind of thing. Not suggesting that you had or have an addiction. God forbid. But if you knew of someone or saw something that affected you personally ..."

As the editor spoke, Donovan flashed on her sister's death and the opioid addiction that led to it. She didn't remember much before the Montgomerys adopted her and her sister—Donovan, three, Emma, six. But she grew up knowing that they were good people, the Montgomerys, and that her big sister would always be there to protect her, to shield her against all the bad in the world.

Then came the hit-and-run accident that took the two people she knew as Mom and Dad, and nearly killed Emma. A senior in high school with her sights set on a full scholarship, she had stayed home that night to study. When an eighteen-year-old Donovan answered the knock at the front door and saw a policewoman standing on the porch, she knew before being told. She read it on her face, her profiling ability showing itself even then.

Donovan remembered that something in her broke as she stared at the officer, something that, through all the years that followed, remained indefinable. She remembered her lack of emotion standing at her sister's hospital bed. She remembered the time it took for Emma to walk again. And she remembered, three years later, watching tears run down her sister's face doubled over in pain at the kitchen table.

After the battery of spinal surgeries, Emma had been prescribed a steady diet of Tramadol. It took four pills to get her through each day, which allowed her to move from chair to bed to toilet with the aid of a walker. Without them, she could not stand, walker or no, and her every move was excruciating.

A year later, her insurance provider changed, and her medication was no longer covered by her policy. The new provider offered counseling and could prescribe a high-dose Tylenol in limited quantity to help her transition. Emma tried both, but the pain became incapacitating. She could barely turn her head, and her hands were so crippled that she had no grip. Very quickly, the sweet, stoic girl Donovan knew to be her big sister changed into a brittle, angry, frightened young woman she barely recognized.

Then one day, Emma seemed her old self, maybe even a little softer than Donovan knew her to be. It took no time to figure out that she had found another means of getting what she needed. This time it was oxycodone. This time it was from a man in a van.

Donovan had tried to talk to her, to get her help, but Emma wouldn't have it. Soon, she switched out oxy for fentanyl: cheaper, stronger, faster. Within the following year, she needed more than the baby blue tablets to keep her steady. Donovan recalled the first time she'd seen her sister shoot up.

"Relax," Emma had told her, "it's just a different way to take it, sis. Same medicine."

Emma had been careful to not let Donovan see this method of ingestion a second time. But that courtesy did not spare the young med student any discomfort. She was there the night Emma began to sweat so profusely that her hair and clothes were stuck to her skin. While both girls tried to deduce what was happening, Emma started gasping for air. By the time Donovan located her cell phone, she had stopped gasping, dead at twenty-six.

A week after her sister's funeral, two things happened in quick succession: Donovan changed the focus of her premed studies to incorporate forensic psychiatry, and she murdered the man in the van.

Donovan's vision blurred as she accessed the memory of her first kill, how he had begged, how good it felt, how methodically and efficiently she'd performed the task.

She knew where to find him, having followed Emma on more than one occasion. There was no moon that night. A camper and abandoned car occupied one end of the lot adjacent to the playground, the large van alone at the other. She saw that he had nodded off with his head against the seat rest. She tapped the glass. He bolted awake, assessed his visitor, and rolled down the window.

Donovan recalled telling him that she was desperate and to please skip the part where he would pretend to not understand what she was talking about. She needed five vials of FuF (the street name for the furanylfentanyl solution that she found in Emma's purse); a friend of a friend told her that he could hook her up. She had cash.

After calculated consideration and having been charmed by her good looks and nerve, he smiled. "Well now, you are one lucky young lady. I just might be able to help you out." He got up and disappeared into the van. She moved to the back and knocked. He cracked open one of the two doors, scowling.

"I'm freezing. I gotta get it in me right now. Please let me in—just for a minute—just 'til I boot up. Please, mister."

Again, he smiled, then opened the door wider, gesturing for her to climb in. She did. He closed the door. It was dark in the van. He did not notice that she wore surgical gloves.

He turned on a lantern, revealing a bunk bed over the front seat, a dinette table to one side, and a sink and two burners to the other.

"Gonna be $150, beauty. Put it on the table," he said, turning on a battery-operated push light glued to the ceiling.

"I heard it was $100." She placed a one-hundred-dollar bill on the chipped Formica.

"You heard wrong. Maybe we can work something out," he hissed, grabbing at her coat.

"Okay, whatever. I don't care. But I need it first. Please."

He exhumed a suitcase from under the front seat and placed it on the table. In it was an array of drugs in a variety of applications from pills to patches. Nestled among them were two stacks of money. He laid out five vials next to the bill, secured the clasp on the suitcase, and set it on a folding chair. "Hurry up."

That was all she needed. The rest was so easy.

A hard punch to his nose with her elbow knocked him backward. He stumbled. She picked up the lantern and butted him in the forehead hard enough to knock him out. Extracting zip ties from her coat pocket, she bound his wrists then ankles.

Planning to gag him with the cheap scarf she had around her neck, the novice killer got another idea. She unclasped the suitcase and took the money.

She remembered thinking, *This will work; no reason to not be poetic whenever possible* as she stuffed the dirty, crumpled bills into his gaping mouth.

Removing a hypodermic syringe from her other pocket, she opened one vial then another, filling the syringe. It was in his arm when he woke.

Donovan brought back each moment as if in freeze-frame: first the terror in his eyes then his breathing becoming shallow as his pupils all but disappeared. She recalled in vivid detail watching the vomit ooze from his lips through the blood money that kept him from screaming. And she remembered when his heart stopped.

As she sat at her polished desk in her Lincoln Square office, the doctor considered how these memories still affected her so viscerally.

True what they say. You never forget your first.

She had wanted to do something like that for as long as she could remember. Every time a child died at the hands of someone they loved and trusted, every time one of her classmates was killed by a drunk driver. It was everything she thought it would be. With that man, standards were set and a code of ethics was locked into place. She would only kill those arrogant enough to think that they had gotten away with murder. Unfortunately for the people she shared the world with, there were plenty of those.

One last thing she recalled about that night: She'd gone from her first murder to seek out a guy from one of her classes that she'd flirted with around campus and had gone out with once just before Emma died. His name was Rick. Whatever he'd expected when he opened the door of his apartment to find her there that night, it surely wasn't her storming him, shoving him to the floor, and taking full advantage of his swift and unexpected erection.

He'd gotten a couple of questioning words out as she tore open his shirt and unzipped his jeans, but he didn't try to stop her, and the words swiftly morphed into inarticulate exclamations of surprise and arousal. He'd had a nice torso—lean, muscular, and hairless. He'd been a competitive swimmer, she recalled.

She was silent as she yanked his jeans and briefs down to this knees. She remembered that his cock, quivering and engorged, was a shade between tan and mauve. The veins stood out, dark against the lighter flesh. She remembered how badly she'd wanted it. She'd grasped it with one hand, pulling it ungently upright, then rucked up her skirt, pulled her panties aside, and impaled herself on it. Pleasure and power shot through her, making her vagina spasm and tighten.

Rick had made a sound like the bark of a dog, then settled into rhythmic gasps as she dug her nails into his shoulders and rode him, trying to shove his cock ever deeper, as if it might flip a switch inside her … or fill a void.

She'd come screaming, putting all of her grief and fury into a blinding, deafening burst of emotion. An anthem for the dead drug dealer's passage to the next realm of existence.

Frenetic sexual energy spent, she'd burst into uncontrollable, wrenching sobs. Rick tried to ask what was wrong, his voice strained and airless. He reached for her, touched her thigh. She wrenched herself away from the touch and shot to her feet. Rick came as she pulled free, his cock pumping semen over his stomach and chest. Donovan smoothed down her skirt, grabbed her things, and left. She thought she heard Rick call out to her as she shut the apartment door.

She'd avoided him entirely the next day, and didn't answer his voice messages or texts. She got over her embarrassment when the news of the dealer's bizarrely karmic murder hit the news. She breathed in all the reports, then went back to Rick for another explosive exhale. This time she brought a condom … and she didn't cry. If he was freaked out by her behavior, he didn't show it. He'd decided he liked to have her on top. She decided she liked that too; it made her feel a sense of control that was sorely lacking in other parts of her life.

Donovan knew that she would not be sharing any of that experience with her readers, but as her editor droned on, she wondered whether or not she could share Emma's story.

"Donovan, are you there? Are you listening to me?"

She fingered the small plastic skeleton smiling up at her from the desk.

"I am, JoAnne. Let me think on it."

Chapter Seven

Donovan had no more than ended the call when Angel appeared at the door. "Mrs. King is here."

Donovan paused for a moment to close one door in her mind and open another. Her ability to compartmentalize had always served her well, and switching focus from the conversation with her editor to meeting a new patient would not be difficult. On this occasion, though, she had to close a couple of doors—one she really hadn't meant to open.

Sliding the statue into a desk drawer, she got up and buttoned her blazer. "Send her in."

The doctor moved from behind her desk to place the patient's file on a small table next to one of the easy chairs used during appointments, then turned to extend a hand to the woman as she entered the room. "Mrs. King. I'm Doctor Montgomery. So nice to meet you. Come in. Have a seat."

The woman shook her hand, then took the seat Donovan indicated. "Doctor, I've heard so many wonderful things about you from Fran. You really helped her work through a difficult time after Ben passed."

Donovan seated herself in a twin of the chair she'd assigned to her patient. The two were angled slightly toward each other on opposite sides of the little table. Scooping up the patient file, Donovan quickly assessed Athena King: fingernails were meticulously manicured; her hair was straightened and tamed, contrasting the psychologist's natural mane, possibly indicating a need to project a particular image; a chic suit that suggested money but that did not fit all that well, suggesting the woman had lost weight and not cared or been able to replace the garment. The birthdate in the woman's file told Donovan that she was fifty-six. Many psychiatric patients wore sadness or fear on their faces, but Mrs. King had a quality that concerned the doctor, a kind of giddy anticipation, like a child waiting in line at an amusement park.

"What brings you here, Mrs. King?"

The woman straightened her skirt across her knees. "It's my husband. Or maybe it's that I don't know what to do with my feelings about my husband. That's probably more accurate." She positioned the short string of pearls around her neck to lie atop her blouse collar, then rolled her wedding band around her finger with her thumb. "He's a politician, you understand. First with the State Board of Education, later with the Illinois General Assembly. I raised three children with the man. I swear I don't know who he is anymore."

She spoke about her husband's infidelities and lack of attention but made it clear that those were not the things that had brought her to seek the aid of a psychiatrist. The problem, as she saw it, was his progressively skewed sense of ethics. Over the years, she watched his righteous indignation at the injustices in the world, especially those aimed at other African Americans, disintegrate into dulled complacency.

Donovan could not put her finger on what was wrong with the session, but the words the woman spoke did not match her demeanor.

"Have you considered couples counseling, Mrs. King? Would your husband be open to something like that?"

"Oh, I sincerely doubt it, Doctor Montgomery. I mean, he doesn't even know I'm seeing you by myself. All of my friends do, but he doesn't. We're like that couple you wrote about in your book. Not *In Full Sight*. The first book, *Red Flags*. You know the couple I'm referring to?"

There it was. Athena King was a fangirl. Which didn't necessarily mean she didn't have marriage troubles. That remained to be seen.

"In your book, that couple—Jack and Charlotte Pennington—had to appear solid to the public because of their social position, but what was going on behind closed doors was another thing altogether. They lied to their friends. They lied to their kids. That's why it was so hard to track them and find their killer when they came up missing. Now, Percy and I—"

"Excuse me for stopping you, Mrs. King, but are you saying that you believe that you and your husband are in some kind of danger?"

"No! Oh, no. Not like that. But the duplicitous nature of our marriage …"

Donovan listened and counseled for another forty-five minutes. She did not cut short the session, but she did refuse to autograph the copy of *Red Flags* that Mrs. King had tucked in her purse, telling her that, though she would be happy to sign it for her in any other circumstance, a session was not the place.

As she walked a disappointed yet still exuberant Athena King to the door, the woman thanked her for her time, told her that she was even more beautiful in person than on TV, and asked when the new book was expected to be available.

Angel witnessed the exchange and, having heard much the same on many occasions, took over when Donovan cordially passed the woman to her. Angel launched into a litany of upcoming book events and a reminder that the website always had the latest information.

As Donovan peeled away, she saw a large spray of lilies on the corner of Angel's desk that had not been there before the session. They were the same flowers that had been on the fireplace in Tristan's suite at the Waldorf, and in the same type of crystal vase.

Donovan turned to Angel for confirmation. While escorting Mrs. King to the door, Angel nodded and directed Donovan's attention to the envelope resting against the elaborate arrangement. She opened it. There was no note, only a linen handkerchief scented with Tristan's cologne.

As Mrs. King walked out, Jordan Payne, assistant prosecutor for the state's attorney general, walked in. The man had annoyingly awkward timing.

"Jordan Payne's here to see you, Doctor Montgomery," the admin said with an ironic smirk. "No, you were not expecting him. Me neither." She dropped the unnecessary relay of information and gave the man a genuine smile. "Hey, Jordan. You want some coffee?"

"Hey, Angel. No, thanks. I'm just going to be a minute. I know she's busy." He reached in the pocket of his light trench coat, extracted a black knit cap with the Cubs logo on the front, and handed it to her. "I remember you said you lost yours, so I picked this up for you in Wrigleyville yesterday. Man, you should've seen Daley Plaza this morning. Some party."

Angel's smile widened. "How sweet are you!"

"I really am."

"And, of course, you were at the game."

"Of course I was."

As he bantered with Angel, Jordan kept his eyes on Donovan, who was still standing between her office door and the lilies. She cocked her head, inviting him to join her in her office. "Come in, Counselor. I think I have a little time before my next appointment."

Jordan ran a hand along his low fade, noticing the flowers as he passed. "Pretty," he said through clenched teeth.

"Yes. They are," she responded, giving them an appreciative glance.

He cleared his throat, then said, "I had a meeting in Ravenswood and thought I'd take a chance that you'd see me before I head back to the Loop."

Donovan watched as he unfastened the button of his tailored suit and straightened his tie. There was a definite chemistry here, but she chose to ignore it. Between political aspirations and her work … and her occasional extracurricular activities, she had, so far, kept him at arm's length. It was safer for both of them.

"Have a seat," she said, gesturing to one of the side chairs facing her desk. The doctor positioned herself behind that barrier.

The attorney, eyeballing the couch and overstuffed chairs also available in the room, acquiesced and sat where instructed.

"What can I do for you, Jordan?" Donovan asked.

He perched on the edge of his seat, legs apart, smoothing down his Vandyke and again adjusting his tie. Donovan had observed this habit on many occasions; it was something he did while thinking through his next move or words. She also knew that he was unaware of it.

"Donovan, my office has asked that I assemble a new task force designed to combat the recent increase of drug activity in Chicago.

You know the stats, I'm sure. What was already a huge problem has turned into a twenty-four/seven, four-alarm fire. I threw your name into the ring. Don't be mad," he added, raising his hands as if to forestall a tart response. "I just thought, given your nearly superhuman profiling abilities, that you might find it in your heart to help us outline a strategy and home in on the most aggressive ways to implement it." Jordan smiled broadly, crossing his long legs. "And maybe use some of that ever-growing celebrity of yours to help shine a light on our efforts."

Donovan leaned away from the desk and crossed her legs as well. Then she crossed her arms.

Jordan adjusted himself in the chair and cleared his throat again. "I mean, you wouldn't have to get too deeply involved. We're just seeking some fresh ideas. Obviously, the old ones are not working. Just some fresh ideas and your face ... your beautiful face."

She fought back an urge to smile ... or grind her teeth. "You know, Jordan, last month you asked me to help with a fundraiser to support local libraries because I write—and sell—books. Remember that?"

He raised his eyebrows, blew out a slow breath, and vaguely shook his head as if not sure what she was referring to.

"You need help with anything else? Strategizing a better social media presence, perhaps? Helping your baby niece earn more Camp Fire Girl beads? Car need any work? Where's this all going?"

Jordan covered his mouth but quickly discarded the empty gesture and laughed out loud. "Okay. Okay, maybe. Maybe I'm looking for ways to legitimize spending some time with you, Donovan. But you have to admit you are a logical person to solicit for something like this."

"You're more than competent, Jordan. Odds are very good the whole task force is first-rate. You've got this."

"Of course. I understand completely. Can't blame a guy for trying, though, right? Seriously, thanks for hearing me out."

He got up. So did she. He walked to the door as she came around the desk. "Jordan." Against her better instincts, she said, "There are more direct ways to go about spending time with a person, ways that don't impact anyone's schedule quite as much."

Hand on the knob, he playfully made a face as if considering the possibilities. "Like dinner?"

"Brilliant! Yes, like dinner."

Loosening his grip on the door, he turned to face her. "Hey, you hear about that young woman they found in Bronzeville this morning?"

Well, that was an unexpected sidestep. "Newsome has asked me to work on the case," she said neutrally. "I just came back from meeting the victim. She was on a slab at Alfie's office."

He nodded his head. "I'm not surprised. Makes perfect sense that the chief would want you in on something this potentially explosive, given the whole Roy Barns connection. But how are you gonna help them find a killer while you're still seeing patients and writing another book?"

"Quickly, I hope."

His eyes twinkled, staring at her with a combination of desire and admiration before letting himself out and closing the door.

Donovan blew out a gust of air and returned to the safe comfort of her desk. Where Tristan's physical distance operated as a sort of safety zone, Jordan put her a bit off, in part because he was closer to hand. If they got … involved, it might prove harder to live the life she'd chosen.

She was jarred from her reverie when Angel buzzed to inform her that the next patient had arrived a few minutes early. Donovan asked that she send him in. She had been seeing the man for more than a year. As he updated her on the steps he had taken to overcome the long list of phobias that had plagued him for decades, she thought about the girl on the slab and the plastic statue tucked into the top drawer of her desk.

I can't see the murderer yet, but you—you were there, little miss. You know who did that to her. And I'm betting you can tell me.

Forty-five minutes later, the phobic gentleman thanked the doctor and told her how much the sessions continued to help. She shook his hand while praising him for his diligence and commitment to getting better. And for the same forty-five minutes, he remained unaware that while she listened and offered advice, Donovan had been simultaneously sorting through the few clues she had on a Jane Doe's murder.

The doctor's final patient for the day canceled. Eager to get home and dig in further on the new case, she collected her things and turned off the light on her desk. She stared at the drawer for a moment before pulling it open and removing the statue. She was in the process of tucking it back into the Hermès when she stopped at Angel's desk to let her know she was leaving for the day.

Angel nodded at the handbag. "Hey, D, you gonna tell me where you got the icky little dolly?"

"Alfie," she said, glancing down at the skeleton with its ghoulish expression. "It was with the body they found this morning."

"*Girl,*" the secretary whispered. "That was some nasty shit."

"Newsome has me working on it."

"Naturally. Can I see it?"

Donovan held it out to the other woman, who gently lifted it from her fingers to roll it around in her own, observing it from every angle top to bottom. "My yaya had a bigger one of these on an icon shelf in her apartment. Scared the hell out of me."

"Your who?"

"*Mi abuelita*, my grandma. She and my two aunts were all into this stuff."

"How so?"

"Prayed to the damn thing, offered it stuff, coins mostly. I remember needing bus fare one time and her taking change from the bowl she put the coins in at the statue's feet. She was genuflecting and bowing her head, promising the plaster skeleton she would repay her. I thought it was funny, so I laughed. That was the only time she ever raised a hand to me."

Donovan sat on the corner of the desk. "She hit you?"

"She slapped me. Didn't hurt; it was just such a shock. I think she shocked herself too. I remember it so clearly. She looked like she'd just dropped a priceless vase or something. While we were both frozen, staring at each other, she said, '*Cariño*, never disrespect la Señora de las Sombras. She can protect you, she can bring you many blessings. But she does not like to be disrespected.'"

"What did she call her?"

"Señora de las Sombras. It means Lady of the Shadows. That's another name of Santa Muerte. Skinny, the Boney Lady, the Pretty Girl, the Powerful Lady, there are a bunch of them. Of course, my yaya preferred the Lady of the Shadows because it's, by far, the most poetic ... and the creepiest. She had a gift." Angel extended the statue to Donovan. "What do you think it was doing at the crime scene?"

"Not sure. Maybe nothing. Maybe something." Rising from the corner of Angel's desk, Donovan took the figurine and slipped it into her purse. The Lady of the Shadows was certainly riding in style today.

"You gonna tell me about that purse? Give me a Tristan update?"

"No."

"Hey, D—"

Donovan stopped.

"Did you ever see *Breaking Bad*?"

Today seemed to be the day for sudden changes of direction. Donovan temporarily gave up on leaving and turned away from the door. "Sorry, no. I just don't watch as much television as I should, I guess. Why?"

"You know that Los Empresarios got much more powerful once El Rey was captured, right?"

Breaking Bad she had no clue about, but she did know that El Rey was the Durango drug lord currently serving time for his lethal activities. The Empresarios cartel had grown exponentially more powerful once El Rey was out of their way, despite the fact that their own leader, El Capricho, had gone missing.

"Yes, I know. I read. What does this have to do with my purse?"

Angel smiled and flipped open a patient file, preparing to get back to work. "Nothing. It has to do with *her*." She tipped her head toward the Hermès bag. "*Breaking Bad* had a pretty memorable scene in one episode about Santa Muerte. Honestly, I think that contributed a lot to her new fame. She's everywhere. Not just old aunts and grandmas. Mostly younger devotees, some decent people, some really scary people. Cartels love her. And, for all we know, El Capricho may still be alive and well and running things from underground. He disappeared shortly after El Rey's incarceration. Word is that he was, or is, a big fan of Santa Muerte. They say it was her protection that kept him from being arrested."

"You believe that?"

Angel looked up from the files. "Look, D, I know you don't believe in that shit. I don't either. But plenty of people do, and that's what matters, right? Especially if those people are cartel. You can end up dead either way."

Donovan drove home, pondering Angel's unwitting wisdom. She was absolutely right; what mattered was not what the people trying bring down the cartels believed, but what the cartels believed, and how deeply they believed it.

That, my girl, she told herself, *is profiling for dummies, and don't you forget it.*

Chapter Eight

The Lincoln Square townhouse on West Winnemac had served as Donovan Montgomery's safe house and sanctuary for over a decade. It suited her. The law enforcement and government buildings she frequented for her forensic work were all located in the Loop. Her home was not. She liked it like that. Likewise, those places were easily accessible from Lincoln Square. She liked that, too. Every aspect of her life had been thought through and streamlined to maximize productivity and focus.

Glad to be home, she turned on the art deco floor lamp next to the door and set her purse on the black leather club chair next to it. Walking across the hardwood floor to the dining table, she flipped on another lamp that cast a warm amber light across the room. Placing her laptop and files on the table, Donovan drew open the drape that covered the large bay window facing the street. She knew that she would be spending the next several hours at that table, and intended to get comfortable first, starting with a hot shower.

Picking up her purse, she extracted two items: the plastic statue and the handkerchief scented with Tristan's cologne that he'd sent with the flowers. Positioning the statue next to the computer, she pressed the handkerchief to her nose and closed her eyes. She could feel him. She could taste him. The primal power of her olfactory sense nearly conjured the man in the flesh. Nearly, not quite.

Knowing that the scented handkerchief would be a distraction to the evening ahead, she put it back in the Hermès bag and moved it to her bedroom, positioning it on one of the glass shelves in her walk-in closet.

After taking off her pantsuit and hanging it with the care that only another obsessive-compulsive could understand—straightening the seams, fastening all the buttons—she entered the adjacent bathroom, tied her long, curly hair atop her head in a knot, and turned on the shower, stepping over the tub's edge into a cloud of sage and lavender–scented steam. Pressing both hands against the tile, she allowed the water to cascade over her, clearing her head of the day's distractions.

Sometime later, she returned to the walk-in closet and removed from one of the built-in dresser drawers a perfectly folded pair of flannel lounge pants and an oversized T-shirt depicting the world-famous Ferris wheel at Navy Pier. Both were worn to cloud-like softness. She slid into them, loving the feel of the fabric against her skin.

Reentering the front room, she scanned the area, checking that all was as it should be: each throw pillow neatly in place, both coffee table books angled just so. She ran a finger across the frame of her prized possession, a Jacob Lawrence painting, and decided that the room was in order.

After lighting a stick of Nag Champa, Donovan turned on a programmed music station that played only techno music—no vocals, no talking—sat in her favorite chair, and reached into a small African Bolga basket containing the glass bong perpetually waiting for her there. She had found that THC unbridled her thoughts better than anything else. It allowed quick access to her subconscious where she could plumb for buried information and thoroughly examine all dark possibilities. But she did not have enough to go on with this murder, not yet.

After one long hit, she changed tactics and went to the liquor cabinet and poured herself two fingers of Woodford Reserve. She noticed her computer across the room. The plastic skeleton was facing her. Hadn't she set it down facing the other way?

Shaking off the absurd alternative and deciding that she had not placed the figure as she thought, Donovan went to the kitchen to get ice for her drink. She'd always found the sound of ice against the side of a well-made glass uniquely relaxing—like bamboo wind chimes in a light breeze. She swirled the tumbler to make it sing and felt the mental stresses of the day uncoil.

Returning to her laptop, she gave the plastic saint a glance, then accessed the National Crime Information Center (NCIC), a Federal Bureau of Investigation database of criminal histories, fugitives, stolen properties, and missing persons available exclusively to law enforcement upon clearance by the FBI. The nature of her work with the Chicago Police Department allowed her that same privilege, and she commonly scanned the site to aid in her profiling and forensic cases.

She intended to take advantage of Chief Newsome's suggestion and visit Ruben Ortiz, the Empresarios lieutenant being held at the Metropolitan Correctional Center on West Van Buren. His insight and opinions on legalizing currently illegal drugs, the cartel's main source of revenue, would make him an invaluable entry for her book. *If you'll talk*, she thought as she perused his criminal record. Of course, the facts on file were only what the feds knew about—Ortiz's record of arrests and prosecutions. It made for an interesting read but offered nothing that Donovan did not expect to find: felony drug charges, extortion, money laundering. He had also been charged with the attempted murders of three men in El Paso several years before, but the charges were dropped when he managed to strike a plea agreement with the prosecution.

Donovan took another sip of her Woodford. "Okay, so sometimes you do talk," she murmured. And he might just talk to her. She was a bit of a celebrity in the Chicago law enforcement and justice system; Ortiz might be one of those criminals for whom notoriety was part of the allure of crime. He might view her interviewing him as a perk—a way to raise his cachet.

Logging out of the NCIC, Donovan pulled up the personal history on file with the CPD then turned her attention to Google, reading the few articles that mentioned Ortiz. Concluding that she knew all she needed to know before interviewing the man, she freshened her ice and reseated herself, giving Santa Muerte, who had not moved, her full attention. "As long as I'm here, little miss, I may as well try to understand you better. Maybe that will help me figure out how you showed up where you did—and why."

When Donovan typed the folk saint's name in the search bar, myriad articles appeared. Journalists had covered the deity and devotees from every angle. Santa Muerte could heal you or kill you, she could make you wealthy or rob you of all earthly possessions. Donovan quickly made an assessment that this cult figure worked the same as prayer or witchcraft; if the person believed strongly enough, they could transfer that energy into actualizing a situation—or at least would interpret events according to their expectations for the saint's or deity's agenda.

One thing above all else grabbed Donovan's attention. Indeed, cartels loved Santa Muerte. There were articles, books, and interviews on the topic. Angel and Alfredo were not mistaken. And this particular "deity" had inspired many gangland killings by or on behalf of drug lords who sought her protection. They clogged the internet.

As Donovan perused article after article, her cell rang. It was Jordan Payne.

She was not sure whether she was pleased or annoyed with the interruption. She made her voice neutral. "Hey, Counselor, what's up?"

"Donovan, hi. Listen, I just wanted to call and tell you that I'm sorry if I came off as anything other than sincere this afternoon."

"Regarding ..."

"I really would like for you to be a part of this task force. My ... uh, other motivations aside, your input really would make a valuable addition. And I genuinely respect your decision to pass. I just want you to know the request was not just some cheap manipulation to work with you again."

"You were born to be an attorney; you know that?"

He chuckled. "I do. But I meant every word."

Donovan swiveled her chair to look out the bay window. "I know. I knew that in my office. You are a lot of things, Jordan Payne, and they're not all stellar. But you're a good man. You wouldn't toy with something so vital to this city. Let me think on it, okay? Let's talk about it in a few days. That good?"

There was a momentary silence on the other end. "That's great. Perfect. We'll talk. Thank you, Donovan." He cleared his throat. "So, now that that's out of the way, how 'bout I swing by? We can chat about other things, maybe watch a movie. I could get us a deep dish from Giordano's on Montrose. Mmm. What do you say, Doctor?"

She smiled. "For such a fancy man, that is a very cheap date you're proposing."

"Nah, not a date. Just two pals sharing a slice. Say yes."

"I can't. I'm still working. Can I take a rain check?"

"Sure. Maybe later in the week."

"That sounds nice. Spinach and artichoke, right?"

"Chicago Classic, naturally."

"Half and half then."

"It's a date. I mean … fine. Half and half it is."

She swiveled back toward the desk. Her eyes landed on the computer and the article she had been reading before Jordan called. The photo depicted a shrine built around a larger-than-life effigy of the cloaked skeleton surrounded by believers on their knees before her. Each held a votive candle lit against the twilight.

"Hey, Jordan, you know anything about Santa Muerte?"

"Santa who? Wait. Muerte is dead in Spanish, right? Someone wants Santa Claus dead? That's harsh."

Donovan laughed. "Santa Muerte. Saint Death. She's a sort of folk goddess. Came up in a case I'm on." She gave him a brief description of the saint and her associations.

"Okay. That's cool. You know, Donovan, sometimes your world is almost too scary for me. But, I mean, I'd be willing to Netflix us a double feature of *The Exorcist* and *Get Out*, if that would make me more appealing."

She rolled her eyes hard enough for him to hear them. "Good night, Counselor."

Before shutting down her laptop, Donovan did a search to see if the murder in Bronzeville had gained traction. It was now the lead story on all outlets. The body had been ID'd. She was Cynthia Vandenberg, daughter of William and Mary Vandenberg, owners of the Fresh Start Drug and Alcohol Rehabilitation Centers freckling the West Coast, the same Bill Vandenberg that Donovan had met at the precinct. Apparently, Roy Barns had recognized her when he was taken to the ME's office.

Dear God, that must've been a moment—discovering that the murdered girl was his goddaughter.

Donovan watched a media clip of the Vandenbergs leaving the medical examiner's office through a gaggle of reporters as she finished her drink. The reporters shoved mics at them begging for a comment on their daughter's murder. A ghostly pale Bill Vandenberg ignored them and pushed through them while practically carrying his wife to the car.

A big man in a dark suit held open the door for Mrs. Vandenberg. Bodyguard? Chauffeur? As she bent to climb in, she turned and glanced up almost directly into the camera, dabbing at her eye with a fingertip before disappearing into the back seat. Mr. Vandenberg walked to the other side of the car and got in as the man in the suit took the wheel. Chauffeur then, though he looked the part of a bodyguard.

It struck Donovan how swiftly the news of the dead woman's identity had made it to the press. The media scrum had begun while the Vandenbergs were still in the ME's office making provisions for the disposition of their daughter's body.

That clip was chased by another, this one of Roy Barns. He, too, was leaving the medical examiner's office but stopped to give a statement to the press. Detective Hadley stood at his side, hands clasped. Barns's voice rattled with emotion as he espoused his commitment to legalizing drugs and fighting the surge of drug-related violence. His face contorted with grief as he tried to find words to express the horror he felt at learning that his best friend's daughter was the unfortunate young woman deposited on his curb in the wee hours of the morning.

Donovan shut down her laptop and went to the kitchen to rinse her glass. The daughter of Roy Barns's best friend is dumped like garbage at Barns's home. If this was about his proposed drug legislation, that made a twisted sort of sense. The fact that the girl was an ex-user might make her seem the perfect sacrifice to Santa Muerte—but perfect for whom?

Donovan's cell phone rang again, jarring her out of her thoughts. Drying the glass, she retrieved the phone and saw that Evangeline Newsome was the caller.

"Chief, what can I do for you?"

"Donovan, I'm sorry to be calling you after hours. You got a minute?"

"Of course. Just a moment." She pulled up the app that controlled her media system and shut off the music.

"What's up?" she asked the chief.

"Have you heard that they ID'd the body?"

"Cynthia Vandenberg, daughter of Barns's buddy Bill. Yes, I just heard."

"Okay, good. Now we have a few more puzzle pieces on the table to work with. But I'm calling about Ruben Ortiz, the cartel lieutenant I was telling you about."

"Have they moved him? I plan to take you up on getting that interview."

"No, he's still at MCC. And now that we know who our vic is, Mr. Ortiz may be more valuable to us than originally thought. I just got word that because all of his nastier crimes were committed in Chicago, they're working on keeping him here until his trial. His attorney's still pushing for witness protection, but right now, he's ours. I gave your name and Hadley's to the feds along with a heads-up that you'd be in touch."

"Because if the murder in Bronzeville and its connection to Barns is drug-related ..."

"... and we both have a pretty good idea that it is, I want you and the detective to meet with this guy. Maybe all the words coming out of his mouth are lies, or maybe he's scared enough to play ball. Anyway, if you can get over there first thing tomorrow, I'd like your assessment of that, the viability of the information he's willing to share. And while you're at it, go ahead and see if he'll cop to knowing anything about the murder. If this murder was a hit and not just some ambitious flunkey trying to get the cartel's attention, he might."

After Evie disconnected, Donovan stood gazing out her bay window, certain down to the soles of her feet that whether the perp was just an overly ambitious flunkey or someone higher up in his organization, Cynthia Vandenberg's murder was a hit. A hit with a message. Question was, what was the message and who was it from? The most obvious answer was that it was from someone who did not want drugs to become legal.

Donovan Montgomery knew from experience that the obvious answer was often not the *real* answer.

Chapter Nine

Donovan spent a good deal of time at the twenty-six-story triangular building on the corner of Clark and Van Buren. Chicago's Metropolitan Correctional Center (MCC) had housed many of the men and women she had evaluated prior to taking the stand. Whether those people were deemed fit to stand trial often depended on her assessments and expert testimony.

Pulling into the lot, Donovan glanced at her cell. It was eight forty-five, fifteen minutes before she would be able to enter the building. Given her familiarity with this federal prison and its check-in process, she took those fifteen minutes to prepare.

Knowing that what a woman—even a forensic psychiatrist—wears when visiting MCC is closely monitored, the doctor had chosen carefully that morning to avoid anything that would show any cleavage, fit too snugly, or could be construed as provocative in any way. She had on a pair of wide-leg linen trousers and a matching jacket that revealed nothing of her shape; her makeup was the bare minimum. Removing a tissue from a small box between the seats, she flipped down the car visor and blotted her lipstick.

No visitors were allowed to have more than fifty dollars on them in denominations no higher than a ten-dollar bill, and anything else brought in had to be visible in a see-through bag. Donovan was prepared for that; her transparent plastic clutch bag contained only her driver's license, keys, and a small handheld recorder for the interview.

At nine o'clock, she approached the sand-colored concrete building and entered through the glass doors to begin a security clearance. Her presence there had been requested by the chief of police, so submitting the visitor form typically required before meeting with an inmate had been waived, but the rest of the regular check-in process remained. This included signing in, showing a photo ID, allowing a pat search, passing through a metal detector, and being scanned with an ion spectrometer used to detect particulates indicating any illicit substances.

The doctor understood and respected all of these protocols and walked through each without comment, while nearby, a young woman was being detained by a guard whose name tag read "Brewer." The woman had a diaper bag on one arm and a baby nestled in the other ... and was clad in a clinging spandex dress of bright red so short as to pass for a tunic. She and Brewer were exchanging words.

"What the fuck do you mean I can't go it? What's the problem? Just let me in." The woman had a prodigious scowl.

The guard gave up a long-suffering sigh and rolled his eyes toward his partner, who had appropriated the diaper bag, preparatory to scanning it. "Did you read any of the literature on how to do this?" he asked.

"What? No! What are you talking about?"

"Ma'am," said Officer Brewer, "there's a dress code. You can't wear that in here."

"Why? What are you talking about? Dude, this is my best dress."

While they argued, the second guard—an imposing Black man named Bell—scanned the diaper bag and extracted a baby bottle. Whatever was in it, Bell apparently did not believe it was milk. He pressed a button on the walkie sticking out of his pocket, mumbled a couple of words, then held the baby bottle up and swished it from side to side to catch his partner's attention.

Officer Brewer glanced at the bottle, shook his head, and turned his gaze on the suddenly silent woman. "Really?"

A beat later, two armed guards appeared, and the woman—baby, bottle, and all—was taken into custody.

Having concluded her own security check, Donovan walked over to the guards. "Liquid meth?" she guessed.

Brewer snorted and shook his head. "How did she think that might work? Seriously."

Donovan grinned. "You might want to run a check, see if anybody in the area is missing a baby."

The guard grinned back, then appeared concerned.

"Kidding," Donovan said and moved on to the next stop.

At a desk just beyond the metal detector, Officer Bernice Westmoreland studied her computer screen while tapping her stubby fingers against a coffee cup. Donovan approached the desk, and the other woman glanced up.

"Morning, Doctor Montgomery. You're looking well. Who're you here for?"

"Hi, Bernice. I'm here to see Ruben Ortiz. Can you tell me which unit he's in?"

At MCC, the guards and employees changed constantly. Officer Westmoreland was the exception. On every occasion Donovan could remember being at this institution, she'd been in the visitors' reception.

"No problem. Let me look that up." She turned back to her computer screen. "Say, you see what our boys did in the Friendly Confines yesterday? 'Bout time, am I right?"

"Go, Cubs," Donovan said, demurely waving a fist in the air.

"Okay, Ortiz is in 23. Just so's you know, Unit 23 is not scheduled for visitors today. Gonna be a prairie up there. Maybe a couple, two, three wandering around, but mostly you'll have the place to yourself."

"Thanks, Bernice."

"You bet, Doc. Watch your back."

Donovan made her way to Unit 23 and took a seat at one of the stainless steel tables on a built-in stool. She had never been in this common area when it was so devoid of visitors and inmates. Only two guards were present, slowly patrolling the area. A handful of phones hanging in polyurethane boxes on the walls and a few silenced television monitors suspended from a cement column were all that decorated the large white room. She saw it as if for the first time.

This isn't a meeting place; it's a tomb.

Minutes later, the subject of her interest entered, flanked by two armed guards. His bright orange jumpsuit broke the monochrome monotony surrounding her. He looked the same as he had in his mugshots and news articles, average in every way, and too young to have already committed so many crimes.

One guard remained at the door while the other escorted the handcuffed prisoner to where Donovan sat. She could see that Ortiz's eyes were moist and red.

Does that baby bottle trick actually work occasionally?

Ortiz spoke, his voice hoarse and more subdued than expected. "They tell me you're writing a book," he said, "and that I'm supposed to answer your questions. But I don't know how much I can talk right now. I'm a little out of it. I just heard that my mother passed this morning in Chihuahua. I guess this shit they're pulling on me and my little brother was too much for her. Anyway, if we can keep this short ... you understand."

Donovan kept her expression flat. What was this, a dodge or a bid for empathy—a reminder that drug kingpins had mothers too? "I'm so sorry for your loss, Mr. Ortiz. It must be terrible to lose your mom—twice. I know she died the first time about sixteen years ago."

He cocked his head back. "Bitch won't stay down," he said, smiling broadly.

Donovan raised her eyebrows. "Look, I get that you don't know who I am, but I work with the police. And part of what they pay me for is to figure out if people are telling the truth or lying, and I'm very good at my job. So, let's cut the crap."

He huffed. "Okay, *jefa*, whatever you say."

"And you should probably wipe that smile off your face, Mr. Ortiz. Your chance at witness protection is gonna fly right out the window if I report back that you are a less-than-credible witness."

The man's forehead furrowed and his smile became a sneer. "They tell me your book is about legalizing our merchandise. I got that right?"

Donovan removed the digital recorder from her plastic purse, turned it on, and set it on the table between them. "I want to gather the justifications and arguments for both sides of that debate. In that you're a major player for Los Empresarios and find yourself with some time on your hands, I thought your insights might be useful. Do you mind being recorded?"

He glanced at the guard closest to the table then turned back to her. "I got a choice?"

Donovan took a deep breath through her nose. "Yes, you do. But if you choose to participate, I can promise your anonymity. I won't use your name or where we met. Keep in mind that everything you do that shows your cooperation with the police might inch you closer to helping your little brother—and WITSEC."

He straightened his spine, adjusting himself on the built-in metal stool.

"The answer is that for the most part, nobody gives a shit. No cartel cares if the shit's legal or not. Mota is already legal. Every Pacheco working at the corner bank or shoe store or motherfucking Jewel-Osco buys weed. You think we care? You think we've lost a lot of money over it? Let me answer that for you. We haven't. We're stronger than ever. Los Empresarios has doubled in reach and power over the last couple years. Ever since El Rey got pinched, we own this shit. We own Chicago. We own LA. We own every small town in middle-fucking-America, from sea to shining sea, *jefa.*"

Well.

Donovan wondered what she might send to Chief Newsome to thank her for setting up this meeting.

"I see. And do you think that would be the case with meth, cocaine, opioids? Legalization wouldn't cramp your organization's ability to make a profit? You'll be getting a lot of new competition."

He made a face suggesting how ridiculous he found the question. "Things remain like they are, great. If your *pinche* douchebag políticos decide to legalize crystal or *goma* or whatever it is, bring it. People still gonna be scrambling to buy their shit from somebody. And we're already in your backyard, *mamacita*. Maybe a few million more customers get hooked, that's all. It's all good."

Donovan watched as Ortiz leaned to one side then the other, rolling his head to stretch his neck. Feeling that she had gotten what she came for on that topic, she picked up the recorder, turned it off, and slid it back into her plastic clutch.

Ortiz, catching the movement, sat up and leaned on the table. "Oh, you think we're done? Cuz I don't think so. I'm writing a book too. Yeah, I'm writing one about the trumped-up bullshit pinning my brother Hector to those two cops who got popped in Chinatown, when I know who did it. I'd like your thoughts on that, *jefa*. I think your insights might be very valuable."

She considered what he was asking. "If you're straight with the feds, they'll let him go. If what you're saying is true and you're able to give them the cop killers, they'll release your brother."

"When? He's sixteen. They're charging him as an adult. He's running out of time. When?"

"I don't know. But the more you cooperate, the better."

He opened his mouth to derail the conversation further, no doubt, but Donovan had more ground to cover with Ruben Ortiz.

She laced her fingers together atop the table and said, "I can tell you what might push things along for you and your brother. If you were to know anything about Cynthia Vandenberg's murder and why someone might have chosen to leave her body where they did, in front of a former congressman's home, that would benefit everyone: the police, the Vandenbergs, you … and Hector. That I can promise you."

He squinted and gave up trying to talk over her. He'd clearly been unprepared for this twist in the conversation.

"I don't know—"

"Bullshit, Mr. Ortiz. You know."

She waited, watching as he pondered his next words.

He opted for bravado. "You got that kind of pull, Doctor?"

Donovan leaned in. "If you're a good boy, you won't need it. But yes, Mr. Ortiz, I do." She leaned back, placing her hands on her lap. "You know, they found a small plastic statue of Santa Muerte at the crime scene. Strangest thing. Can you make any sense of that, Mr. Ortiz?"

He relaxed. "That sounds like Eddy. He goes for that shit."

And with that, she knew he was about to give her what she wanted. A deal had been struck. "Eddy?"

"Yeah, you should talk to Eddy. Now, Eddy definitely does not want to fuck around with legalized drugs, but he's an exception to the rule." He smiled. "He is an exception to all the rules."

"Who are we talking about?"

"Salvador Eduardo Ignacio Zunigas. They call him 'El Tortuga' cuz he likes torture and takes his time. He's a *lugarteniente*—a lieutenant—like me, only I'm sane and he's not. Funny you'd bring up Skinny. Eddy's quite a devotee. So, I gotta think he knows something about that poor girl they found. Now, most *traficantes* making offerings to Muerte usually cut off the head, sometimes the hands, drain the blood. But Eddy, he goes for the heart. It's like … a trademark. Eddy thinks that shit is real cool."

"You don't?"

"Hell no. Gives me the yips. But I wouldn't do anything to cross Lady Death. Hey, if you're gonna kill somebody anyway, you may as well get a little holy protection out of it. You think it's something new, cutting off people's heads, cutting the skin off their faces, cutting out their hearts? It's not. It happens all the time. Only this time they found the body. And that's because somebody wanted them to. Now, I don't know what went down, you know, but I'm just saying ... Eddy's got flair."

"And he's still on the street. So, are you saying that you believe that's why he's been able to avoid arrest? Because of his devotion to Skinny?"

He shrugged. "Rumor has it that's how El Capricho keeps slipping through their fingers. They say she's got his back. El Capricho is a true believer. Personally, I think Eddy's just a copycat."

Ortiz scratched his chin with his shoulder. Donovan dipped her head to lock eyes with him. "You're being very helpful, Mr. Ortiz. I *really* appreciate it."

Understanding her innuendo, he sat at attention.

"Just one more thing. Where can I find Mr. Zunigas?"

She stared him down as he flexed his jaw, thinking, buying another moment while deciding whether or not to give her more.

"You know, there's this hotel in Chatham where some of Eddy's crew hang out. I think it's called the Liberty. Maybe they'll hook you up, I mean if they don't kill you. Cuz they know you're here. These dudes already checked you out, *mami*. Count on it. But if you live, maybe somebody could set up a meeting. Eddy would fucking love to be in a book."

Donovan came to her feet, thanked him for his time, and turned to go.

"Hey," he called from behind her, "if they don't cut out your tongue or throw acid on you or nothing, you tell Eddy's boys I said, 'You're welcome.'"

She turned back to him at the exit. "I hope for your sake they don't do any of those things. If they do and I'm not around to look into your brother's case, he's going to spend a long time in prison, bullshit charges or no."

In her car, Donovan called Angel and asked her to find out what she could on Salvador Eduardo Ignacio Zunigas. She did not tell her that she was on her way to Chatham.

"Listen, I have to make a pit stop before coming back to the office, and I don't know how long it will take. But Ange, if there's a mug shot of this guy, text it to me."

Chapter Ten

Once in her car, Donovan tried to remember how to get to Chatham. It was one of Chicago's most dangerous, depressed neighborhoods, and she'd never found herself needing or wanting to be there. Her meeting with Ruben Ortiz had changed that.

She googled the Liberty Hotel. Nothing came up. She programmed the Prius's GPS for directions to the area and thumbed the ignition. Finding the Liberty Hotel would not be a problem, partly because of her tenacity and partly because Ruben Ortiz wanted her to find it. Donovan knew that he had not given her a nonexistent destination. He had given her a real one that housed at least some of Zunigas's crew. She was a threat ... or an offering.

Turning from Van Buren onto Clark, Donovan reflected on how quickly Ortiz had given up the Chatham location. She could divine his thought processes; in his mind, the gamble had him winning either way: the snooping bitch would get herself killed, or she would actually get an interview with El Tortuga for her high-brow book, which would make him a hero. If she survived the interview, she'd help him pry Hector out of prison; if not, he'd just contrive to swing a deal with the DA through someone else.

She grinned. Ruben Ortiz clearly did not understand who he was dealing with.

Her cell rang. It was Hadley. Eager to get where she was going and mentally prepare for whatever she might be walking into, she let it go to voice mail. No sooner had the phone stopped vibrating than it started again. Again, it was Hadley.

Well, cowboy, I guess this is who you are. Mister Persister.

She hit the phone pickup button on the steering wheel. "What can I do for you, Detective?"

"Morning, Doctor Montgomery. I sure hope I didn't catch you at a bad time."

"Well, I am on my way to an appointment. Driving as we speak."

"Oh, gracious. Do keep your eyes on the road. I'd never forgive myself if you got in some fender bender because you were good enough to take my call."

"I've got a hands-free system, but yeah, phone calls can be distracting. Talk soon."

"Just one thing. Is there any way you could delay your appointment for a short while? I'd really love to sit down with you for a minute. Go over some things."

"I'm afraid that's out of the question right now. You know, Detective Hadley, I have every confidence that you're on top of this case. Please keep in mind that I am a forensic psychiatrist, not a detective."

"You are. Yes, ma'am, I know you are. But Chief Newsome seems to think we'd be better off looking into this particular case together. And I've got to tell you, I'm one hundred percent sure she's right about that."

"Yes, well—"

"I mean, we've got to find out who did this horrible thing ASAP. And given your expertise … well, you and I working together might just make the difference between success and a murderer going unpunished. Where you headed? I think you're gonna want to get in on this."

Get in on what? Donovan was as intrigued as she was annoyed.

She had no intention of telling him where she was headed. He should be solving the murder, but the Chatham date was hers and hers alone. Still, his hard pursuit meant that he might be able to figure out where she was going. He, too, would be talking to Ortiz. He might extract the same information. She deduced that Ortiz would see more to be gained without involving the detective. But Hadley was sharp—and persistent. Postponing her date with Eddy's crew might be smarter than postponing Detective Beau Hadley. If she didn't visit Eddy right away, he'd bide his time. Wait in his lair like a trapdoor spider.

Beau Hadley would not bide his time.

"Where are you, Detective? If you're at the precinct, I can swing by now before my appointment."

"That's the thing, ma'am. I'm not. I'm at the Museum of Science and Industry. It's over here on, uh, Lake Shore Drive. Now, what's the matter with me? You probably know what street it's on, being a native and all."

She paused before speaking, as his whereabouts caused her jaw to clench. "Seriously, Detective?"

"Yes, ma'am. I am sorry. There's been a little situation. Look … do you think you could get here in, say, another ten minutes or so? If I can wrap things up here, I'll wait for you."

"You'll wait for me?"

"Gotta run. Do please drop by here before your meeting. Thank you, Doctor."

A parade of questions ran through Donovan's mind. If she ignored his request, would he find her behavior suspect or merely be insulted? If he did find it suspect, would he be curious enough to dig more ferociously to know where she went instead? Would he find her? Could he?

You won't let this go, will you, Detective? I know I wouldn't.

Jackson Park was nestled deep in the beautiful Hyde Park neighborhood that housed the Museum of Science and Industry. It took thirteen minutes to get there. As Donovan made her way along Lake Shore Drive, she took in the postcard-perfect view of Lake Michigan to one side and the stunning architecture of the fourteen-acre museum on the other.

Pulling into the underground parking structure, she received a text. It was from Angel—no message, only Eddy Zunigas's mug shot. He had his head cocked coyly to one side with his chin slightly lowered: doughy face, wispy champagne-colored hair, and black eyes shaped like playing card diamonds under thin arched brows. He was like a creature from a fairy tale, or another planet ... or a nightmare.

Donovan and the image on her phone stared at one another for a moment before she tossed the cell in her purse and headed for the entrance.

The sooner I get done here, Eddy, the sooner you and I can get acquainted.

Chapter Eleven

The museum's entry hall was a cavernous open space dotted with attractively lit displays around its periphery and packed with people. Some stood reading plaques, some stared at their brochures, and others engaged in animated conversations as they navigated the crowd en route to the next point of interest. It reminded Donovan of schools of fish amicably coexisting between and amid the pools of sunlight in an aquarium exhibit.

She paused for a moment, assessing her surroundings, then called Hadley. "I'm here, Detective. I'm in the entry hall. Where are you?"

"Fantastic. Say, you made good time. Listen, I'm gonna be another minute or so. Why don't you meet me at the U-505 submarine exhibit? I'm wrapping things up here with the director. I'll find you."

He hung up.

This better be good, Hadley. This better be very good.

The U-505 was an infamous German U-boat captured off the coast of West Africa near the end of WWII by Allied forces. It took up most of the museum's first level, and Donovan could not help but be momentarily awed by the grandeur of the beast. She had seen it before when visiting as a tourist, but that had been a lifetime ago. She remembered being intrigued by the story of how the Allies had pulled off their heist in such a way that the Germans thought their U-boat had been sunk. It was no less a marvel now. She wondered if this was where Tom Clancy had gotten the seed idea for *The Hunt for Red October.*

There's hope for you yet, Montgomery.

Stepping past the museum's re-creations of the interior of the sub—the small galley, a kitchen only large enough to accommodate one person at a time, the thirty-five bunks that served as lodging for fifty-nine sailors who were forced to take turns sleeping—the doctor mused over what that kind of living situation would do to a person's psyche. She read that all but one of those men survived and were eventually transported to a POW camp in Ruston, Louisiana, where they had a lot more room plus food, medical care, and exercise. But for the inevitable interrogations, it seemed like a lateral move.

The momentary intrigue of her surroundings did not quite dissolve her annoyance at having been summoned by the newbie detective. His attitude toward her, while publicly admiring, seemed dismissive in practice. As if her time and her pursuits were not as important as whatever he had going.

And what is it you have going, exactly?

She found a seating group between the submarine and related wall displays and took a seat in a padded swivel chair. A moment later, she spotted Detective Beau Hadley exiting through a tucked-away unmarked door at the opposite end of the exhibit hall. He was accompanied by two men and a woman. She watched as the four exchanged goodbyes and shook hands before they parted, the men and woman disappearing back into the private areas of the museum. The detective returned his Stetson to his head, poked a trifold brochure into his jacket pocket, and scanned the long gallery as he headed back in her direction.

Donovan did not rise, even when he saw her, smiled, and waved. Reaching her, he dropped into an adjacent chair and removed his hat.

His smile never wavered. "Thank you for coming. I owe you one."

"Indeed. And twenty-two dollars for parking. Lucky for you this was Free Pass Day. Why am I here, Detective?"

She could see that he was carefully constructing an answer. He glanced up at the steel marvel in front of them.

"One of the people I was here to see told me that our being able to hide that thing from the Germans at the end of WWII helped us win the war." He shook his head. "It's the length of a city block and weighs three times more than the Statue of Liberty. How is it possible that we could hide something like that?"

Donovan was reaching the very limit of her patience with his boyish wonder and oblique communication style. "Detective ..."

Hadley got up and, once again, positioned his hat on his head. "Let's get out of here. We're losing time."

What the hell? The doctor stood and adjusted the collar of her trench coat, hoping the expression on her face would curdle his brains. "I just got here."

A new smile spread across the man's face as he guided her past the tourists and back toward the entry hall. While on the escalator, he stood close to her and spoke loudly enough to be heard over the din of voices filling the cavernous space.

"Been a busy morning. I was at the precinct when I got the call that my services were being requested here at the museum. There was a breach in their security system that had several alarms going off simultaneously, and some poor old fella dropped dead at just about the same time. He'd worked in their maintenance department for the better part of thirty years. Poor old guy. Anywho, looks like the events were unrelated. Just weird timing. The fire department has been and gone, and the museum's security team is sorting out the SNAFU with the alarms."

Moving through the entry hall, they exited into the parking structure.

"Belt and suspenders," he said. "You know that expression, Doctor Montgomery?"

Donovan stopped dead in her tracks, crossed her arms, and stared at him. "Excuse me?"

"My daddy used to say that when he wanted to be extra sure about something; belt and suspenders. Guess that's what they were doing by calling me in." With breathtaking quickness, a sober expression replaced his smile. "Right before being called here, I was able to get confirmation that Cynthia Vandenberg recently broke up with a guy she'd been seeing for a while. Fellow's a foot soldier for Los Empresarios. From what I hear, he wasn't happy about that breakup. But Cynthia was looking for a fresh start, committed to getting clean and turning her back on all of her drug affiliations. From what I hear, he didn't take that well either."

Donovan softened her stance and slid her hands into her coat pockets. "Retaliation? Is that what you're thinking? That maybe this has nothing to do with Barns?"

"No. I definitely think this has something to do with Barns. Her being deposited there was no coincidence."

She glanced out over the parked cars, thinking.

"Nah, you don't think it's a coincidence either, Doctor Montgomery." He stepped away from her, inching farther into the lot. "Where're you parked? I was hoping to hitch a ride."

She turned back to him. "Don't you have a car, Detective? How did you get here? And sorry to be blunt, but why couldn't you have told me this over the phone? Why did you feel the need to drag me away from my work?"

He looked down at the cement and gently pushed around a cigarette butt with the toe of his boot. "That's the thing, ma'am. I would have. Would have done just that. But while I was dealing with the museum's concerns, I got another call. A body has been found next to a dumpster behind a taqueria on Twenty-Sixth Street in Little Village. The guy was cartel. Small-time, but cartel. Shot at close range with a two high-caliber rounds. One eye's been removed. When I heard that, I thought of you. Thought how we're in this together and how I'd like for you to take a look with me. What do you think? Will you come check it out?"

And you couldn't have mentioned it over the phone? "You think there's some connection?"

He pushed back the Stetson, releasing a wave of thick golden locks. "Hard to say. These cartel folks kill one another all the time. There's just something about the timing I find bothersome."

Bothersome. "I will say, removing an eye was an interesting touch."

"Yep. Downright Shakespearian."

Donovan's eyebrows rose.

"What? I do read, Doctor Montgomery. Look, I've already asked them to keep the body where it is until we get over there. And I'll have somebody from the precinct drive me back. What do you say?"

Begrudgingly, Donovan pulled her key fob from her purse. "Follow me."

As he climbed into the passenger seat and she positioned herself behind the wheel, she could feel him staring at her.

"They tell me that sub in there nearly won the war for the Nazis before we seized it," he said as they both fastened their seat belts. "Ironic, seeing that thing today. You know, I've been reading up on this drug trafficking business, and turns out that the cartels are using subs to move their product."

She glanced over at him then started the car. "I've heard that."

"I hadn't. Subs! Smaller than that one, 'course." He nodded toward the museum. "Got 'em maneuvering through the Caribbean and along the Pacific Coast straight into the US. It wouldn't surprise me to find out that someday soon, they're trafficking right through the Great Lakes and straight into Chicago. Yes, ma'am. The folks behind this drug business are no different than those Nazis. This is just a different war."

Donovan made a mental note: *It may seem like he's babbling, but he never is. He's thinking, sometimes out loud. And he's calculating each response.*

"What's the name of the taqueria?" she asked, pulling out onto the street.

"Lupe's," he answered, opening Google Maps on his cell and cranking up the volume so she could hear the directions.

They did not talk for the first few minutes of the short drive from the museum to Little Village. The only voice was that of the robotic female voice giving them periodic directions. At first, Donovan found the lack of conversation a little odd. In her experience with the man, he always had something to say. But after assessing his constant adjustment of the cell to maximize her ability to hear it, she realized he was staying quiet so that she would get them there as quickly as possible.

"Detective, we're good. I know the way. Just give me the address."

She noted that he seemed relieved, his shoulders relaxed, his smile returned. He gave her the address and, for the last five minutes of the drive, he read to her from the museum brochure that he had stuck in his jacket pocket. Too late to alter the outcome, Donovan regretted having told him that she knew how to get where they were going.

They drove under the terra-cotta arch that read *"Bienvenidos* a Little Village" on Twenty-Sixth Street, marking the neighborhood's main drag. Donovan knew the area to be touted for a diverse assortment of shops, evidenced by the Western wear, sequined *quinceañera* dresses, bakeries, and Mexican grocers lining both sides of the thoroughfare. She took in the colorful murals adorning the buildings. Everything looked friendly. But the doctor also knew that was not always the case in this part of Chicago.

The restaurant was easy to find. Three police cars and a coroner's van were still onsite. The building sat apart from its neighbors, distanced by dirt lots to either side. Yellow tape and fold-out barricades surrounding the eatery, including the adjacent outdoor dining area and parking lot. Patrons and passers-by stood near the tape, staring at the action taking place behind the restaurant.

Donovan scanned the faces. Some looked disgusted. She could not tell if the disgust was aimed at the crime or the cops. Others seemed as if they were watching a movie that they had seen one too many times.

Doctor and detective walked across broken asphalt toward the back of the building. There, the asphalt ended and a carpet of gravel covered the ground. A coroner's van stood idle a few feet from the body. The back doors of the van were open, flanked by two attendants, one leaning against the vehicle, the other texting someone or playing a game on her cell, Donovan couldn't tell.

Hadley approached the policeman standing nearest the dead man. Donovan followed.

"Sturgis, am I right?" Detective Hadley smiled at the police officer while extracting surgical gloves from his pocket and putting them on.

"Yes, sir, Dan Sturgis. Impressive. Lots of names to memorize."

"Great with names. That's why they hired me."

The officer returned Hadley's grin.

"This is Doctor Montgomery, Dan. She's a forensic psychiatrist, works with the department."

Donovan exchanged nods of greeting with Officer Sturgis.

Hadley knelt next to the dead body and continued his introduction. "She's famous. Written some great books on profiling. Helps solve a lot of crimes."

The officer turned to Donovan again, uncertainty creasing his brow. "Oh. That's great. Congratulations."

Donovan tried to smile at the man, then frowned down at Hadley. She remained standing, positioning herself on the opposite side of the victim, who was lying on his back in a pool of blood. His left eye was missing.

Officer Sturgis spoke to the detective. "We left him exactly as we found him, sir, just like you asked."

"I appreciate that. What do we know?"

"A little more than we reported earlier, sir. His name was Chevy Velasco. Had a rap sheet couple miles long—selling, petty theft, public intoxication, tagging, assault, you name it. He was a foot soldier for Los Empresarios. Shot with a Glock 23, close range. Entered under a shoulder blade and exited between the left pec and breast bone. Everything's been dusted, and Yvonne took a bunch of photos."

"Straight through the heart."

"Yes, sir. We retrieved the bullet."

"Just one?"

"Yes, sir. Found it lodged in the dumpster here." The policeman tapped against the chipped green paint on one of the rusted dumpsters, showing the detective and doctor where the bullet landed.

"And the eye?"

"No sir, we didn't find that. Made a thorough sweep for it, too."

"Was he packing?"

"Yes, sir. A Taurus .357. It's in his jacket."

Hadley retrieved the gun, smelled it, and put it back in the man's pocket.

"Any idea about the time of death?"

"He lived alone in an apartment on South Spaulding. We'll check with the neighbors, see what they know. The owner of the taqueria was here when they closed. They close at midnight. He didn't see anything out of the ordinary when he left around one a.m. He did recognize the victim as a regular, though. Says Velasco threw a punch at a guy here last night, Hispanic, about the same age, he figures. He broke it up and everything calmed down, so he thought. A cook found the body this morning when he showed up to open around eight thirty."

"Any idea what upset Mr. Velasco?"

"No, sir. Owner says it was just one punch. Both men stayed after it was over, so the owner figured they sorted it out, whatever it was." The officer pointed at the body. "Maybe not."

Detective Hadley thanked Officer Sturgis. "I'll give you a holler if we need anything else."

Now alone with the body, Hadley motioned to Donovan. "Join me? Please," he added.

She knelt beside the dead man's head directly across from the detective.

"What do you see?" he asked her.

Donovan took a moment to assess the corpse, aware of Hadley studying her. She met his gaze, then reached into her coat pocket, pulled out a pair of disposable gloves, and worked them over her fingers. She pressed her thumb against the victim's cheek, the one under his existing eye.

"The skin is beginning to discolor," she said. "That can start as soon as thirty minutes to an hour after death, but weather can affect it, and it was cold enough last night to slow down that process. In the early stages of lividity, usually less than four hours, the skin can still be blanched when you press it." She again pressed her thumb against his cheek. "Here, the discoloration doesn't dissipate. That indicates six to ten hours ago."

She moved her fingers to the dead man's jaw, then to the skin around his eyes. "But adding to that, rigor mortis is already starting to set in, so closer to that ten-hour mark than six. Always shows up in the face and neck first." She sat back on her heels and said to the detective, "I'd say the murder took place sometime between two and three in the morning. Of course, Alfie will be the official word on that."

Hadley winked. "See, now that kind of deducing is one of the reasons I wanted you here. Okay, he's cartel—probably low on the ladder. Shot in the middle of the night, nothing arbitrary about it. He either answered a call to come here or he made the call to meet someone. Feels like an ambush to me, so I'm leaning toward the former. Then there's that missing eyeball to consider."

Dried blood freckled the dead man's neck and chin from the gunshot to the chest, and blood still moist and glistening beaded from the empty socket like gummy red tears on his cheek.

Donovan mulled over the situation. "Fresh wound. He wasn't stabbed in the eye. It appears that it was scooped from the socket with something smooth because the lid is still intact."

Hadley nodded. "I agree, which has me thinking it was planned. And the eye wasn't found, so whoever did the scooping took it. Maybe still has it."

"Could be a trophy."

"Crossed my mind. Sets this apart from your everyday gangland antics."

"Not necessarily," she said. "Shot through the back." Donovan tilted the body on its side enough to see the entrance wound visible on his leather jacket. "Close range, indeed. Alfie can tell us if there's any stippling on the skin, but I'll bet that there is. Looks like the barrel was probably touching the jacket. The size of the exit wound would support that theory." She let him roll back to his original position, noticing, as she did, the several tattoos on his neck.

"Yep. Again, we're in agreement. Then there's this gash on his forehead."

Hadley got up and reenacted what he considered had taken place. "He shows up. Maybe he knows who called him here, maybe he doesn't. Could be the fellow he had a row with earlier. Maybe he called him up and asks if he wants to finish their conversation in the parking lot. Not sure. But my sense is that he wasn't ready for this. Gun still in his jacket. So he shows up, looks around, nothing. Maybe something hits the dumpster —a rock or bottle ..." He scans the gravel around the bin. "Here ya go. Could've been this crushed can." The detective slid the can into a small evidence bag pulled from another pocket. "He spins around to see what it was, so now he's facing the dumpster, and his assailant sticks his gun into his back and pulls the trigger. Then ..."

"... he falls against the dumpster and cuts his forehead. That works," Donovan finished his thought as she approached the bin and scanned the metal lip. "This might be blood," she said, pointing to a dark splotch. "After hitting his head, he fell to the ground, and the killer or killers removed the eye."

Hadley stood at her shoulder, peering at the possible blood as she pulled off her gloves and deposited them in the dumpster. The detective took a few photos of the dumpster with his cell, then scraped some of the mystery substance on a slide produced from the same pocket as the bag.

"Someone," he observed, "was very angry with Mr. Velasco."

"Clearly. But why do you think this has anything to do with Cynthia Vandenberg's murder?"

He removed his gloves and placed both hands on his hips. "Well, there's no *concrete* reason to think so. These cartel folks can find plenty of excuses to off one another. And the punch he threw might have inspired retaliation." He stepped closer to Donovan. "But she knew these guys, at least some of them. Could be somebody was unhappy about her getting killed. Or the way she was killed. Or the message that it sent, which might have something to do with legalizing the drugs they're in the business of selling. I don't know."

Donovan could read his thoughts. He was fishing. Asking, *Am I way off, or am I onto something?*

"It's worth consideration," she said.

Hadley smiled. "Something to think about. Well, let's get you on your way. Get you to that appointment."

He escorted her away from the scene and toward where she'd left her car at the front of the restaurant. Her initial annoyance at meeting with the detective had dissipated. The body behind Lupe's offered some interesting possibilities, perhaps even pieces to the puzzle she was compelled to solve. More importantly. it provided her a crash course into the mind of Beau Hadley.

"Alfredo showed me the plastic saint you found with Cynthia's body," she told him.

He looked at her for a moment then back toward the crime scene as they stepped onto the asphalt. "Creepy little thing, isn't it?" he said. Again, he made eye contact with the doctor. "What do you make of it?"

"I'm not sure. You must've noticed the tattoo on Velasco's neck."

"I did. Same saint. Cynthia had one too. I think they're all the rage. All the most fashionable cartel members have them tucked between inked images of lost loved ones and Jesus Christ."

Donovan grinned, pulling her key fob from her pocket. "I'll admit I hadn't heard of that folk saint before yesterday. How 'bout you?"

"No. No, ma'am, I most definitely had not."

"You talk to Newsome about it?"

"I did. It didn't seem as significant to her as it did to me."

"So, you were intrigued."

"Yeah, well, it wasn't any more 'Midnight Horror Show' than the rest of the murder, but it was thought-provoking. Seemed to mean a lot to Mrs. Chavez, Barns's housekeeper. She was adamant about us keeping it with the girl as some sort of protection for her soul."

At the car, Donovan turned back to the detective, resting one hand against the door frame. "You need to convince the chief to look into that aspect of this investigation further. There may be something to it. It could be that someone near where the murder took place put it next to the body as some kind of protection. But it might have been meant as a signature, or another message, or an addendum to the initial message, which could be that Barns needs to back off his push to legalize drugs."

"You don't think it was placed there by the killer or killers as protection," Hadley pressed.

Donovan calculated her response. "It may have been. But maybe the protection was not meant for Cynthia Vandenberg. Maybe it was meant for the killer."

Hadley's brow furrowed. "I'll do what I can. The force has been working overtime on this wave of drug busts taking place in the city. Unfortunately, I'm still the new kid. I only have Newsome's ear to a certain degree. But I'll bring it up to her again. If you think it's important, then I think it's important."

"Good. Thanks. And one more thing. There's a cartel lieutenant named Eddy Zunigas I believe may be well-acquainted with Ruben Ortiz. You might want to follow up on him and his whereabouts prior to the murder."

"You think he's involved?"

She slid into the car before answering. "I don't know, Detective. I study crime scenes and bodies for forensic evidence. I don't solve crimes."

He glanced up at the sky, then back at her. "That's not what I hear." He cocked his head to one side and asked, "Why did you just give me that name? Forgive me, ma'am, but you're not what anyone would call a natural-born team player. If you've got something I don't, why hand it to me?"

She had debated that question long before offering Hadley the information. Holding his gaze, she gave him a partial answer. "Because I want you to solve this case so that I can finish my book and tend to my patients."

The corners of his mouth twitched. "Of course."

And I want to level the playing field so we'll know who gets there first, you or me. She left that part unspoken, but Donovan thought she could see the whole truth reflected back at her from his bright blue eyes.

"Say, you wouldn't care to join me in visiting Mr. Ortiz, would you? I'm headed over there now."

Donovan closed the car door and lowered the window. "Been there, done that, as they say. I met with him earlier this morning. I'd just left him when you called."

Detective Hadley's signature smile returned as he bowed his head to her. "Of course you did. That's where you got that name, Eddy Zunigas. And that, Doctor Montgomery, is the other reason I want you in on this with me."

As she put the car in gear, he reached in, lightly touching her shoulder. Donovan glanced back at him. "With me, Doctor. *With* me."

She gave no answer to that but merely shot him an ambiguous smile, rolled up her window, and pulled out onto Twenty-Sixth, heading back through the terra-cotta archway.

You're right, Detective. I'm not much of a team player.

Chapter Twelve

Driving toward 55 North, Donovan sorted through the last two hours in the company of Detective Beau Hadley. It had proved to be time well spent, giving her a more informed perspective on how the case was being handled. Though razor sharp and equally determined, the young detective was also new to Chicago, the tidal wave of drug deaths and seizures facing the city, what it was to work short-staffed in such scenarios, and dealing with Chief Evangeline Newsome.

Based on these factors, she made a decision: what happened to Cynthia Vandenberg and why was indisputably the department's job to resolve. The doctor would guide Hadley when he sought guidance. She would answer his questions, for the most part. But if, ultimately, he could not make things right by the girl, Donovan would do what had to be done. Either way, whatever waited in Chatham, she would be taking care of it by herself.

I-94 brought her to the South Side neighborhood, which, at first blush, resembled any number of other small communities nestled in the less metropolitan parts of Chicago: twentieth-century architecture comprised of brick walls and sashed windows, ragged, antiquated, yet exuding an old-school Mayberry-like charm.

Driving down East Seventy-Fifth, she spotted the large wood-framed neon sign for Lem's Bar-B-Q. Jordan Payne had represented two men involved in a murder that took place in the area the year before and told her that the only reason he could imagine going back to Chatham would be for Lem's ribs. She figured it would be as good a place as any to ask for directions to the Liberty Hotel.

She turned into the first slot of the eatery's small parking lot adjacent to Frances's Cocktail Lounge and Grill. Getting out of the car, she assessed the street: a liquor store, some empty buildings, a bakery, more empty buildings. As she started for Lem's front door, a female voice called out, "Ooh, my! Hey, fancy lady, what you doin' here?"

Donovan located the voice. It belonged to a woman crouched on the sidewalk in front of Frances's. Propped up against a rolling metal door closed to protect the front window of the bar, she scowled at Donovan. To her right sat a small dog tethered by a bungee cord, and to her left was a large bag brimming with an assortment of items and an empty one-gallon water container with the top cut off. She wore several layers of sweatshirts against the cold; the top layer was a Carnegie-Mellon University shirt with a faded logo and a variety of stains.

"Fancy pants! Come all the way to Chatham for a bucket of tips! Mm-hmm. You be careful. Gonna get that sauce all over that Black Barbie face of yours."

Donovan dismissed the rant and started again for the front door. The voice got louder.

"You hear me? Hey, Black Barbie! Hey!"

The sweet-spicy smell of authentic barbecue coming from the vaguely rectangular building made Donovan think that Jordan was probably right. The line was short at this time of day; there were only a few people outside a lobby so tiny, it could hold only a handful of patrons. The line moved quickly, and Donovan soon found herself inside, working her way toward the counter. Other customers gave her obviously expensive trench coat and boots a bemused once-over, but no one commented.

When she reached the polyurethane window, she smiled and said, "Hi. I'd like a bucket of tips, please."

While she waited, a man entered the lobby, standing to her side in the narrow space.

As she paid for the bucket and took it down from the pass-through, she engaged the cook. "Thanks. Listen, I'm looking for the Liberty Hotel. How do I get there? Do you know?"

The cook shook his head then turned to the woman working next to him. "Never heard of it," she said before unloading a tray of fried chicken into a food warmer.

Before the doctor decided her next move, the man beside her moved closer. "This must be providence," he said, smiling.

Having heard that very line many times, Donovan turned to give him a "you did not just say that" look, but the man stepped toward her again. "Sorry, miss. I just heard how that sounded. I'm a happily married man. But I've never even been to Chatham, let alone this establishment, and I thought it odd that you mentioned that particular hotel. I just passed it, my business partner and I, earlier this morning."

Donovan tilted her chin up an inch and looked the man in the eye. "Is that right? Well, that is providence."

"I thought so. We're land developers—Atlas Development—and we've been canvassing the area." An expression of concern crossed his face as he looked away for a moment. Shaking it off, he continued. "The hotel is on Cottage Grove Avenue, the south end. I remember because that particular stretch is … pretty … well, let's just say it's in need of help."

She smiled. "Thank you. You just saved me some time. Best of luck with your project."

Donovan approached the door. The man leaped to open it. "Miss …" She watched as he sorted through the next words to come out of his mouth. "I … I don't know what you want with that place. Certainly not my business. But just in case there's some less-than-urgent reason that you're thinking of visiting that hotel, maybe you should rethink your visit."

She understood everything he did not say and thought it was kind of him. She nodded. As they cleared one another's paths, her stepping out of Lem's and him stepping back in, he added, "If you are determined to go there, just … stay near your car, okay? I'm not sure that we didn't see a carjacking around there this morning—in broad daylight."

Again she nodded, and thanked him again. After a moment's hesitation, he nodded too, and disappeared into the restaurant.

Before getting in her car, Donovan walked over to the woman crouched against the metal door in front of the cocktail bar. She appeared to be sleeping with her eyes at half-mast. The doctor knelt beside her.

"Hey, friend, can you hear me?" she asked while petting the little dog. The dog lifted his head against her gentle touch. The woman slowly opened her eyes fully and tried to focus. She did not speak, but Donovan could see the hint of a grin attempt to curl the corners of her chapped lips. She appeared to be dreaming.

Donovan placed the bucket of rib tips next to the woman and stood up. Before getting in her car, she glanced back. The woman had roused herself and was feeding the dog from the bucket. She saw Donovan, and the two women held each other's gaze in motionless silence. The older woman adjusted her seat on the concrete and took out a tip for herself.

"Child," she said calmly, "you get out of this hood now. I mean it. This here … this is the *good* part of Chatham."

South Cottage Grove Avenue proved to be an easy one and a half miles from Lem's. But the drive made clear the warnings of the man at the counter and the woman on the sidewalk. People moved like zombies. Trash littered the road.

This place is broken.

Driving down the street, Donovan spotted a two-story building with a weathered wooden sign bolted to the roof. It was typical of old hotels, and she thought it might be the Liberty but was unable to make out the words on the sign. She pulled over to the curb as she drew level with it. The words "Christ Church of the Ascension" was barely visible behind the tagging spray-painted across it.

Donovan took in the sad edifice. Some of the windows were boarded up; others remained shattered and uncovered. A chain-link fence surrounded what was once a parking lot but now was home to mattresses, tires, and other refuse strewn across a blanket of weeds. Shifting her foot to the gas, she pulled out into the road again.

Roughly a block and a half ahead, a figure staggered out of a building on the right-hand side of the road. Though a few cars were parked along the street on both sides, no other people were out and about. The figure stood out. As she neared the person, she saw that it was a thin African American man in a red T-shirt. He turned toward her down South Cottage Grove Avenue and made his way tentatively along the grimy sidewalk. Wary of his surroundings or just unsteady on his feet? Donovan couldn't tell. But the closer she got, the faster he moved.

Head down, arms wrapped tightly around himself, she assessed that he did not want to be seen, that he was trying to hurry past her car unnoticed. He'd almost drawn level with her when his legs betrayed him. He took a misstep and tumbled from the curb into the street, hitting the ground only a couple feet from her front bumper.

In the time it took for him to stand up, Donovan was at his side with a firm grip on his skinny arms. He was a young man—midtwenties, she estimated—wearing stained Dickies and a cheap pair of slip-on tennis shoes. The T-shirt hung loosely over his bony frame. Her proximity also informed her that he had not bathed in some time. His clothes clung to him, stained with sweat. A series of small scabs studded one cheek as if he might have taken another fall recently. Mucus glistened on his upper lip. She slid her hands to his and turned them palms up. Track marks scored his ashy flesh from elbows to shirtsleeves.

The young man stared vacantly while making a weak effort to break her grasp. She squeezed more tightly. Acquiescing, he stood limp, no longer looking at her but through her with pupils the size of fleas nested in the center of his cloudy reddened eyes.

Donovan deduced that heroin was his drug of choice. She also knew that he had just had a fix. And more than likely, he'd purchased it and shot up in the building she'd seen him exit, now less than a block from where they stood.

"Are you all right?" she asked, letting go of his wrists.

"I have nothing," he answered in a clear, round voice. "I swear to you, I have nothing."

That surprised Donovan. She could tell by the way he enunciated and chose his words that the young man's intellect had, so far, tolerated his experience. He was smarter than his appearance would have anyone believe. She could not yet assess how smart but evaluated that he had not been in that place for very long.

"I see. Well, you are not from here, and you don't belong here. College educated. Upper-middle-class background. I don't know if you think I'm a cop or a thief, but I assure you I'm neither. I'm a doctor. Those track marks are bad, but they aren't scarred over, not yet. Usually a person with your current preoccupation would scar both arms before looking for other places to stick that needle. My guess is that you haven't been using for very long. Probably only graduated from smoking to shooting recently. Started recreationally, weekends, parties. Turned into something else while you weren't looking. Three months? Four months?"

Peaceful now as the drug coursed through him, the young man's brow lifted and he cocked his head a little to one side. "Wow. What kind of doctor are you? A psychic doctor?"

"No, it only seems that way sometimes. I'm a forensic psychiatrist. I figure things out."

He tried to smile. "That's cool. Hard to believe, but I was working on becoming a doctor myself," he said, tears welling as he spoke. "Undergrad studies, biological sciences. I mean, that's what I was doing before … leaving. And, no, I'm not from here. I don't even know how I got here."

Over the young man's shoulder, Donovan could see something move on the steps of the building he had exited—a dog, she thought, or maybe a child.

"What's the name of the building you just left?"

"Liberty Hotel. There's nothing there that you need, Doctor. If you're looking for a room, drive a little farther. You'll be better off in Chesterfield."

"The Liberty Hotel?"

"That's right. And justice for all." His lips tightened into something that was not quite a smile.

"Did you score the H you just shot from that building?"

After a moment's hesitation, he frowned. "Yes, ma'am."

The figure she'd noticed down the street had moved from the steps and onto the sidewalk. It was a man, a tiny man with a hump on his back wearing jeans, a white T-shirt, and a knitted cap. He waddled a few yards down the sidewalk and stood facing them. Donovan fished a business card from her inside breast pocket and handed it to the would-be med student.

"My name is Donovan Montgomery. What's yours?"

"Cameron. Cameron Nessel."

"Well, Cameron Nessel, I'm writing a book about the pros and cons of legalizing street drugs, and I'd like to interview you for that book. I'll pay you for your time. And, if you're interested, I'd like to help you get back on your feet. You haven't been here that long. It's not too late. I promise."

He slid the card into the rear pocket of his Dickies and lowered his head. "Thank you."

Again, her eyes went to the other man who had begun walking in their direction. The young man turned to see what had grabbed her attention. She could feel the sudden tension in him.

She seized his arm and shook his hand. "Nice to meet you, Mr. Nessel. I do hope to hear from you *soonest.*"

She perceived that it was grief and shame that twisted the muscles in his face. "Nice to meet you," he whispered. "And ... and, yeah. I'll—" He patted the pocket where he'd put her card.

Assuming the dwarfed man had something to do with her meeting and wanting the young man gone before he approached, Donovan fished a twenty-dollar bill from her pants pocket and placed it in his hand. "You know, I passed a sandwich place about a block from here. Go get yourself something to eat, okay?"

Choked with emotion, he started to respond.

"Go on. Go eat while you're still high. We both know where that twenty's going if you wait. You gotta eat."

Those seemed to be the magic words. He shot another glance at the dwarf and took off without further comment.

Chapter Thirteen

Donovan moved toward the small man as he moved toward her. African American, approximately three feet tall, and of indeterminable age, his dwarfism bowed both legs and arms, keeping his jeans and T-shirt from fitting properly. The knitted cap on his average-sized head covered dreadlocks punctuated by beads of different colors.

When they met up with one another, they both stopped.

"You know him?" the guy asked.

"I was just asking for directions. I'm looking for the Liberty Hotel."

"Yeah? Well, the Liberty Hotel has been looking for you. What took you so long?"

"I had to make an unexpected stop. How do you know who I am?"

He stepped back, scanning her from top to bottom, guffawed, and turned to walk next to her. "Lucky guess. We've been waiting for you, Doctor Montgomery."

"Who has?"

He looked surprised. "Couple of guys from Eddy's crew. You want a meet-and-greet, you've got it. No problem. Things go just right, these men will be able to set something up, get you a sit-down with Zunigas. You'd like that, right?"

She found herself in front of the dilapidated two-story brick building that she'd seen the med student leave moments before. To Donovan, it did not look up to receiving guests, but dim light filtered through a smudged glass door, suggesting that someone was in residence. Over that door hung the only sign claiming the place as the Liberty Hotel—the two words stenciled in large black letters above the metal frame.

"Yes. Yes, I would," she said climbing the three concrete steps to the entrance. "I was hoping to see him today."

The man placed his hands on the ground and mounted the steps on all fours, then smiled, exposing a mouth full of tobacco-brown teeth. "That's not how it works," he said, then ushered her inside and closed the door behind them.

They stood on chipped linoleum tiles. Floral water-stained wallpaper covered the lobby walls. The place smelled of urine and ammonia. A short check-in counter stood to one side behind it, with rows of room keys hung on hooks. A large White woman with sponge curlers in her hair perched on a stool between the counter and the wall of keys. Hers was the first White face Donovan had seen since entering Chatham. The woman read from a magazine and did not look up.

"How is it that you were expecting me?"

"Ortiz set it up," he answered, leading her to a narrow flight of stairs. "Cops aren't the only ones he's talking to."

The dwarf led on, stepping up onto a semicircular landing at the bottom of the staircase. As Donovan followed suit, the woman behind the counter barked, "Watch your step," in a voice that sounded like a long belch.

Donovan turned. The White woman had not looked up from her reading. Was the warning about the staircase or something else?

"Follow me," the man said, dropping and taking the stairs two at a time: hand, hand, foot, foot. Righting himself when they reached the top landing, they walked the narrow hall in silence.

Donovan took the opportunity to fish out a pair of disposable gloves and slid them on. She always carried plenty in the deep pockets of her trench coat. In her line of work, they were often necessary, and given her penchant for murder, proved to be invaluable. She might not need them for whatever waited for her down the hall, but Donovan almost hoped that she would.

Her escort stopped at Room 207 and knocked. *"Abre la puerta.* She's here."

A giant of a man opened the door. Standing well over six feet, he was an imposing Latino with broad shoulders, a flat menacing expression on a square face framed by an incongruous bowl haircut. He stood in the doorway, effectively blocking her from the room.

He miss the memo?

From behind him, another man said, *"¿Qué coño te pasa?* What the hell is wrong with you? Let her in."

Big Guy moved aside with his hand still on the knob. As she stepped past the muscular man, Donovan could hear the lock softly click. She did not have to turn to know that her tiny escort was now gone.

Another Latino with a pencil-thin mustache sat at the foot of a bed that looked like pigs had tangoed in it. She guessed he was in his late thirties or early forties. A striped polo shirt strained to cover his ample belly. Next to him on the bed was a suitcase, an old-school

American Tourister. The lid was closed but the clasps were open. Logic informed Donovan that the suitcase contained drugs, some of which had just gone into Cameron Nessel's arm.

Big Guy positioned himself, feet apart, between a dresser and a set of empty ironing board clips mounted on the wall by the bathroom door. Strewn atop the dresser's veneer top were a needle, spoon, throwaway lighter, and rubber tubing. The anger roiling Donovan's stomach threatened to divert her from the task at hand.

Focus, Montgomery. Anger is unproductive. Focus.

She smiled at both men. A big, bright, sunshine smile that caused both men to raise eyebrows in surprise.

Yes, I know. I'm supposed to be scared shitless. Surprise. I'm not.

The man sitting on the bed stood up. Between labored breaths, he said, "*Hola, Medica.* Come in. Have a seat." He gestured to the bed. The only options for seating were the bed and a beat-up office chair.

Donovan declined. "Thank you, I'll stand. I won't take up too much of your time."

"We're gonna take as much time as we need," he wheezed, rubbing his chest. "I understand you would like to talk to Señor Zunigas. Why is that?"

He attempted to straighten himself and began popping his knuckles one at a time. Perhaps it was meant as a threatening gesture, or perhaps it was something that he did unconsciously before every act of brutality. But by the smirk on the Big Guy's face, Donovan had little doubt that she had been set up. That was disappointing. Still …

If they're planning to kill me, why are we talking?

Regardless of the reason for the interview, Donovan took the opportunity to calculate her options for a quick and messy escape. Casually, she took off her trench coat and placed it on the desk chair. "Please forgive the gloves. I'm a bit of a germaphobe, I suppose." She slid both hands in the pockets of her blazer to minimize the visual distraction of the pale blue latex. "And thank you for seeing me. I'm here because I'm writing a book about the pros and cons of legalizing street narcotics, and I want to get the cartels' take on the subject."

Big Guy stepped forward, pulled a folding knife from his pants pocket, and snapped open the blade, holding it close to his hip. Wheezy held up a hand to stop him. He did not bother trying to convince her that Eddy Zunigas was not a member of a cartel. His allegiance was public record.

She turned to assess the knife, then returned her gaze to the mustached man. The civilized part of the conversation had concluded.

"You let your gorilla play with sharp objects?"

Big Guy reached out with his free hand and gave Donovan a shove. She staggered toward the bed, pulling her hands from her pockets to keep herself from colliding with its occupant.

Wheezy chuckled. His laugh sounded like air escaping a balloon. "You wear latex gloves to an interview? Just like you, we're protecting ourselves. You have gloves, we have knives. Wonder which is better protection? Now, explain to me why you want to talk to Zunigas."

I want to tap dance on his grave.

She'd love to be able to just say that, but that would be rude and tactless and probably start a fight. If there was a real chance of getting past these two goons and actually talking to Zunigas, she had to try diplomacy one more time.

"Okay. Your boss and every other cartel member has skin in the game. I'd like to talk to him about that. Mr. Zunigas—El Tortuga—is a very powerful man," she pandered, "and the book will be so much better for his input. It would make him even more of a celebrity than he already is—just like El Capricho."

She was peripherally aware of Big Guy tapping the blade of his knife with his index finger. She shrugged. "Why don't you see what your boss wants to do? Any way that he's willing to talk to me is great, over the phone is fine."

Wheezy's forehead beaded with sudden sweat. His tiny eyes squinted. She read his thoughts on his face: *Eddy might like that. He might love it. Would I be a hero if I brought her to him?*

"And let's have Señor Lurch put away the knife," she added. "It's not necessary."

This provoked more laughter from her adversary. "Maybe not, but it's lots of fun. Bitch, you do got balls. I'll give you that. You come up here from wherever-the-fuck to set shit up, think you can just meet up with El Tortuga. Who are you supposed to be—Queen of Chicago? Nice of Ortiz to send you over, though. We haven't eaten yet. But Eddy asked me to find out what this is about before we fuck you up. You ain't going anywhere, not to Zunigas or the fucking bottom of a shallow grave until I get an answer that makes some kind of fucking sense."

Donovan remained silent, calculating distances, possible quickness. She assessed Wheezy again. Or lack of quickness. She gave Big Guy's knife a second glance.

"Bitch, talk. Don't worry about that fucking blade. If I kill you, that ain't the way you gonna die anyway." He removed a small glass bottle from his pocket. "This is acid. Get people to talk—*excelente*. Burn their brains out—*excelente*. Get rid of a motherfucking corpse—*perfecto*. We got plenty more. Your call. Give me one good reason not to use it."

Guess I'm gonna have to set up that meeting some other way.

Donovan executed a backward kick, leading with the heel of her ankle boot. It connected with Big Guy's groin. The first kick doubled him over, the second—a roundhouse that caught him in the side of the head—took him down. The knife tumbled from his hand, ending up beneath the dresser. She let it go and whirled to face his partner, who covered his surprise with a sneer and came at her.

She let him come, grabbing his wrist with one hand and his nose with the other. A sudden two-fingered yank ripped through soft tissue and cartilage and sent a spray of blood everywhere.

He roared in pain, clutching his bleeding face with one hand. The other still held the bottle of acid.

Hearing sounds of the gorilla's recovery from behind her, Donovan went for the knife. It had skidded beneath the chest of drawers, its hilt sticking out from the shadows. She'd just scooped it from the floor when the big guy wrapped his arms around her from behind. She reversed her grip on the knife, put her thumb on the pommel, and drove the four-inch blade deep into his side.

He let go of her, trying to cover the wound with both hands. She hadn't been able to aim the blow and had caught him in the ribs. This time, she did aim, for his throat. She didn't miss.

One hundred percent certain that he would not be getting up again, Donovan turned back to the man writhing on the bed in a fetal position. It was clear to her that he would not be moving quickly in any direction as preoccupied as he was with his hemorrhaging nose.

"Hey!" Her voice was as sharp and commanding as she could make it. She wanted the guy's attention. "Your big buddy is dead. So you're going to tell me where your boss is. Where is Zunigas? And what does he know about Cynthia Vandenberg? Hey!" Donovan tapped the bottom of his shoe with the toe of her ankle boot.

He responded with a groan and opened one rheumy eye to glare at her.

"Give me your phone," she ordered. "Right now. Put it on the bed. Do it!"

Trembling, he let go of his nose and removed the phone without releasing the bottle or rolling off of his side. He placed it on the bloody mattress, somehow managing to angle himself toward Donovan.

He was smiling. The bastard was smiling. Blood covered his lips and teeth. He lifted his arm, the bottle of acid still clutched in his hand. Guessing his intent, Donovan scooted backward across the room. But she'd misread him. He broke the thin neck of the bottle against the wall and poured the contents over the cell phone. As smoke and fumes enveloped the space around him, he put a bloody hand to his chest and lay back, looking as if, content with his act of fuck you, he'd just decided to take a nap.

"Hey," Donovan said again, though she knew that he could no longer hear her. She approached the bed warily, nonetheless, until she could see that his ruddy complexion had turned an ashy blue.

Bad heart. No pun intended.

The doctor pressed her fingers to his wrist. She checked the carotid artery in his neck. Nothing.

"Well, that was an unfortunate bit of timing," she complained to the dead man.

After a moment's thought, she uncurled his hand and placed the knife in his clammy palm. She moved to Big Guy's body, checking each pocket for his cell. She came up empty and got down to search for places it might have fallen during their fight.

Nothing.

"You choose today to lose your phone? What'd you do—leave it in the car?"

Like you'll answer me. Unbelievable. Body count—two, cell phones—zero.

As the rotten egg smell of sulfuric acid wafted through the hotel room, the doctor gingerly put on her coat and slipped out into the hall.

The barren hallway seemed narrower than when she'd first passed through, as if the walls had gotten closer. There seemed to be no other tenants, but she doubted that to be the case. They were just in hiding. The noises coming from Room 207 hadn't brought them out because those were the sort of noises they expected to hear from 207: struggle, anguish, death.

When Donovan came down the stairs into the lobby, she found the woman at the counter had fallen asleep. She still held the magazine, but her head was tilted back and her mouth hung open as she snored. Through the glass of the front door, Donovan saw her diminutive escort once again seated at the top of the concrete steps.

Standing between the landing and counter, hands in pockets, she paused to consider the situation. Then, keeping her gloved hands hidden away, she pushed open the door with her butt and stepped outside.

The little man jumped up when he saw her, his surprise clear.

She smiled at him. "Sit down. Let's chat."

He took one step toward the door trying to see in. The smoky film covering the glass obstructed his view. Unsure of what to do, the man cautiously complied.

Donovan sat next to him, tilted back her head, and laughed. "You don't know how many times I've seen that same look when I walk out of situations like this. Always a shocker. Did you think something bad was going to happen to me up there?"

Ignoring the question, he glanced over his hump at the door as if convinced one of the men would appear. "Where are they? What do you want?"

"Which question do you want me to answer first?"

He scowled.

"Okay, well, they're dead, and I want some information."

He spat on the concrete step below. "Bullshit."

"No. Both are true. I need to know who you work for. You work for the two dead men upstairs or somebody else?"

He nervously scooted away from her while thinking.

"Look, I don't want to kill you too. I just need to know. It's a simple question. Who do you work for?"

His eyes darted from her to the street, back and forth. "Bitch, I live here. I work for me. Those Mexicans paid me to deliver you. I did that. That's it. End of story."

"When we met, you mentioned someone named Eddy, Eddy Zunigas. You sure you don't work for him?"

"Shit," he said, wagging his head, hands clasped between his knees.

"You knew that I wanted a meeting with Mr. Zunigas. I still do. Can you help me make that happen?"

The guy looked as if he was about to cry, but he rallied and turned to face her directly. "I don't work for Eddy ... not exactly."

"Still earning your stripes?"

"His crew deals from Liberty. I live here."

"And you've tried to make your services a plus for their organization, right?"

"Something like that. They asked me if I was interested. Told me who they were working for. This cartel is a big fucking deal. Los Empresarios? Shit, I was stoked." He grinned. "You may not believe this, but I don't get that many job opportunities. Saying yes was easy."

"And saying no would be dangerous."

The man looked out into the street. Swallowed.

"So, what are your duties, exactly? And what's your name?"

"It's Titus, but everybody calls me Lumpy ... or Quasimodo. Not sure which is worse."

"Well, Titus, what do you do for Mr. Zunigas?"

"Usually I get the food and whores. Sometimes I take the junkies upstairs. If somebody comes by looking to score, anybody they don't already know, I tell the Mexicans and one of them comes down. Today I was supposed to deliver you."

Donovan took her hands out of her pockets and folded them on her lap. The blood had begun to dry on the gloves. The man stared at them, dark skin blanching.

"Call him. Call Zunigas for me."

He gave her a dubious look. "Bitch, I don't have his number. Shit, I've never even met him. He's like some fucking rock star. I don't even have the numbers of the two Mexicans." He rubbed his eyes with the heels of both hands. "I liked it like that."

She got up. "Okay. I believe you. Now, if you're clever, Titus, you'll believe me. They'll be out here to check on things when they don't get the drug money, and when they do they're going to walk into what I left up there. Now, they don't want any police involvement, so the odds are good that they'll just clean up the mess and go about their business. All in a day's work. But they're going to want to know who did it. That's where you come in."

"Oh, yeah? You hiring me?"

"No, I'm instructing you. Now, you could get on the next Greyhound bus headed for Anywhere Else, USA. That would be the prudent thing to do. But if you choose to stay—and I've got a feeling that you will—you let them know that Donovan Montgomery did drop by and that she still wants a meeting with their boss."

"What's in it for me?"

She got up and started down the street in the direction of her car. "I don't know. Maybe your life, maybe not. I'm thinking that depends on how well you play it. But if it were me, I'd make myself seem useful. You have a good day, Titus."

She pulled off the gloves, making sure they were inside out, and stuck them in one pocket of her trench coat, then removed her cell from the other. "Angel? Hey. Listen, that appointment of mine went longer than I anticipated ... Yeah. I'm not going to come into the office today. Everything good on that end? ... Excellent. Thanks, Ange. I think I'm going to swing by the dry cleaners, then drop off the car at Salvador's. It's time to get it detailed. Hopefully he can squeeze me in today while I'm playin' hooky ... No, I didn't forget the interview at WGN in the morning. I'll be there ... Okay. See you tomorrow."

The doctor checked the condition of her trench coat, impressed that it had remained virtually unscathed.

Glad I wore the black instead of the beige.

Chapter Fourteen

Driving to the television station, Donovan sorted through the points she wanted to make during the interview. She was not concerned. Sit-down interviews were preferable to having microphones thrust at her walking from point A to point B, but both were part of being a high-profile personality. Having been to WGN on several occasions to discuss various murder trials for which she served as an expert witness and to promote the books she penned on criminal profiling, she knew what to expect. But early in her career, the doctor had decided that it was prudent to know exactly what she wanted to say and not allow the interviewer to sidetrack or derail the theme of the conversation.

On this occasion, she would be interviewed by the station's most celebrated host, Patricia Parker. Pat had a reputation to uphold. They didn't call her the Rottweiler behind her back (and to her face) for nothing. Donovan came to the interview prepared to answer questions regarding her upcoming book and the general debate around legalizing drugs, but she was also prepared to shut down any discussion of the connection between the former congressman, his politics, and the corpse found in front of his house.

She also wanted to include a message to Cynthia Vandenberg's killer—specifically that he should stay as far out of the attention of the Chicago PD (and Donovan Montgomery) as possible. Reverse

139

psychology often worked with criminals who'd come to believe they were "protected" or that the law enforcement types arrayed against them were dim bulbs.

Pat Parker had beguiled or bullied many of her subjects to say things they hadn't meant to say. Donovan suspected this was why, though the police had tried to keep it under wraps, the existence of the folk saint's icon had gone public. Pat Parker had uttered the words "Santa Muerte Murder" while teasing Donovan's appearance on her show, and the press had glommed onto it. Donovan was less than eager to visit that topic, but she knew that there would be no way around it. She wasn't sure who had leaked the presence of the statue, but her money was on Selena Chavez. The poor woman made an easy target for a reporter of Parker's experience.

Heartless, bloodless, naked bodies just aren't salacious enough, I guess. Gotta spooky it up.

Donovan wasn't superstitious, but she took the fact that she claimed a parking spot close to the WGN front entrance as the previous tenant was leaving a good omen. At the reception counter, Donovan was greeted by a cheerful production assistant sent to usher her to the Green Room, where guests waited to be called to the set.

"Morning, Doctor Montgomery. I'm Lisa. Please follow me." She appraised Donovan admiringly. "I read *In Full Sight* twice. It's so nice to meet you."

The young woman moved so quickly, Donovan had to just about power walk to keep up.

Lisa tapped the earpiece of her headset and said, "I've got her." She paused, then said, "Yeah, I'll check with her." She turned to Donovan. "You want to visit makeup, Doctor Montgomery?"

"No, thank you, Lisa. Maybe they can just powder me closer to airtime."

"Perfect." She escorted the doctor down a long carpeted hallway, stopping before a half-open door labeled, appropriately, Green Room. "Here we are, Doctor. Bailey will be in to powder you here, I think. When he heard you were going to be on-set today, I thought he was going to explode. Don't be surprised if he asks for an autograph." She grimaced. "Sorry."

"No problem. I'd be delighted."

No sooner had the production assistant left than the makeup man came in. He stopped, gasped, and put a hand to his mouth. "O-M-G," he whispered as he approached. "Girl, sit."

He gestured to a chair situated in front of a mirror framed with lights that mimicked the spectrum used in the studio lighting. Donovan complied. Bailey deposited his makeup kit on the counter beneath the mirror, opened it, and produced a sponge and a translucent setting powder formulated to work under studio lights. He dabbed at Donovan's forehead and nose as he spoke.

"I'm Bailey. And I am a fan."

Donovan smiled. "Thank you, Bailey. That's sweet."

"What a horrible thing, that young girl getting killed like that." He continued dabbing then stepped back to assess his work. "But I told my friend James that if there's anybody who can get to the bottom of it, it's Donovan Montgomery."

Donovan looked up at the man, but before she could explain that she was not a detective, he said, "I know. I know what you do, and I've seen that little Beau Hadley talking about the case on TV. What a cutie-pie. All that blond hair. Mm-hmm. But *you* are profiling the bad guys. And when Donovan Montgomery is profiling your backside—you been profiled. You are gonna have this foul thing sewn up in no time."

Another production assistant came in and marched over to the couch. He seemed harried and tense.

With disappointment on his face, Bailey put the sponge and makeup back in the case and stood up. "Wish I'd brought one of your books with me. I'd have had you sign it. Maybe next time. Anyway, break a leg. Go get the bad guys." He winked and left her in the hands of the production assistant, who did not introduce himself but launched right into his pre-broadcast guest prep.

"So," he said, approaching her chair, "you were scheduled to talk about the book because the topic is grabbing a lot of media attention right now, but the Vandenberg murder is going to take up a lot of space." His expression was wry. "Sweeps week, you know. Bad for the victim, good for ratings." He checked his watch, clasped his hands together, and said. "Any questions?"

Donovan shook her head. "Not my first rodeo."

"Okay, you'll go on in five. So, let's get you to the set."

The first Pat Parker segment was just going to commercial when Donovan and her escort reached the staging area. The moment the director said, "We're out," he walked her past cameras and crew to a seat in the chair across the news desk from the anchor, who was already seated and smiling.

The two women nodded to one another. Someone clipped a lavalier microphone to the lapel of Donovan's blazer. Following a quick test of the mic, the crew scrambled back to their places.

At the director's cue, the newswoman addressed the camera and introduced Donovan, welcoming her back to the broadcast.

"Doctor, we're all eager for the release of your upcoming book, *The War on Legalizing Drugs: Its Impact on American Addiction.* When can we expect the release?"

"Hi, Pat. Thanks for inviting me back. I believe I heard October."

"Excellent. Just in time for holiday gift-giving, right?"

Donovan gave her a vague smile and no comment.

"The topic of the book has become a lightning rod of controversy of late. And, in that we'll be electing a governor in November, an October release might be perfect timing. The public might want to get better acquainted with the subject matter prior to voting, since one of the candidates, Roy Barns, is a major advocate for the legalization of street narcotics." Parker's face slipped into an expression of deep concern as she turned to address the camera. "Of course, it was on the former congressman's doorstep that the naked, ravaged body of Cynthia Vandenberg was found only two days ago."

Donovan raised her brows at the woman's wording and the theatrical delivery. "Actually, the woman's body was found on the street in front of his house, not on his doorstep."

"Next to the trash bins. Right?"

"Yes."

"We'll get back to the Santa Muerte Murder in a moment. But first I'd like to have you share with us the import of this next book of yours, which focuses on the current push by some to legalize drugs, including cocaine, methamphetamine, even heroin."

"That is correct. It will document both sides of that debate."

"Though many of us have heard the more vocal supporters speak out on this—most notably former congressman Barns—some of our viewers may still be scratching their heads, wondering how such legislation would be a good thing. Can you frame the debate for us?"

Donovan nodded. "Sure, it is a hot-button topic, Pat, and I think that's understood on both sides of the debate. Hopefully, the book will help shed some light. But in a nutshell, the 'Yes' side of the debate posits that decriminalizing these narcotics would not only help reduce the current overcrowded and understaffed prison system, but would dramatically reduce other criminal activities associated with the pursuit of illegal drugs like smuggling, burglary, theft, and murder. Also, the money saved by the reduction in special law enforcement programs, raids, and the like could be put into prevention, treatment, and rehabilitation. In other words, they propose to treat addiction like a disease rather than a crime. In addition, if the police force is not tasked with arresting users—sometimes for minuscule amounts of a drug—it frees them to turn their attention to other crimes that take place every day."

The anchor leaned forward, elbows on the thick, clear plastic desktop. "Treat addiction like a disease, you said. What would that entail?"

"Well, more addiction assistance programs, educational efforts, rehabilitation centers, and other medical and support services that are, inarguably, painfully lacking here in Illinois. Oregon is doing this already. Other states are starting to look more closely at the pros and cons of changing the way we look at drug use. To treat it more like we treat alcohol and alcohol addiction. An adult can buy and consume alcohol legally, but that doesn't mean it's legal to drive under the influence or that we can't or don't treat alcohol addiction."

"I'm sure you're aware, Doctor, that opponents argue that legal access to these narcotics would only cause people with a habit to walk more briskly to an early grave while inspiring those who now only get high socially to become full-fledged addicts. All of which would cause more crime, more deaths, and more broken homes."

"You've just defined the 'No' side of the debate. That side contends that drug users are the problem and should be punished. The 'Yes' side counters that the drugs are the problem but that their use should be treated where they can be, and managed where they can't. And, of course, they've also argued that criminalizing drug use—and drug users—has not so much as dented the demand, and that, perhaps, there are other avenues to explore. They also argue that criminalizing drug use simply creates another set of criminals who make money from controlling access."

Parker nodded emphatically, gesturing with a sheaf of notes that Donovan knew were more prop than prompt. "Which brings us to the cartels. What about them? What happens to the cartels if drugs are decriminalized? Wouldn't that change their legal status as well? Wouldn't they be able to work in the daylight, as it were?"

"Theoretically, yes. But they'd also cease to have a monopoly on the product—which would be regulated. They'd have to exist alongside legal competition, adhere to health and safety laws."

Parker leaned back in her chair. "That's an interesting point. I wonder how they'd feel about that?"

"That's one of the things I'm looking into."

"You are?" The newswoman sat forward again, sheaf of "notes" in both hands. "So, you have been in communication with the cartels on this?"

"I have."

"And?"

"It's not as cut and dried as it might seem. At the end of the day, these are businesspeople. They have different business models and different ideas about what will or will not be beneficial to them."

"Businesspeople?" Parker widened her pale gray eyes in feigned shock. "I think most people would say they're cold-blooded killers, ruthless murderers in the business of destroying the country, body and soul, not to mention our economy."

The doctor enjoyed watching the newswoman bait a hook. "Pat, no one is denying the cartels are in a position of power. But legalization might deprive them of that position. Inarguably, it presents a complicated set of variables."

"Complicated? How so? Seems pretty straightforward to me. If legalization means increased competition and lower asking prices for their goods, I would think cartels would not be terribly happy about it. I mean, we're talking about their livelihood, right? Drug trafficking is their bread and butter. Taking away that revenue source could produce unintentionally negative results."

Donovan gave her interviewer a bemused smile. "So, your argument is we shouldn't legalize drugs because the cartels won't like it?"

Parker sat up straight, momentarily speechless.

That's right, Pat. You just backed yourself into a slippery corner.

"That's not ..." Parker began, shook her head slightly, then said, "That's not what I meant and it's not *my* argument, in any case. I'm just—"

"Playing devil's advocate?" Donovan suggested. "I know. And you're usually pretty good at it. What did you mean, if not what you said?"

Parker played with her papers for a moment, patting them into order, and pulling a smile back over her lips. "I meant that if the cartels lose out because of legalization, they might resort to violence—"

"That hasn't happened with the legalization of marijuana to any degree."

"Well, no, but that's a different—"

"Or alcohol, for that matter."

Parker's lips drew into a razor straight line before her smile returned. "Well, I guess we'll have to wait for your report on how the cartels feel about this push for legalization. Do you have any predictions?"

"Just that they'll adapt or they won't. And if they don't, they lose. But these are people who know that when a door closes it might be wise to open a window." Donovan turned her head to face the camera. "Businesspeople will always *find a way* to do business. If they're smart, they'll do it *without* calling attention to themselves."

Message sent. If Eddy Zunigas and his ilk were smart, they'd find a way to open a window instead of burning down the house. IF … *if* they were the ones trying to beat local politicians into submission.

Donovan shrugged, turned her attention back to Pat Parker, and smiled. The other woman stared at her, waiting for more, wanting more, but Donovan had said what she'd come to say. So, after an uncomfortable amount of dead airtime, the broadcaster leaned back, crossed her legs, and chuckled warmly.

"Sounds like that could be the topic of yet another bestseller, Doctor Montgomery." She faced her own camera again, all business. "As we mentioned a moment ago, one person who has been especially vocal on the topic of legalization is former congressman and current gubernatorial candidate Roy Barns. In his run for governor, Mr. Barns has, in fact, made this issue central to his platform." She looked back at her guest.

Donovan let a beat go by before she smiled and asked, "Is there a question in there, Pat?"

Parker's lips twitched. "You interviewed the congressman a few days prior to the Santa Muerte Murder. Is that right?"

Donovan wasn't at all surprised that Pat Parker knew of her interview with Barns. It was hardly a secret. She nodded. "I did," she answered agreeably. "He's a high-profile and eloquent proponent for legalization."

"Some have suggested that his eloquence and very public presence may have led to the brutal murder of Cynthia Vandenberg."

I wonder who?

Keeping her expression neutral, Donovan lifted her jaw ever so slightly, a move the cameras may or may not catch but Pat Parker surely would. She met the newswoman's gaze, her own as cold as she could make it. "That's quite a supposition. You have anything to base it on?"

Parker's smile was long gone; the raptor reporter likely thought she was about to swoop in for the kill. "It's been reported that police found a statue of the neo-pagan death saint, Santa Muerte, with Ms. Vandenberg's remains."

Donovan's hackles rose, sending a hot chill down her back. "Reported by whom? That is not a detail the police have publicly released,

Pat, and they have their reasons for not releasing it. You know how these things work in an open case."

Parker ignored the jab. "I notice they've also kept a lid on the fact that Cynthia Vandenberg is the daughter of William Vandenberg, one of Congressman Barns's closest friends and a major campaign donor. You're a profiler. Do you see a connection?"

"What I see is privileged information. It's an ongoing investigation. If you want to know what they do or do not wish to release to the public, I suggest you ask the homicide chief, Evangeline Newsome."

"Privileged. So you have been brought in officially as a profiler on that case, is that right?"

"I have."

Parker spread her hands in her patented "Whiskey Tango Foxtrot" gesture and asked, "What *can* you tell us?" in a tone that demanded to know why she'd been forced to ask the question.

Donovan tilted her head back and laughed. "Not one thing," she answered, her own tone telling the newscaster she shouldn't have asked it at all. "Good grief, Pat, you know the drill. You know how tightly the CPD holds information in an ongoing investigation. I'm surprised you blurted out that tidbit about Santa Muerte. I'll bet Chief Newsome is too."

"Well, regardless of who leaked it, the icon of the folk saint and the ritualistic nature of the crime are public knowledge at this point. The young woman was naked, her heart yanked from her chest, and every drop of her blood drained."

It crossed Donovan's mind that this woman would be well-suited to a different sort of reality television other than the news.

"The two are not necessarily connected, Pat. Many people believe in Santa Muerte as a protector, benevolent to those who call on her and ferocious against their enemies."

"Can you at least give us some insight into why the icon might have been left with the body?"

"I really can't. I find idle speculation often leads to absurd conclusions. It could be something as simple as a desire to taunt the authorities."

The newswoman tried again. "It has been well-documented that there are many cartel members devoted to this particular narco-saint. It seems a logical conclusion that the Vandenberg murder may well have been committed by one of the cartels. Wouldn't you agree, Doctor Montgomery? Maybe as a message to Mr. Barns to back off?"

"The force is looking at all possibilities."

"But as a profiler, would you agree that is the logical conclusion?"

"As a profiler, I would say that you are working very hard to generate ratings," Donovan said amiably. "I'll leave the concluding to the investigators, Pat. My findings will be given to and released through the department at its discretion."

Forced smiles were exchanged as the newswoman reminded viewers to watch for Donovan's book and get their preorders in as soon as they were made available.

Thinking the interview was all but over, Donovan made what she intended as a closing statement. "Thank you, Pat. I appreciated the opportunity to sit down with you today. Hearing both sides of a debate allows everyone to make more informed decisions. Whether we legalize narcotics federally, gradually by state-by-state legalization, or continue to criminalize their use, it impacts all of us."

"Either for the better or the worse."

"Time will tell."

Donovan fully expected Parker to announce a break and the next segment to be set up, but instead, she asked another question.

"Doctor, tell me, if Cynthia Vandenberg's killer or killers are watching this broadcast right now, and they may be, is there anything you'd like to say to them?" She nodded to one of the cameramen. Following her cue, he raised his hand so that Donovan would know to which lens she should aim her words.

The doctor knew what the newswoman was hoping for: a sound bite worthy of clogging the airwaves and making it onto social media— something foreboding, something titillating. She could add such a flourish to the message she'd already sent; she could stare intensely into the camera and profile the murderer: "This is an act that betrays extreme cowardice ... and stupidity." She could issue a threat: "That icon is the stupid trick that will get you caught."

She could, but she wouldn't. Instead, she glanced at the cameraman wiggling his fingers at her while hunched behind the green-lit camera, then turned back to the newswoman, smiled sweetly, and said, "No."

Pat Parker's eyes widened and her face turned red even under the wash of studio lights. Then she laughed as if Donovan had just told the most wonderful joke, before informing the viewers that they'd be right back after a commercial break.

Parker stood up, glaring at Donovan as she smoothed out her blazer, then sauntered over to the news desk without a word. A production assistant bounded onto the set, quickly removing the lavalier from Donovan's lapel and placing it on the chair. The doctor took note of the small plastic flowers displayed throughout the hair buns anchored to either side of the girl's headset.

"That was—hilarious," the assistant whispered, leading her off-set. "Seriously, that was awesome. That's totally gonna go viral."

"You think so?"

"Oh, for sure. There are absolutely going to be GIFs. Swear to God. Like just you saying, 'No,' then a close-up of Pat's reaction. Hi-larious. Let's get your things. I'll walk you out."

Collecting her purse, Donovan stopped. "What's your name?"

"Oh. Sorry. Melanie."

"Tell me, Melanie, is there any paper nearby, something that has the WGN logo on it?"

"You mean, like a souvenir? Sure. We have like scratchpads with the logo on them. They're all over the place. I know Mike has hundreds of them up front."

At the reception area, the assistant leaned in and grabbed a notepad. The young man sitting at the desk looked up. "Hey, Mel."

"Hey, Mike. Here ya go, Doctor," the young woman said, handing it to her.

Taking a pen out of her purse, Donovan wrote, "To Bailey. Thank you for making me look so good. All the best. Donovan Montgomery." She then removed the top page on which she had written the note and handed it to the girl. "Melanie, will you be good enough to see that Bailey, the makeup man, gets this?"

"Wow. Sure," the assistant said, already headed back through the lobby. "You are truly most excellent, Doctor Montgomery. It was über-nice to meet you."

On the drive back to her office, Donovan turned on the radio. The two dead bodies she left in Chatham had not yet made their way into the news feed.

She rolled down the window and turned on some music, wondering if Eddy's cleanup crew had taken a murder and a heart attack as karmic retribution.

Angel was standing at a file cabinet when Donovan entered the office. After getting updated on messages and appointments, Donovan riffled through the three pieces of mail set aside for her perusal. "This is it?" she idly asked.

"That's it. Hey," Angel smiled, "that was the single most unique ending to an interview I have ever heard you give."

Donovan scowled and grinned simultaneously. "Yeah. I usually try to wrap those things with something a little more salient, more poetic. I just wasn't willing to take the bait."

Angel returned to her desk with the files she had pulled and sat down. "Take the bait? Girl, you were the bait. Like you were some big, juicy worm that was going to catch her a Pulitzer or Peabody or something."

"Well, she was just doing her job."

"I ever tell you about my cousin Hector? He slaughtered pigs on a farm in Yucatan. I mean, it was nasty, but he was just doing his job."

"Now that was poetic," the doctor said, leaning against the door to her inner office.

"Girl, that chewed-up old rag doll did not deserve any poetry," Angel added under her breath while leafing through the files.

Donovan stepped forward and patted her old friend's shoulder. "Poetic and colorful, very colorful."

"Seriously, though," the secretary continued, "the interview went really well, I thought. You kept her—"

Just then the outer office door opened and Donovan's first patient walked in. Donovan disappeared into the other room as Angel greeted the man. She asked him to take a seat and let him know that the doctor would be with him in just a moment.

When the second of her two sessions concluded, Donovan called Chief Newsome.

"Hello, Doctor Montgomery. What can I do for you?"

"I saw Ruben Ortiz yesterday morning, and I talked to Detective Hadley after."

"And I understand you were on the news today. You're a busy girl. What's your take on Ortiz?"

"I think he's willing to talk, and I think he may well have already given us what we need to solve the Vandenberg case. That's what I'm calling you about."

"I'm all ears."

"The *tchotchke* that was found with the body … "

"Santa Muerte, yes, I know. The press is loving that shit. Love to know who leaked it. I hope it was Mrs. Chavez. Anybody else I'd have to put on report. What about it?"

"On a hunch, I asked Ortiz if he knew much about that particular narco-saint. The cartels are fond of her, I understand."

"And?"

"He isn't a devotee, but he gave me the name of another lieutenant for Los Empresarios who is. His name is Eduardo Ignacio Zunigas. Goes by Eddy or El Tortuga."

"Why am I hearing this from you and not Hadley?"

"You will be. I shared the info with him yesterday. I'm not sure Hadley explored that angle with Mr. Ortiz."

"Okay. Let's move on. Why do I care about Eddy ... uh ..."

"Eddy Zunigas. Because you and I both know that there is a very good chance this murder was either committed by some loose cannon cartel member or was a sanctioned hit. And, in that cartels and Santa Muerte seem to go together like gin and tonic, somebody might want to find the fellow and ask him what he knows."

"Donovan, I appreciate the tip. And we're aware that there might be some ... creepy significance to the little deposit left with the body. But the police force is running on fumes right now. If Hadley wants to talk to Zunigas, he has my blessing. But we need him—and you—focused on Barns, his stance on drugs, and the fact that the daughter of a family friend and major contributor to his political efforts was left at his curb."

"Evie, the two things are related, if for no other reason than that the most violent objection to Barns's stance on drugs will almost certainly come from the cartels. And if you're looking for a perp who would rip out a human heart, drain blood, and leave a little *tchotchke* with the remains, you might want to take a deep look at the guy they call El Tortuga because, to quote Ruben Ortiz, 'He likes torture and takes his time.'"

"Got another call. Hold on. It's Hadley. Donovan, I hear you, okay? Hey, we give 'em enough time, these Empresarios might kill each other off and take care of it for us."

"Trust me—we don't want that."

"Speak for yourself. Anyway, right now I've got the man they found yesterday in Little Village and another two they dug up in Chatham this morning, so the plate can only hold so much. You feel me?"

Donovan carefully considered her next words. As much as she wanted to know more about what the police had discovered in Chatham and how they discovered it, she chose to say, "I do, Chief. Thank you for your time."

"Hadley's got this. I'm glad you two have agreed to share the field of play. I knew you would. When can I expect your findings on Ortiz?"

"Next thing on my to-do list. You'll have them by tonight."

Donovan archived her frustration with the speed and vague direction of the investigation as well as her curiosity about the bodies she'd left in Chatham. If Newsome and Hadley were looking at them through the same lens they were the hit in Little Village, she might just have thrown them a curveball. She hadn't considered that possibility in the moment and now found herself wondering if she could do anything to minimize the effect.

She wrote her assessment of Ruben Ortiz with extra care and, when that was done, she had Angel courier the documents to the precinct. Taking a moment to make a few additional notes about her meeting with the inmate, Donovan closed her laptop and stared at the plastic skeleton on her desk.

"You are one pain in the posterior, you know that?" she told the little icon, then picked it up and rolled it back and forth between her fingers. "What's really going on here, tiny miss? Did you come from a good guy or a bad guy? Hm? Are you a saint or a devil? And tell me, Ms. Muerte, were you there to protect that young woman—or to protect somebody else?"

She placed the figurine on the opposite side of the desk. "Either way, that was some pretty dark protection."

Chapter Fifteen

After a day that provided more questions than answers, Donovan was eager to get home, flip on some music, pour a glass of something red, and decompress. But as she walked through the front door of her townhouse, the mellow tones of Marvin Gaye rolled into the little foyer to greet her. Clusters of lit candles decorated the living room, and the faint musk of bergamot and sandalwood ignited her senses.

She had company.

Without a word, Donovan placed her purse and coat on a club chair, slid off her blazer, and stepped out of her Sarah Flints. She moved toward the bedroom, slowly unbuttoning her blouse. Leaning against the door frame, she took in the tableau presented in her bedroom.

Tristan lay naked across the velvet spread covering her king-sized bed, his skin glistening like bronze satin. He sat with his back against her pillows, sipping from a flute of champagne. Candles filled this room as well, and a bottle of Dom Pérignon rested in a silver bucket at the bedside with an empty flute next to it awaiting her arrival.

When their eyes met, Donovan thought she felt the room shift and was reminded of how dramatically this man affected her, a Pavlovian response she chose not to fight, though she knew she should.

Tristan gently placed his glass on the teakwood nightstand and poured her drink. "Welcome home," he said, extending the crystal flute.

Guiding her blouse from her shoulders and allowing it to drop to the floor, Donovan stepped closer to the bed, leaving the blouse behind her on the plush carpet. She could feel her vagina tightening hungrily, growing moist with a dew of desire.

"My client got called away," Tris told her. "We had to reschedule. I'm flying back to Georgia later tonight. But that's hours from now, and you did give me a key."

Before taking the glass of champagne, Donovan unhooked her bra and unzipped her pants, shedding both. Only her panties remained. When she was close enough to the bed for Tristan to touch her; he slid his hand beneath the lace of her panties, running his fingers through the lush, curling mat of pubic hair. He cupped her pussy for a moment, then curled a fingertip up inside her, stroking gently over the mouth of her vagina. She could hear how wet she was. When she moaned, he slipped the finger in deeper, using it to pull her to the edge of the bed.

Donovan moaned again and spread her legs a little, allowing him to probe deeper. "How did you know when I'd be home?" she murmured, letting her body flex to the rhythm of his strokes.

"Never ask a magician how he does his tricks," he responded, uncurling a second finger inside her. "Just enjoy the magic."

As much as she reveled in this intimate touch, she wanted more. She pulled his hand away, regretting the loss of those skilled fingers. Then she placed her champagne glass next to his before slipping off her panties and swinging herself onto the bed.

Straddling Tristan's thighs, she looked down on his fully erect penis. It inspired awe no matter how many times she saw it like that, moving, pulsing, as if it possessed a life of its own, apart from the man.

"Magnificent," she purred, running a fingertip up and down the smooth chocolate shaft, around the flared bell of the head. She leaned down to kiss the tip, letting her mouth linger.

"O-ohh," Tristan groaned. "Oh, yes, you are."

She straightened, smiling, and he reached up to cup her breasts, caressing the nipples with his thumbs. She let him do that for a long moment, then murmured, "I am so ready for you, Mr. Liaquat."

"Are you?"

"See for yourself." She drew one of his hands down between her legs, letting him feel the wetness there, feeling every movement of his fingertips as they explored.

"Well, well," he said. "It seems you have a condition, Doctor. I wonder if I might have the remedy."

He withdrew his hand and used it to raise his cock so she could mount it. The other hand continued massaging her breast, thumb brushing over the erect nipple again and again.

She loved this heady sense of balancing on the knife edge of control and chaos. She loved the way he sometimes took her and sometimes gave himself up to be taken. And right now, she was not—*not*—going to think about how much she *shouldn't* love it.

She rose up onto her knees, lowering herself until her vulva mantled the thick head of his cock. She would consume him slowly, she thought. One soft bite at a time. She was just taking that first "mouthful" when a knock at her front door broke into the moment. She hesitated.

Tristan groaned in frustration. "No, baby. Just ignore it," he rasped, and thrust upward, pushing himself inside her.

She tried to get back into the moment, started to take him in again, but when the knock was repeated, followed by the doorbell, she knew that whoever was out there had effectively hit her pause button, bringing frustration and pain.

"I'll see if it's someone I can banish to the outer darkness," she said.

Feeling as if she had an aching hole between her legs, she tore herself away from Tristan and snatched a silk kimono from the hook on the back of her closet door.

She moved from bed to door with the strains of "I Want You" playing in the background. Peeking through the peephole, Donovan found herself staring at Jordan Payne's manicured Vandyke.

Jesus-Lord. Of all the people and of all the times ...

She wanted to just go back to Tristan, shut the bedroom door, and pretend not to be home, but he'd no doubt seen her car in the driveway that ran alongside the townhome, as well as her shadow in the sidelight next to the door. Hell, he might even have seen her arrive home.

Reluctantly, she opened the door. The man's hands were full, a Jiffy Pop popcorn tin in one and a pint of Ben and Jerry's ice cream in the other. Jordan lifted both arms, showing her what tidings he brought with the pride of a cat presenting a dead bird to its owner.

They exchanged stunned expressions—she because of the ritual offering, his because of the kimono, the music, the candles, and her flushed annoyance.

His expression of delight faded. He blinked and stammered "I ... I thought I'd surprise you."

"You succeeded."

"I thought ... we had a tentative movie night scheduled."

"I see. Well, yes, 'tentative' is the operative word. I'm ..."

His gaze moved from her to something behind her. Over her shoulder, she saw a naked Tristan leaning against the bedroom door frame with his arms crossed. His ardor had not diminished much.

"As you can see, I have all the company I want. So, sorry, no movie night." She smiled at Jordan and shrugged. From the corner of her eye, she saw Tristan shoot the other man a cat-eat-cream smile before he disappeared back into the bedroom.

Jordan offered Donovan a tentative smile. She thought he would dismiss himself, but he did not. He simply brushed past her into the foyer, all bounce and enthusiasm. He headed straight for the kitchen and deposited the treats on the quartz top of the island between the kitchen and front room.

Tristan came out of the bedroom, appearing like a thunder cloud. This time he was wearing pants.

Donovan noted that his fly was up but the top button remained undone.

Oh, God, save me from the mating dance of the alphas.

Jordan and Tristan now stood facing each other as Donovan closed the front door and joined them. Jordan extended his hand to the shirtless stranger. Tristan took it. The men shook hands, holding a bit longer than necessary for a polite greeting. Donovan thought their interaction was like they were arm wrestling, which, in essence, they were.

She needed to get control of this situation and heartily wished that Tristan had stayed in the bedroom. She was pretty sure that it was him showing himself and that last gloating smirk that had inspired Jordan to barge into her home as if he had some sort of tacit right to do so.

She opened her mouth to send Jordan on his way when he asked Tristan, "You wanna run back in there and grab a shirt, brother?"

Tristan raised his eyebrows. "Now why would I do that? The pants are coming off again soon as you're gone." Turning to Donovan, he added, "Baby, are we supposed to tip the Instacart guy? I've never done this before. When did you have time to order snacks?"

Donovan barely kept from rolling her eyes. "Okay. Enough of that. Tristan, this is Jordan Payne from the prosecutor's office. Jordan, this is Tristan Liaquat."

She did not offer any exposition as to what role Tristan played in her life. She did not feel obliged to do so, and it seemed pretty damned obvious ... at least on the surface. Truth to tell, she wasn't one hundred percent sure what role either of them played.

"So, Jordan," she said, "thanks for the thought, but you really should have—"

She left what he should have done unsaid when her cell phone rang from the purse she'd left in the living room. She happily excused herself to answer it. It was Hadley.

Donovan turned to head for her bedroom, glancing aside at the two men facing off between her kitchen and living room. "I have to take this," she told them. "Bye, Jordan."

She picked up as she closed the bedroom door. "Detective?"

"Doctor, I do hope I didn't catch you at a bad time. I seem to have a knack for doing that. Do you have a minute?"

She pulled out the cushioned seat from her vanity, sat down, and crossed her legs. "Detective, I can honestly say that you called at the perfect time. What's on your mind?"

"The body of a second young Hispanic man's been found in Little Village. Apparently, this young fella turned up next to a railroad track not that far from Lupé's taqueria."

The earlier promise of hot sex and the hopefully waning testosterone battle in her front room went on the back burner as Donovan rose and began extinguishing the pillar candles Tristan had placed about the room. "Any similarities to the first vic?"

"Well, I understand that they didn't find any ID so we're going to have to sort out who he is before we know whether or not he's cartel. But I'm pretty sure we're going to find out he is. Might even be connected to the other guy."

"What makes you think so?"

"Shot close range, .40 caliber just like the first guy, and they tell me that one of his eyes has been neatly removed. Listen, I know it's after hours, but how would you feel about swinging by to take a look? I'm on my way over there right now."

Donovan pivoted, scooped her bra from the floor, and headed for her walk-in closet. "I'm getting dressed as we speak," she told him, suiting action to word.

"Oh, man. I really did call at a bad time."

"It's all good. I'd just gotten into my comfy clothes. Text me the address and I'll see you shortly."

She pulled on a sweater and jeans, donned a pair of boots, and shrugged into a fleece-lined jacket. When she opened the bedroom door, she couldn't figure out if she was surprised or not to see Tristan and Jordan in a face-off over her kitchen island, elbows on the gleaming surface, spoons in hand, eating from the pint of Americone Dream between them. They ate in silence, giving each other side-eye glances.

Laugh or scream. She couldn't decide and settled for grinding her teeth as she stepped farther into the room.

Wonder if they'd notice if I just walked out the door.

Tristan saw her and straightened, frowning when he saw how she was dressed. "Hey, baby. Where're you going?" He set his spoon on the quartz countertop.

"It was melting," Jordan explained, swallowing his last bite.

"Yes, that's why they invented freezers," Donovan said wryly. "I have one, in fact."

The two (allegedly grown-ass) men faced Donovan, like a couple of nine-year-olds caught playing with matches.

"Where're you going?" Tristan asked again.

"Same place we all are," she answered. "Out."

"But—"

"That was Detective Hadley. I'm needed across town. Jordan, I'm afraid movie night will have to be postponed … indefinitely. Tristan, honey, I know you have to catch a plane. Let's all leave together, okay?"

Without debate, they did. While Tristan was dressing, Jordan extinguished all the candles.

"So, this guy—" Jordan whispered. "Is it serious?"

Tristan's voice sounded from the bedroom, warm with victory. "I have a key."

Donovan simply raised her eyebrows and buttoned up her jacket.

She checked the time when she got into her car. At a quarter to ten on a moonless night, she put both peacocks in her rearview mirror and followed the directions the detective had sent to her phone. She didn't tell them she was off to meet two more men, one of them dead and missing an eye.

Chapter Sixteen

Hadley's directions led Donovan to an industrial stretch of Little Village she had never explored. Once she turned off of Twenty-Sixth, a few miles away from the quaint boutiques and authentic Mexican eateries, she entered a maze of dimly lit streets. Lampposts planted too far apart cast long shadows along the empty sidewalks.

The GPS instructions told her to make a left at the next turn. It gave no street name. She turned left and found herself facing a broad alley of uneven tarmac lined on the left side with the rear entrances of machine shops, textile manufacturers, pallet companies, and the like, each illuminated dimly by lamps anchored above their loading docks. Three rows of train tracks paralleled the street on the opposite side, a seemingly endless band of steel extending as far as she could see.

Donovan slowed the car, taking in the desolation surrounding her. Torture, dismemberment, a bullet—anything could go down in a place like this and no one would be any the wiser.

What a brilliant little find.

Just over a block away, flashing red and blue lights informed her that she had located the crime scene. She pulled up and parked behind Hadley's car next to the train tracks. Three police cars and a coroner's van were stationed on the opposite side of the alley behind a two-story brick building with Peterson and Sons Medical Supply Co painted across the rear face.

Hadley stood near a white tin utility shed between the buildings and tracks, taking pictures with his phone. Donovan could see the silhouette of a body at his feet. Police canvassed the area with flashlights, scouring the weeds and gravel.

The police had set up fold-out barricades several yards apart from one another on the tarmac. Yellow crime scene tape connected the heavy plastic barriers. The tape seemed unnecessary to her, given the location and lack of traffic. Donovan approached a uniformed officer standing on the far side of the tape line.

"I'm Doctor Montgomery," she told him. "Detective Hadley called me." She glanced in Hadley's direction. He saw her, pocketed his phone, and waved.

"He's expecting you, ma'am. Here, you can step between these so you don't have to limbo under the tape." The officer smiled and separated two of the portable blockades.

Donovan passed between them. "You think somebody's apt to wander over here?"

"Well," he said glancing over at the body, "somebody did."

"*Touché*," Donovan responded, then turned and walked carefully across the gritty tarmac toward the shed.

As she approached the detective, he put away his phone and touched the brim of his hat. "Doctor, thank you for coming. I'm glad you found us tucked away back here. I just landed a minute ago myself."

"What do we know?" she asked, extracting disposable gloves from her jacket pocket and pulling them on.

The detective echoed the movement. Together, they knelt in the dirt in the shadow of the shed, both focused on the one-eyed corpse. The body lay face-up. Still-moist smears of blood encircled the empty left eye socket, gleaming wetly in the security lights of the Peterson and Sons warehouse. His open leather jacket revealed a once-tan shirt, asymmetrically patterned in deep crimson blossoms where bullets had penetrated his chest.

Hadley tipped his hat back and tugged at his forelock. "No cell, no ID. They're running prints. I've got a feeling we'll get lucky, but let's see." He unbuttoned the bloody shirt and gingerly lifted both sides, ungluing it from the red paste. Donovan studied the exposed bullet holes, smelling the tang of iron.

"Two shots. One exit wound." The detective pointed to the extruding tissue in the middle of the victim's chest. "The other's an entrance wound. Single round defect." He then indicated the other bullet hole surrounded by a concise ring of abraded skin. "Practically on top of each other."

"Hmm. So once through the back to take him down, and the second to finish the job." Donovan made a "V" with her fingers to either side of the entrance wound. "You said it was a .40 caliber. Are we sure of that?"

"They found both bullets."

"Ah. Where?"

"One hit that tin shed. It went through the fella's back. And the second one …" He rolled the corpse on its side to show the doctor underneath. In the blood-soaked dirt was a small hole. "The other bullet was stuck in the ground."

"Straight through. Barrel pressed against his chest."

"That's how it seems."

Donovan tilted the victim's head to either side. "Bruising. Even has a fresh cut on his chin. There was a struggle." There was also a tattoo. Sister Muerte again.

"Which would explain the second bullet," said Hadley. "I would've expected a head shot, but ..."

"... but the murderer wanted the eye undamaged."

"That's how I read it."

"The left eye again."

"Significant?"

She pursed her lips. "Could be. Left eye ... the sinister eye."

"Sinister?" He looked puzzled. "That like the evil eye?"

"Not really. Historically, it just meant the left side of something. But in the way that humans have of making the unusual threatening, the word 'sinister' took on a ... well, a sinister meaning. Left-handed people were different—hence scary, hence probably demonic."

"I'm left-handed," Hadley observed, then, "I guess that explains why my elementary school teachers tried to make me right-handed."

The two stood up and removed their gloves. Beau Hadley called over the attendants from the coroner's van, letting them know they could load the body and asking for a trash bag for the gloves. One went to retrieve a plastic bag while the other brought over the waiting gurney.

"That man hasn't been dead more than a couple of hours, probably less," Donovan said as they watched the body being loaded into the van.

Hadley nodded. "I understand that this part of town shuts down on the early side. Even if these companies are still in business—though they look pretty outta here to me—but even if, they would probably have been closed and empty."

"Who found him?"

"A man called it in. Wanted to remain anonymous. Could've been a kid walking along the railroad tracks. Maybe a vagrant."

"Or the killer, wanting to be sure the police saw his work. It takes a certain amount of hubris to stamp your murders by removing an eye."

Hadley studied the doctor's face. "They *want* us to catch 'em?"

She scanned the bleak terrain. "Or they want us to know who they are. Of course, it might just be somebody who collects eyes."

Hadley chuckled.

"No, I'm serious. When the cops discovered all of the horror trophies in Ed Gein's house back in 1957—lampshades, chair seats, belts, a long list of things he made from human skin—the authorities also found boxes of body parts he had collected, everything from noses to genitals."

The detective's mouth fell open.

Donovan grinned. "Well, you and your team will figure it out. How about car tracks? Footprints?"

Hadley seemed to shake himself, then said, "No to both. I was counting on some wheel impressions. Both parties must have parked up on the street in front of these old buildings. I'm sure you saw the tattoo."

"Hard to miss. Our girl Muerte gets around. Have we checked what's in that shed?"

He glanced over at it. "Yeah. It's empty. We dusted anyway. So the first young guy was cartel. I'm eager to find out if this fella is as well."

"I agree with your instincts. This is most certainly a related killing. But is it tied to Cynthia Vandenberg's murder? We have nothing to suggest that, except that we know she broke up with a Los Empresarios foot soldier and had the club logo tattooed on her arm. That's not much."

"I know. Once we figure out who this man is, we'll know more about his affiliations, maybe even a list of ex-girlfriends. I've just ..." He trailed off, his eyes going unfocused.

She watched him sorting through his thoughts for a moment, then prodded him. "You've got a gut feeling, right, Detective?"

He nodded. "Yes, ma'am, I do. I really do." He sheepishly made eye contact from under the brim of his Stetson. "Yeah, I know. Hunches are—"

"Me too," she admitted.

Hadley exhaled, then smiled, adjusting the Stetson ... which didn't need adjusting.

"What are you thinking, Detective Hadley? Or should I ask what's your gut feeling?"

"Retaliation, I'm thinking. Somebody is unhappy about Cynthia Vandenberg's death, unhappy enough to kill off as many Empresarios as they can, in which case, we're going to see more of these, specifically targeting the men responsible for her death, or the men working for the man responsible for her death. Something like that. So—"

"So who would do that? Not Barns."

He glanced sharply at her. "Gut feeling?"

"Gut feeling."

"Okay, not Barns, then. Bill Vandenberg?"

"That makes better sense," she said. "Why don't you find out where Mr. Vandenberg was earlier tonight while you're gathering intel on the vic?"

"Yep, good idea. I'm on it."

"You find out anything about Eddy Zunigas?"

The change of subject seemed to catch him by surprise. "What? Oh, no. No, not yet. I talked to Newsome."

"So did I. Is she offering you any more muscle?"

"Not exactly."

"Not exactly? What does that mean?"

"She's offering me her well wishes."

Donovan shook her head and stepped away from the crime scene toward her car.

Hadley accompanied her. "You know, Doctor Montgomery, the entire time I served on the force in Weston County, I saw two dead bodies. One was a hit and run, and the other was a crime of passion; the wife had her husband killed and thought she could get away with it. The family had a lot of money so it was a high-profile thing, but honestly, looking back it could've been an episode of *Murder, She Wrote* compared to this stuff. Chicago is a very different city."

Donovan stopped at the door of her car and turned to face the man. "I'll give you that. And we do have a surplus of murders. But most of our victims aren't missing body parts."

She unlocked the car and climbed in. Before she could close the door, Hadley leaned down to talk through the open frame.

"Listen, thanks again for coming out here tonight. I'm gonna head back to the precinct to go over everything we have so far. I'll keep you posted."

He rose, tipped his hat, and turned to his own car.

"Detective," she called out. He turned around. "Mind if I join you?"

The look on Hadley's face reminded Donovan of someone walking in on a surprise party in their honor. "No, ma'am. I don't mind that one bit. I'll see you there."

Chapter Seventeen

The doctor and detective arrived at the precinct in tandem. They passed a policewoman stationed at the front counter then snaked through a dozen desks on their way to Hadley's. Hellos were exchanged between them and various officers working that night.

Hadley placed his Stetson and jacket on a hook affixed to the cubicle half-wall and asked Donovan if she would like a cup of coffee before they got started. She declined.

"Yeah, it's not really coffee, is it? More like the dishwater left after you've washed a coffee cup."

She slid off her jacket and hung it on the rack. "That's a terrifyingly accurate analogy."

As he accessed digital photos that pertained to the case and spread hard copy files across the large calendar pad to the right of his computer, Donovan observed the man's clean, uncluttered workspace. Everything had been laid out in a row along the back edge of the desk: paper clips, pens, stapler. A coffee cup bearing the precinct logo rested on a cork coaster illogically sitting in the same row as the pens and stapler instead of next to where either hand would easily grasp it. There was exactly half a cup of coffee in it.

Donovan recognized the profile. "Okay. Looks like we're the obsessive-compulsive twins. Obviously separated at birth."

He grinned. "I had that feeling about you, Doc. I guess it takes one to know one."

She gave his desktop an assessing glance. "Not in your case. I've learned to hide it better, is all. Bet you stacked your blocks and lined up your stuffed animals, too."

He nodded. "You got me."

"And you got yourself on a career path that has you sorting through clues and methodically demystifying the mysterious."

"Can't argue that."

Add an adrenaline addiction and an unacknowledged death wish, and you have a recipe for a detective far more suited to Chicago than whatever bucolic haven you escaped.

"No, you really can't."

She noticed a family photo on Hadley's desk. The photograph was of a handsome White couple flanked by a little girl and two teenage boys filled a wooden frame positioned at the corner of the desk. A mop of golden locks cascaded over the forehead of one teenager, and the smile across his face was attention grabbing. Donovan noted that the family photo was facing the chair, not the room. It was the only personal item on the desk, and a singular red flag available for her psychological assessment. She knew at a glance that attachment—that family—was Beau Hadley's Achilles' heel. She wished she could warn him about that, but knew it would fall on deaf ears.

She turned instead to his computer screen as he eased into his chair. The screen came to life, displaying a virtual wall of photographs showing Cynthia Vandenberg's ravaged remains from various angles: her wrists, bruised from her struggle and slashed to drain her blood; her breasts pulled to either side of her torso to expose her empty chest cavity; the expression on her face. Other photos showed the distance from where the body had been deposited in relation to the street and house.

Before she could comment, Hadley's cell rang. Donovan bent over the desk and studied the images while he took the call. A moment later, he slid the phone into his pocket and leaned back in his chair. "So, that was Stevenson. They ran the prints."

Donovan remained at the computer but turned her head to face him. "And ..."

"It seems our most recent one-eyed corpse is Jorge Perez. Mr. Perez had a rap sheet long and broad as a beaver's tale. And just like Chevy Velasco, he, too, was a foot soldier for Los Empresarios. Now, I'll wager those two knew one another. What do you think?"

Donovan stepped back from the screen, straightening her spine. "I'll back that wager."

He smiled at her, nodding, then jumped from his seat as if ejected. "Holy cow, what is the matter with me? Here, let me get you a seat, for goodness sake." He moved a chair from the opposite side of his desk and positioned it next to his.

"Thanks, Detective. I am eager to revisit some of the news clips."

"Absolutely. Me too."

Two clicks later, they were watching footage of the crime scene from a local news report. A reporter passionately informed the public of every grim detail known to them at that point. The victim had already been ferried away, so the camera focused on the trash bins, the house, and the blood staining the ground where the corpse had been found.

"Look at that. Look at her getting a close-up of that kid's blood. Yes, ma'am, that was a good day for the press," the detective said, disgust slightly curling his upper lip.

"I'd like to see whatever clips you have of Barns, Detective. Are those handy?" Donovan asked, guiding him back to the reason for their late-night work session.

"Right. Sure." He closed the video and scrolled to the next. "Here we go. This was broadcast earlier today."

The caption under the clip read, "Former congressman and gubernatorial candidate Roy Barns pledges fight against drugs. Demands justice in Santa Muerte Murder."

In the video, Barns stepped out of his front door and walked toward his car, which was parked at the side of the house. Surprised and seemingly annoyed by the reporter's intrusion, he chose to stop at his car door to answer her questions, which consisted of how he was holding up and what they knew about the murder investigation thus far.

Hadley shook his head. "That's horrible. Those aren't questions, those are a bid to make him crumble on live TV."

Donovan glanced from the screen to the detective then back. "I can see that you're on his team, but I'd advise you to step back, Detective. There's a chance he's not a great guy. Keep every scenario open. We don't know everything yet."

Hadley's gaze locked on his keyboard as he considered her words. He did not make eye contact with her, but he did nod and pause the clip. "Yeah. I know better. Thanks for reining me in. I guess I am invested in this case in a different way than I have been with others. She was so young, the Vandenberg girl. That crime was so—ghoulish."

Donovan looked again at the family photo on his desk then back at the man.

"Anyway," he said clearing his throat, "here we go."

In the clip, they watched an emotional Barns speak about his continued fight against the glut of illegal narcotics overwhelming Chicago as well as much of Illinois and beyond. And he vowed to, if not eliminate it completely, dramatically reduce the drug-related violence associated with it. He then committed to helping the authorities in finding and punishing Cynthia Vandenberg's killer or killers to the fullest extent of the law.

But as he spoke, he seemed strangely distracted and almost incoherent: spitting out certain words, whispering others, stammering. His eyes darted left and right as he talked, and he never faced the reporter directly, never once looked directly into the camera.

When it was over, Beau Hadley froze the piece. Donovan and he stared at the image of Barns for a moment before Hadley let out a gust of breath.

"Wow, he gave her a lot more than he had to, that's for sure."

Donovan nodded. "He's a seasoned politician. He knows how to turn an ambush into an opportunity. He decided to use the air time to his advantage."

"Doctor Montgomery, we've heard Mr. Barns say those same things over and over again for the last seventy-two hours, practically verbatim. But here ... here something's different. I mean, I get that the guy's looking beat up, road weary, and a full ten years older than earlier in the week. But ... I don't know. You think he's taking something for his nerves maybe? Help me out, Doc. What am I missing? If he's that unsteady, why not blow the reporter off?"

"Because he thought he was up for it but wasn't. Because not speaking to her would show weakness ... or worse. Because, as he is running for governor, it would be a shameful missed opportunity to act like a leader. None of the above—all of the above."

Donovan turned back to the screen and the inanimate form of the congressman. She studied him, allowing herself to sort through any unexplored information, deducing, assessing. She, too, found Roy Barns's physical condition unsettling.

"It strikes me," she said slowly, "that though he didn't say it directly, he seems to be connecting his fight against drugs to finding Cynthia's killer. That inadvertently implies that he's decided that the two are linked in some way. I also find it curious that on this occasion, he didn't chase his commitment to fighting the drug epidemic with a push to legalize street narcotics."

"Right. That *was* weird. That's his thing. Maybe he's just over-whelmed. I mean, the guy's best friend's daughter, a girl he watched grow up, was found dead at his curb ... and she wasn't just murdered, she was mutilated. If that happened to her because of his policies, well, I suppose anybody would be stammering and unfocused. It could be that it's getting harder for Congressman Barns to convince his constituents—and himself—to get behind legalizing drugs right now. I'm thinking the subtleties of that forward-thinking idea might be flying right over the heads of most folks, what with this particular murder and all."

Donovan listened to Hadley's summation. She did not disagree with anything he said. Still, the expression on Barns's face, his shifting eyes, his general demeanor was atypical for the man. Though Hadley seemed content with the conclusion he reached, Donovan was not.

"What else do we have?" she asked. "Let's take a look at the Vandenbergs."

Hadley clicked open the footage of Mr. and Mrs. Vandenberg leaving the medical examiner's office after identifying the remains of their daughter, Cynthia. Donovan saw the detective's lips thin and jaw tighten as he watched the couple navigate the crowd of reporters and cameras vying for their reaction. This time, he kept his commentary to himself.

Watching as the two made their way to their waiting car through the shouting mob and microphones, Donovan asked Hadley to pause it. She peered closer at the husband and wife, at their faces, at how they were with one another.

A plainclothes detective passing behind Hadley's desk stopped dead in his tracks. "Whoa," he said, drawing near to see the computer screen over Hadley's shoulder. "I don't mean to butt in, but isn't that Dillard?"

Donovan and Hadley looked up at him.

"Is who what?" Hadley asked. "Detective Diaz, that's William Vandenberg, the father of the Santa Muerte victim."

"Must you call her that?" Donovan murmured.

"Sorry. I've just heard it so many times over the last three days."

A uniformed officer—a sergeant—seated at a nearby desk had risen and come to join Diaz in Hadley's cubicle. His name tag read Moore. "I'll be damned," he said, leaning in for a better look. "Diaz is right. That's him. Guess he's gone into the chauffeur business."

"Yeah," said Diaz. "Or private security, maybe."

Hadley glanced at Donovan, then swiveled his chair to face them. "I hate to sound like the new kid on the block, but could one of you fill us in on what you're talking about?"

"Sorry, Detective," said Diaz. "It's just that we both know that guy. Not the dad, the guy in the black suit next to Mrs. Vandenberg. The driver. That's Jerry Dillard. He retired from the CPD a couple of years ago. I didn't know him all that well. Moore did, though. But I've heard the stories."

"Yeah, there are plenty of stories," said Sergeant Moore. "And Dillard's the villain in all of them. Somehow the creep retired with honors and a full pension. How did he pull off getting a plum gig for a corporate exec?"

Detective Diaz made a face. "Hard to kill a cockroach. Guess he's working for the murdered kid's folks now. I'd heard he ended up as a rent-a-cop at some industrial park in Evanston. I guess he's come up in the world."

Hadley pushed his chair back, forcing the men behind him to step away. He then got up and planted his posterior on the wood veneer top of his metal desk. "How about you gents fill us in?"

Donovan added, "And please do tell us what inspires all the animosity toward this retired officer."

The two exchanged glances. The doctor could read the reluctance on their faces. Why? Did they secretly admire the guy or was it a case of not wanting to talk trash about a one-time colleague?

After only a moment of consideration, Sergeant Moore said, "For starters, because he got away with killing a Hispanic couple in their apartment while executing a no-knock warrant and shooting a seventeen-year-old Black kid who was on his knees, gun down and hands in the air when Dillard and his partner cornered him. Dillard told the kid to run. He did. And when he did, Dillard shot him in the back."

"And his partner ...?" Donovan asked.

"Didn't report it," said Moore, "but he did tell another cop, and word spread pretty fast."

"Dillard went through a lot of partners," Diaz added. "Everybody knew about his penchant for offing so-called 'criminals.' Through the creep's entire career, no one crossed the Blue Line. They just stopped agreeing to partner with him. I turned down that honor myself, actually."

"No one crossed the Blue Line," Hadley repeated.

"No," Diaz admitted, "but nobody condoned his violence and racism, either. Not openly, anyway." He turned his attention back to the frozen tableau on Hadley's display. "And there he is helping Mrs. Vandenberg into her car like a gentleman."

Donovan could almost smell the acrid tang of his disgust. She returned to the video. Mrs. Vandenberg was frozen, looking up into Dillard's stony face, wiping tears from her eye.

She'll get little compassion there, Donovan thought.

After a minute of silence, Sergeant Moore said, "Sorry we crashed your meeting, Detective Hadley. It's just that nobody around here would expect a guy like that to fall into a soft job for a rich family."

He and the plainclothes officer excused themselves and went about their business.

Hadley smiled broadly at Donovan. "Well now, that was just a little gift from heaven," he said, reaching for the cold coffee on the cork coaster. "We need to chat with Mr. Dillard."

Donovan cocked her head. "Yes, you do."

His smile dimmed a little at her correction. "Well, apparently he's a little trigger happy and likes to execute extrajudicial sentences. Maybe somebody liked that about him."

"You mean maybe *Vandenberg* liked that about him."

Hadley took a sip of his coffee, wrinkling his nose at the taste. "Well, you have to admit, based on what we have so far, Mr. Vandenberg does seem to be the logical employer."

Donovan nodded silently. *Extra-judicial sentences.* It bothered her that that phrase put her in company with Dillard—or whoever had shot those two young men and stolen their eyes.

Chapter Eighteen

Donovan arrived at her office the next day eager for the normalcy and routine of meeting with patients. She listened to the radio on the drive in. Encouragingly for her, there continued to be no mention of the Chatham murders. Hadley, she trusted, would be talking to Mr. Vandenberg, Dillard, and hopefully would be able to smoke out Eddy Zunigas and get Newsome to put more resources at his disposal. Things seemed to be under control, and the doctor's ability to compartmentalize allowed her to refocus attention on her practice, at least for the moment.

When she entered the office, she and Angel exchanged smiles and nods.

"Hola, D."

"Morning, Ange. How many people am I seeing today?"

"Well, if there are no surprises, you're seeing Mr. Saunders followed by Mr. O'Connor." As Donovan passed her desk, she added, "You have about fifteen minutes before the Saunders session."

Both patients were on time. Both sessions went smoothly. But when Donovan said goodbye to Mr. O'Connor and opened her office door, she caught Angel silently giving her a signal. And from just beyond her assistant's desk, she could see Athena King sitting in one of the waiting room chairs.

Angel got up and went into Donovan's office, nudging the doctor to join her. She closed the door. "Surprise!" she said brightly.

"That's the woman who wanted the autograph."

"Right."

"Oh, Angel."

"I know, but I think maybe you should talk to her again."

"Why?"

"That lady out there is in trouble: vague, weepy, unsteady verbally and physically. D, I'm telling you, this time, it's for rizzle."

The doctor shook her head. "I hope you're right about this, Ange. I sincerely hope she has something pertinent on her mind. Fans are nice, but this is a medical practice."

"I know, Donovan. But—"

"Seriously, I would have referred her elsewhere. I'm trusting you on this."

Angel extended the woman's file. "Good. My instincts say you should."

Donovan would know within a moment with Athena King if Angel had miscalculated, but having known her for thirty-plus years, the doctor knew that Angel seldom did, especially when it came to assessing people.

"Okay, Ms. Torres. Let's do this," she agreed, taking the file.

Angel opened the door and gestured for the woman to enter, which she did. The doctor invited her to take a seat in one of the overstuffed chairs against the wall as Angel removed herself, closing the door behind her.

Donovan saw that the older woman appeared to be more frail than the last time they met, her clothes less crisp, her hair less contained.

"Hello, Mrs. King," she said, sitting in the adjacent chair. "What brings you in today?"

The woman lowered her head. "I'm so thankful that you said yes to seeing me, Doctor, especially without an appointment." She fiddled with her pearls. "You probably think I made the other appointment just to meet you. I'll admit I was starstruck, but those things I told you about my husband and our ... eroded relationship—those things are all true."

Donovan observed the woman's cloudy eyes and hollowed cheeks. "Okay. Do you want to explore it further? Is that what's brought you back here?"

"Not exactly." Athena King clasped her hands and then released them, planting her palms on her knees and taking a big breath. "No, I came here today because I've had a kind of revelation about my life, about what might become of me if I don't deal with the frustration." She leaned closer to Donovan. "You know, it feels like apathy, but it must be pain, pain so deep that my brain can't process it anymore. I don't bounce back like I used to."

The woman went on to recount the details she'd mentioned three days prior. She remained convinced that her husband Percy was in the throes of another affair. But this time, he didn't seem concerned about hiding the infidelity. And this time, she didn't care. She talked about the youthful anger that had once fueled his fight against social injustice slowly becoming nothing but a desire to keep his seat on the State Assembly. She no longer cared about that either.

"He's gone. I don't know who he is. And I don't know who I am either. I'm just so tired."

Donovan agreed with Angel's assessment. This was a very different Athena King. The element lacking in their first encounter was present here: sincerity.

"Still not open to couples counseling?"

The woman's glazed eyes turned slowly to Donovan. "I don't want counseling. I don't want to talk to someone else about this trash. I don't want to hear him lie to one more person. I don't want to beg him to tell me what he's up to. I just want out."

Tears fell. Donovan moved the tissue box between them closer to the arm of the chair.

"Lord, I must look a fright." Reaching for her handbag, Mrs. King extracted a compact as mascara stained her delicate face. "My friend Jane keeps telling me that I should just get a divorce. Says people do it all the time. Jane's been divorced three times, mind you." She tried to smile. "Doesn't matter. I'm not interested. And Percy ... Lord, he would rather see me dead than drag him through all of that."

Donovan stared intently at the woman. "Is that right? Do you mean that?"

After glancing up at the doctor, she turned back to her compact and continued dabbing at the corners of her swelling eyes. "He's not a killer. Not that I know about, anyway." She returned the powder and mirror to her purse. "Doctor, you are a vibrant, twenty-first-century woman, but I am old and an old-school Catholic. And so is my husband. No, divorce is not an option."

"Then what do you mean by finding a way out?"

The woman struggled to find words.

"Are you suggesting suicide, Mrs. King?"

Athena King slid back in the chair, wrapping her arms around her small waist and rocking back and forth. "I think about it all the time. It's all I can think about. If the morning came and I didn't wake up, that would be a great relief. It surely would. But every time I reach for that little gun Percy keeps in the nightstand I think about my children, my grandbabies, and what I'd be leaving them to deal with. So, I think I'm here today to see if you have some way of making that seem like ... like a less attractive option."

Donovan's clinical assessment of Athena King was that she may well be suicidal, as opposed to those who wield the possibility as nothing more than an idle threat.

"Okay. I would like to try. Why don't you let me help you get checked into one of the hospitals I work with here in the Loop? One week of supervised solitude might give you a whole new outlook. And it might help us get to the bottom of this."

A faraway expression that Donovan interpreted as contemplation washed over the woman's face as if considering the possibility.

"No, I won't be putting myself away, Doctor, not in a hospital, not in a sanitarium," she said, snapping back from the moment. "But ... taking a short vacation might be a very good idea. Thanks for the suggestion."

Donovan did not like that idea. Going off by herself might afford Mrs. King all the space she needed to make an irreversible decision. The doctor talked about therapy and suicide hotlines. The woman listened.

"Well, thank you, Doctor. I'm not exactly sure what brought me back here, but I felt compelled to see you, if I could, while I felt strong enough to try. I ..." She shrugged, shaking her head as if the thought was frivolous. She adjusted her pearls, an ironic grin curling her lips still moist from crying. "Maybe I wanted you to see that I am actually crazy and not just some sad, old celebrity hound."

The woman rose. Donovan did as well.

"You're not crazy, Mrs. King. You have simply been living in an untenable situation for too long. As to how you leave that situation, well, you have myriad options. I'd like the chance to help you explore them." The two stood facing one another. "Meanwhile, I'd like for you to visit with your grandchildren. Will you do that for me? If they're too far away, call them, okay?"

The woman nodded sheepishly. "Yes. Yes, that's a very good idea. Thank you."

She stepped toward the door, then stopped, turned, and took Donovan's hands in hers.

"I know you're busy. I know you have regular patients and a book you're working on, and I've heard your name wrapped around this horrible murder business at Shirley and Roy's house. Still, you took the time to see me. I can't thank you enough. You've given me more to think about than you probably realize. Sometimes just saying things out loud gives us a fresh perspective."

Donovan felt as though someone had poked her. "Shirley and Roy's house? Do you know Roy Barns, Mrs. King?"

The older woman released her hands to rummage through her purse for her car keys. "Oh, we used to know them, Shirley and Roy. That was a lifetime ago." Having found the keys, she shook her head. "But for the past three days, you can't walk two feet in any direction and not see him. When I came in here the other day, I hadn't heard about the murder. But by the time I got home, they were reporting on it. It brought back a flood of memories. That's all. We were all so young then, young and hopeful."

Donovan casually stepped between Athena King and the door. "How did you know the Barnses?"

A wistful smile appeared on the lady's face. "Through the Freemasons, of all things. Roy and Percy were two young Black men with political ambitions, Percy for the State Assembly, Roy for the moon, it seems. They joined around the same time. First African Americans to be admitted to that particular chapter. Helps to have connections, Black or White."

"Wow. Small world," Donovan said casually. "Have you reached out to Mr. Barns since the murder?"

"Heavens, no. I haven't talked to Roy in years. Haven't thought about him but for when he's on the TV campaigning, but even then he doesn't seem like anybody I ever knew. Then this. I can't imagine why that young girl was left there the way she was, but I'll admit that seeing him all day, every day has certainly made Shirley's memory vivid for me. I liked her, Shirley. Such a sweet little thing. So full of life. And to die that young, that way—fell off a balcony at her husband's campaign headquarters, if you can believe it. Death by misadventure, the police said."

Donovan made every effort to remain relaxed and conversational. Internally, she'd gone on point. "Do you believe it was something else?"

"Not really. It's just that she and I used to go to all of those Masonic dinners, the functions they'd let us women participate in, and she was always so bubbly. Then she changed, became sullen, aloof. Sometimes she didn't show up at all. Next thing I read, she'd fallen from the balcony at Roy's campaign office. It crossed my mind that she might have taken her own life. But then I'd think about those two little boys she had at home, and suicide just didn't add up. Anyway, it was probably an accident like the papers said. I just remember thinking that something smelled a little funny about it. To be Black and politically affluent you have to fight hard to get there and harder to stay. One dirty financial move or shady business transaction would've been all it took to rob Roy of everything he'd worked for. I suppose a bad marriage would've finished him even faster."

She brushed off the memory and stepped closer to the door. Donovan placed her hand on the knob, smiling warmly.

"My God, Mrs. King, you surely don't think Roy Barns had something to do with his wife's death?"

The woman stopped squarely in front of Donovan. "Oh, no. *No*, but I thought that somebody else might have. Someone trying to protect something, though I can't imagine what." Her eyes twinkled. "You know, Doctor Montgomery, Percy always said I had too much imagination. That I should have put it into writing murder mysteries. Anyway, like I said, that was a lifetime ago."

Opening the door for Athena King, the doctor said, "Let me repeat: You're not crazy, Mrs. King, and I'm very glad you came in today. If it's all right with you, I'm going to have Angel schedule you another appointment for three days from now. I'd like to see you twice a week until we get things sorted out. Sound good?"

The woman agreed. Donovan stood at her office door, asked Angel to make the woman's next appointment, then watched her leave. Angel turned from her desk. "So, were my instincts right?"

"As usual, Angel," the doctor said, returning to her office. "Dead right."

The news clip Donovan had watched with Hadley the night before flashed through her thoughts, the congressman's darting eyes, his fractured speech. She knew that she had just been given a present, and she was eager to open it.

Chapter Nineteen

She had done her homework. She already knew about the death of Shirley Barns. But Donovan decided to open again that chapter of the former congressman's life. By sharing her struggles as a politician's wife, Mrs. King had given the doctor a reason to reexamine another woman's similar situation. Maybe Shirley Barns had experienced the same pressures. Maybe somewhere in that story was a clue as to what had happened—and was happening—to Roy Barns.

She positioned herself at her laptop, and between police files, Google, social media, and old newspaper stories, Donovan pieced together a profile of the man that was slightly different than the popular, accepted one.

Initially, everything she pulled up matched what was believed to be true about him. He'd had a wife and young twins when he became a congressman with a platform built on ridding Chicago of its ever-expanding drug trade. By his second term, the Mexican cartels that hid in each shadowed corner of the region had stepped out into the light, their foothold undeniable, their reach seemingly limitless. Chicago became "home port" for trafficking. With every drug-related crime and death, Barns grew more passionately committed to killing the beast threatening his kids and community.

But before the end of that second term, headlines started to change. In interviews, he pivoted toward finding other ways to fight drugs and preemptively protect Chicago's youth, such as sports and church involvement. He stopped pushing to entrap the pushers, and spoke, instead, about the responsibility of parents to create a more structured family life.

Within months of that shift in tone, he began asking Chicagoans to consider the benefits of legalizing street narcotics, a controversial idea that had just started to be discussed by policymakers across the country. Donovan found the first such headline dated July of 2014. In May of 2015, Shirley Barns died.

The doctor read headline after headline: "Congressman's Wife Tumbles from Campaign Headquarters," "Fall Claims Roy Barns' Wife," "Wife of Gubernatorial Hopeful Roy Barns Falls from Seven-Story Building." She read a dozen such accounts of the tragedy. But one *Chicago Sun* piece, in particular, caught the profiler's eye, "What Really Happened to Shirley Barns?"

Shirley Barns, 36-year-old mother of twins and wife of Congressman Roy Barns, fell from the balcony of her husband's campaign office sometime after 10:00 p.m. Wednesday. Campaign workers discovered the body Thursday morning on the concrete patio prefacing the 7-story building located near the corner of 60th and Sacramento in Chicago Lawn on the city's South Side. The extent and cause of her injuries have not yet been released. Chicago police have only reported that Mrs. Barns suffered a broken neck presumably from the fall.

Those who worked with her say that she commonly stayed to lock up when all the volunteers and employees had left for the day. Yesterday was no exception, though no one can understand why she would lean on a balcony railing she knew to be in disrepair. But Shirley Barns's wedding ring was found near the body, suggesting to some that she may have stepped outside for some fresh air, the ring slipped off, and she grabbed for it without thinking. Others have speculated that she took her own life. Despite her injuries being consistent with a fall, authorities are pursuing an investigation before ruling out foul play.

Shirley Barns was transported to Holy Cross Hospital where she was pronounced dead on arrival. Congressman Barns, who was out of town at the time of the accident, was unavailable for comment.

Donovan read it twice.

In subsequent articles, it was clear that the press wanted to make something more salacious out of the fall but was unable to come up with a motive or suspect. Roy Barns refused to talk about it. Her death was ruled to be an accident, just as Athena King had recalled.

Later pieces reported that the congressman enrolled the twins at the Howe School, a military academy in Indiana, where he visited weekly. His constituents loved the decision. Public sympathy for his loss and applause for giving his sons such a patriotic start in life made Roy Barns even more popular. And after serving his term, he retired from Congress, officially announcing his run for the governor's seat with a platform focused on the legalization of all drugs—touting that as the best way to fight the war on drug violence.

Donovan had been putting together the puzzle that was Roy Barns throughout this crash course of interviews and news stories. She only needed one more piece to complete the picture. Turning her attention to the Federal Election Commission (FEC), she pulled up Barns's campaign finance records. As she suspected, there had been a substantial increase in corporate and private donations in the months directly prior to Shirley's death, and they continued to grow through his current run for governor.

"Starting to look like you were bought, Congressman," she said to the screen in front of her. "You get more political clout, and Los Empresarios gets you to step back, re-couch your position, taking some of the heat off them. Let's play 'what if.' What if Shirley found out? And what if someone knew that and feared she was going to talk? What if they killed your wife, Roy, and you got scared—scared enough to get your kids out of Dodge just in case they weren't done making their point? What if?"

Donovan figured that Roy Barns could be asking those same questions, especially after Cynthia Vandenberg's murder. She knew that were she to be on the right track, he too must be trying to figure out the rules to that deal he'd cut with the devil seven years earlier. What had he done to piss them off, and who was next?

She closed the computer and readied herself to pay Mr. Barns a visit. As she made notes and gathered files, Angel opened the office door, doorknob in one hand, a small square package in the other.

"*Mija*, go home," Angel ordered. "Whatever you're doing, you can do it there. And by the way, this just came for you." She jiggled the box.

"It was just outside the door in the hallway. Very mysterious. You want it or you want me to toss it in the dumpster on my way out?"

Donovan glanced up from her desk, first at Angel, then the box, then back to her notes. "That's okay, Ange. Just set it on the corner of the cabinet here. Never know. Maybe I have a secret admirer."

"Mm-hmm. You do, except he's not secret and he usually sends flowers ... or expensive handbags."

The two exchanged grins.

Angel put the box on the desk. "I'm not leaving 'til you do, so hurry up," she said, closing the door behind her.

The doctor zipped closed the courier bag housing her laptop and files then grabbed her trench coat, purse, and leopard-print insulated lunch bag, the contents of which had remained untouched.

Navigating around the desk toward the door, she glanced again at the package. Close enough to read a shipping label, she realized that there was none. An inexplicable wave of foreboding crept through her. She stared at the box for a full thirty seconds before setting down the things in her arms and picking it up. It felt like lightning in her hands; her flight response threatened to kick into high gear. But it was also extremely light—too light to contain something like a pipe bomb.

She set it back down and removed a letter opener from a drawer, carefully slitting open the packing tape sloppily sealing the cardboard flaps. Lifting out a wad of crumpled newspaper that padded the contents revealed a folded piece of yellow notebook paper on top of a small Tupperware bowl that smelled faintly of food. Donovan sniffed the plastic.

Enchilada sauce?

She placed the bowl on the desk next to the box before unfolding the note. Written in sloppy longhand, large uneven letters filled the lined page.

That was crazy shit you pulled. You are 1 tough bitch but you gonna need to get the fuck out of my shit. This is between me & Barns. Not U or nobody else. I handle things how I see fit. This little present is my way of saying that if I hear your name crossed up in my business again that pretty brown secretary of yours is next. I figure her safety will motivate you more than if I came at you. U got chops. She don't. And you can tell whoever you want about my present cuz I got Skinny on my side. You don't. PS—You look great on TV.

—El Tortuga

She knew before opening the nicked plastic vessel what it held. Who it belonged to was the only question. Gingerly prying off the rubber lid, the smell of food grew stronger. Donovan stared down at a human heart. Dried red smears marked the inside of the container. She sniffed.

Definitely enchilada sauce. The organ was sitting in an unwashed plastic bowl.

As she gazed at the still-moist contents, it occurred to her that Eduardo Zunigas may well go down as the nastiest killer she'd ever encountered. In her years with the police force (and long before), she had brought to justice sadists, necrophiliacs, and perverts of every stripe. But what made Eddy a standout to Donovan was his belief that he possessed superhuman, otherworldly support from a deity that crippled all who opposed him and celebrated the crude butchering that seemed to be his calling card.

At least, that was what he believed, and he acted on that belief.

The note conjured in her all the things to which the doctor usually gave little head space to: anger, fear, disgust. But she allowed no time for any of it to take hold. Her professional analytical programming took over. Donovan knew that clinically speaking, a classic antisocial narcissist had written those words and killed those women. That diagnosis would inform every calculated move she made from that moment forward.

She would deal with Mr. Zunigas accordingly.

"Too bad, dude," she told the plastic container. "You could've really benefitted from a first-rate psychiatrist. But alas, that will not be the context of our relationship." She resealed the Tupperware and returned it to the box. "You and I are going to have to grab some face time, Mr. Zunigas. I do love exploring uncharted territory."

Nonetheless, as she gathered up her belongings and the "gift" to leave, her thoughts were not nearly so sanguine: How real was the threat to Angel's life ... and who was missing a heart?

Her cell rang, provoking a muttered curse and a reshuffling of the telltale box.

"Hey, Doc." Hadley's voice seemed to have lost its bounce. "I hope I didn't catch you at a bad time, but another body's been found at the congressman's house. This one ... um, inside."

The air in the room seemed to hit absolute zero. "Mrs. Chavez?" Donovan asked.

"Afraid so," the detective responded. "How did you—"

"Your voice. It wouldn't sound like that if the victim was a stranger. Is ... is the body missing a heart?"

"Yeah ... How did you—"

"I'm pretty sure I'm holding it in my hand. I'm on my way."

"Jesus, Lord," she heard him say as she cut the connection.

Donovan removed the water bottle, apple, and plastic container of salad from her insulated lunch bag and placed the box containing the heart inside. Zipping it closed, she considered what to do with the note. Unsure whether or not she was willing to hand it over to the police, she stuck it in her purse.

"You've just made this very personal for me, Mr. Zunigas," she said, grabbing her things. "Game on."

When she opened her door, Angel was standing in the middle of the waiting room, already holding her sweater and purse. "Finally! Let's go."

The two walked out together, Donovan waiting for Angel as she locked the front door. Walking to their cars, which were parked side by side, she casually asked, "Hey, Ange, are you still planning to go to your sister's this weekend?"

"Yeah. I'm really looking forward to it. I haven't seen my little niece and nephew for like two months."

Donovan smiled at Angel over the roof of her Prius. "Listen, I've got this," she said glancing back at the office. "Why don't you leave early? Go tonight. Get a jump on the weekend. You deserve it, Angel."

Her assistant's placid expression morphed to one of vague concern— or was that suspicion? She stared at Donovan for several seconds, then smiled, throwing an air kiss at her as she climbed into her car.

"Awesome, D. Thank you. I'm gonna do that. Boom! Road trip!"

Chapter Twenty

Because it was five fifteen p.m., after-work traffic forced Donovan to lose a little time getting to the crime scene. As she approached Prairie Avenue, a police barricade kept her from turning onto the street. TV vans clogged the area outside of the yellow tape. Because of the media, she stayed in her car. An officer approached. She rolled down the window.

"Doctor Montgomery?"

"That's right. I'm here to see Detective Hadley."

"Yes, ma'am. The detective wanted both ends of the street blocked off for obvious reasons. Hold on. Let me move a couple of these drums so you can pass."

Before Donovan could roll up her window, a reporter approached the Prius. "Doctor Montgomery, WLS News," the young woman said into a microphone, a camera aimed at Donovan on the shoulder of a young man standing directly behind the reporter. "What do you know about the Chavez murder so far?"

The doctor put up the window without comment. With the barricades moved, she slowly made her way down the street to the congressman's now-infamous house. A small crowd of people stood behind the additional yellow tape sectioning off the driveway and yard. Neighbors, of course, no doubt wondering what had become of their quiet upscale neighborhood. Donovan parked and negotiated passage through the medics and cops to the door.

Inside the stately home, Donovan observed the front room and dining area to be intact. At first glance, no one would know that anything out of the ordinary had taken place. The only aberration was the blood-soaked body of Selena Chavez spread out on the hardwood floor.

Hadley knelt next to the body along with Officer Spencer, the same young cop who had been among the first responders to the Vandenberg murder. As Donovan stepped toward the two men, both stood up. Hadley turned to her. Spencer glanced at Donovan then turned away, covering his mouth before vomiting into his cupped hands. Hadley grabbed Spencer by the arm and guided him toward the kitchen.

"Go clean up. Take some deep breaths and sit down if you have to." He turned back to Donovan. "He's not used to this kind of thing. Not that I am, but … holy cow, twice in one week. And this gal reminded him of his grandma."

He motioned to the insulated bag slung over Donovan's shoulder. "Is that …?"

She nodded and handed him the bag.

"How—"

"It was hand-delivered to my office just before you called. Angel found it in the hallway outside the waiting room door. Neither of us saw who delivered it. I brought it as it was brought to me, in a dirty Tupperware container inside a cardboard box. Maybe you can pull some prints off of the box or plastic other than mine, though I'm doubtful. Any prints here?"

"No prints. Still checking. No forced entry." He met her gaze, his own puzzled. "Why you? Why wouldn't they send Mrs. Chavez's heart to Roy Barns?"

She'd known the question would be asked; she and Eddy Zunigas were the only ones who knew she'd wrought havoc within his domain. Now she simply said, "To scare me off, I imagine. They left the rest of the body for Mr. Barns. I'm sure they know what a profiler does and aren't terribly keen on it."

Hadley nodded. "Yes, ma'am, that's a safe bet. I doubt they realize you don't scare that easy."

Donovan and Hadley stared down at the woman's body. Her cotton blouse had been unbuttoned, not ripped, and the extraction performed with more precision than Cynthia Vandenberg's. Mrs. Chavez's chubby arms and neck showed only speckles and smears of blood, but her olive green stretch pants were drenched in red below exposed broken ribs and a hollowed chest. A rag bloated with fluid had been wrapped around her nose and mouth.

"Ether," Donovan said, catching the distinctive sick-sweet scent.

"Yeah, I can smell it too. Can't say it doesn't make me wanna gag, just like poor Spencer."

"Such a primitive choice."

"Lots better ways to knock someone out. But at least someone did before they ..." He took a breath. "Looks like whoever did this slit her open with something sharper, more precise than on Cynthia."

"Scalpel."

"Yeah, something like that. Think someone medical stepped in for this?"

"No reason to think that. Scalpels are easy to come by. Plus, it would make the process much easier for the killer. No, it looks to me like this was less of a sacrifice and more of a warning."

To me, she added mentally. Actions have consequences; she remembered her father telling her that more than once.

Hadley pulled her away from that train of thought. "I agree," he said. "Her blood wasn't drained. Still has her clothes on. Even so, they left the little skeleton lady for us. So, why do this? Seems like the same scene, only it isn't. Copycat?"

Donovan gave a glancing thought to the note in her purse and redirected the conversation back to the key chain with its Santa Muerte fob nestled next to Mrs. Chavez's open chest. "You dust the key chain?"

"Yeah. Nothing."

She pulled out a glove and snapped it on, bending to touch the folded-back skin from the old woman's wound and then the soaked band of her stretch pants. "This is fresh. Couldn't have happened much more than an hour ago."

"You sure?"

She studied the woman, lifting her arm an inch off the ground, manipulating her jaw slightly. "I am. Pallor mortis has set in, but not dramatically. The skin will lose its color when a person's dead for more than an hour. And algor mortis is evident but not pronounced. That's the cooling of the body. Within another hour or two she'll have what's called a 'death chill.' She's only slightly cooler than the room at this point. But it's the primary flaccidity of her frame that tells me she hasn't been dead for much more than an hour. Longer than that and rigor mortis would begin to seize her joints and musculature."

He shook the dumbfounded expression from his face. "Right. That's what I thought." He scanned the team of professionals working in organized chaos around him. "And in broad daylight. What kind of ghoul does this?"

Donovan ignored what she took to be a rhetorical question. She knew exactly what kind of ghoul had done this, but was reluctant to share the information—even if she carefully sanitized it. Why? Because it connected her causally to Selena Chavez's murder and to Eddy Zunigas? No. She was already connected to Crazy Eddy through Ruben Ortiz. It was entirely reasonable to assume that Ortiz had passed on to Zunigas an unhealthy respect for her ability as a profiler.

The truth was, Eddy had made this personal. Donovan Montgomery now wanted Eddy Zunigas for herself.

"Have you talked to the neighbors?" she asked.

Hadley nodded, sliding the strap of the lunch bag over his shoulder. "They've talked to us. Lots of questions, no information. No one saw anything. We're going to push harder, but right now, it feels like that may be the truth of it. Most of these folks were still at work an hour ago."

She stood and faced the detective. "Who found her?"

"Barns. He'd just gotten home from his campaign office. What a thing. Poor guy."

"I'd like to talk to him."

"Well, ma'am, he was quite a mess there for a while. Kept talking about his twins, that he had to get to them. They're in some Swiss college. I offered to have them flown home and he started screaming like he was in a horror movie. That's when the paramedics got him to his room and gave him a horse-sized shot of Ativan. I think he's probably down for the count, but you can give it a try."

Donovan peered past the cops down the hall. "It can wait. But that man is really fucking with my book outline."

Hadley gave her a frowning face of bemusement. "How so?"

"I checked into Barns's background today, mostly the press surrounding his wife's death. A few months prior to Shirley Barns falling from that balcony, there was a big uptick in corporate and private donations to her husband's campaign. Those donations seem to align with the change in his stance from targeting the cartels to legalizing street drugs. I think he was bought. I think his wife found out. I think, maybe, somebody took care of Shirley Barns to shut her up and make a point with her husband."

Hadley folded his arms and repositioned his feet, his piercing blue eyes open wide and laser-focused on the doctor. "Go on."

"Well, if I'm right, it could be that Roy Barns cut a deal with the devil that he was willing to keep, even after, or maybe most especially after, his wife's 'accident.' But he moved his kids out of harm's way just to be on the safe side. The more he preached legalization, the more money he got. And now he is the front-runner in the gubernatorial race. Though it, unfortunately, cost him his wife's life, the barter is paying off. Then, out of the blue, Cynthia Vandenberg is deposited at his house."

"He says he can't figure out why."

"That clip of him we watched the other night at the precinct, eyes darting all over the place, stuttering. The man was a nervous wreck ... possibly medicated."

The detective rubbed his chin, nodding slowly. "You're thinking he doesn't understand why his loved ones are being targeted when he's playing ball."

Donovan tilted her head. "You're sharp, cowboy. That's exactly what I think is happening. And now ... here's Mrs. Chavez. No wonder he fell apart when you offered to bring his kids home."

Hadley blew out a gust of frustration. "Thanks for the compliment, but what the hell is happening? Why these butchered bodies? I mean, if that scenario is accurate, what *did* he do wrong? Did whoever bought him change their minds about what they want, or is there a new player?"

"An interesting idea, Detective. What if Roy Barns thinks these murders and his previous alliance with the cartels are connected—only they're not? What if another more ... colorful criminal is blowing up the arrangement because of some completely separate vendetta?"

"Eddy Zunigas?"

"Eddy Zunigas. You think I'm right, don't you—about Zunigas being behind this?"

He stared at her, then the body, then the Santa Muerte fob. "Yes, ma'am, I do believe you are right about that."

She leaned in, meeting and holding his gaze. "I promise you, I am."

Hadley's lips parted, but no words came out.

She considered, for a split second, showing him the note. The proof. Why not give it to him? Get El Tortuga behind bars? She could explain away his comment about the "crazy shit" she'd pulled in any number of ways that made sense. Why not speed this up?

Because, she told herself, *it puts the focus on me, not the crazed terrorist who actually believes his diabolical tchotchkes make him invincible. Because while the press goes wild pumping up my celebrity, Eddy Zunigas will end up in custody, where he will join Ruben Ortiz in running his deadly empire from the safety of his prison cell.*

She did not desire that kind of fate for Eddy Zunigas.

"No matter how low you go, there's always someplace lower, Detective," she told Hadley. "Please keep that in mind. Even the fleas have fleas. So, where are you with Vandenberg and Dillard?"

Hadley blinked as if she'd just jarred him awake. "Yeah, um, we've questioned both of them in regard to the one-eyed men. Their stories check out. There's nothing to hold them on."

"Did Gail take pictures of everything here?" Donovan asked, referring to the police photographer present in the room.

Hadley nodded. "Uh, yeah."

"She get plenty of that thing?" she added, tilting her head toward the plastic death saint.

"Yep," he said, his voice barely above a whisper. "You think there's a reason this one's a key chain?"

"Oh, I don't know. Probably just handy. Might just as well have been a candle or a lapel pin, so long as it had that image on it. Detective, where are you with the Santa Muerte angle? Where are you with Eddy Zunigas?"

Hadley's face flushed and his lips curled. "He's a 'person of interest.' Personally, I think he's *very* interesting. I was working on that when this happened, but I haven't been able to find him. Not yet."

Good news.

Funny how things changed. Before today, getting more law enforcement eyes on Zunigas would have been her fondest wish. "Does Newsome have anybody working with you on that?"

With lightning speed, his face took on an expression she had never seen on it. Anger, the quiet kind that can lead to aberrant behavior, the kind Donovan understood.

When he spoke, his voice was hard and tight. "No, ma'am. No one."

That was the proverbial other shoe falling. Eduardo Zunigas was no longer the Chicago PD's problem. With her failure to act, Evangeline

Newsome had unwittingly put a very effective resource on Hadley's team—one he didn't know he had.

Donovan patted his arm. "Don't fret, Detective. I've got a feeling that this nightmare is going to get resolved real soon. I have a sixth sense about these things."

On Hadley's face, anger melted into bemusement. "You going all psychic on me, Doc?"

Donovan smiled, took out her keys, and started for the door. He followed.

At the bottom of the front steps, she turned, narrowing her eyes. "You know, Hadley, I'm going to want that back." She gestured at the leopard-print lunch bag containing Mrs. Chavez's heart. "Just the bag. Not the Tupperware."

Hadley regarded the bag gently bobbing against his hip as he descended the steps. Reminded of the cargo, he gasped, removed the bag from his shoulder, and held it like a jeweled crown on a velvet pillow.

"All due respect, ma'am, I don't think that would be advisable. But …" He stopped next to her at the bottom of the steps to dig around in the pockets of his jeans. He pulled out his wallet, then handed her an Amazon gift card.

Incredulous but amused, Donovan took it. "Now who's going all psychic?"

He chuckled. "Somebody gave that to me as a thank you. You ought to get yourself another bag, ma'am. I don't think you're going to want this one back."

"Thank you, Detective Hadley, but if you call me ma'am one more time, I may consider how cozy your heart would be in my new bag."

The detective seemed torn between laughter and gobsmacked surprise.

"Oh, don't worry," she said. "I'll likely just call you 'cowboy' until you begin to moo."

Laughing openly now, Hadley stammered out, "Yes, ma'am. Sorry, ma'am—aw, damn it."

He saw her to her car, chuckling a bit still. "Thanks," he told her as she slid behind the wheel.

"For what?"

"For you know what. This is … harder than I expected. I was pretty blown out when they called me in on this." He nodded at the façade of the Barns home, still wearing a veil of strobing colors from the emergency vehicles and cruisers. "You helped me through it."

"Gallows humor, cowboy. It's how we roll." She bid him good night and pulled slowly away from Roy Barns's house, already considering her next move.

Chapter Twenty-One

Once on the road, she called Alfredo Ramos to let him know that Mrs. Chavez and her heart would be arriving shortly—and separately.

"Oh … I … my God. Why her? Why … " There was a moment of silence, then he added, "You're working on that, aren't you?"

His atypical response reminded Donovan that her friend had shared an extended conversation with the woman. He felt protective of her, protective enough to put back the plastic totem that had so troubled her when they discovered Cynthia Vandenberg. And though she had always known him to be a kind, thoughtful human, his business—like hers—did not lend itself to bonding with those he encountered through his workplace. This lady had affected him differently. Donovan could hear it in his voice. She could not pretend that Selena Chavez's death had not changed the balance of objectivity and subjectivity in her own mind.

In an effort to soften an already harsh blow, Donovan explained the differences in this murder from the first, primarily that Mrs. Chavez's blood had not been drained, nor had she been stripped, and that it was clear to both her and Detective Hadley that she had been rendered unconscious prior to her death, as they could both still smell the ether hanging in the air.

"Ether? Who uses ether?"

"Like you said, I'm working on that."

"I see. All right," he said stiffly. "So, other than her heart being cut out"—he breathed out audibly—"other than that, Mrs. Lincoln, how was the show?"

Donovan winced. "One more thing, Alfie. I want you to know before you see Mrs. Chavez that they found another Santa Muerte token with the body."

"God. Did they ..." He stopped himself.

"Most likely. Although, it was on a key chain, so I suppose it might have belonged to Mrs. Chavez. At the very least, they staged it."

Alfredo cleared his throat. "A distinction without a difference," he said harshly.

Donovan turned onto Bryn Mawr Avenue, nearing her home. "Listen, Alfie, before I let you go, have you been brought anything we haven't talked about in the last forty-eight hours or so?"

She did not bring up the two bodies she left in Chatham but was hoping that he would confirm what she believed to be true, that Zunigas's crew had done the cleanup and that the bodies never made it to the medical examiner's office.

"You mean besides the two one-eyed corpses? Well, I've finished up on the first one and am expecting another shortly. But you know all about those. Nothing else. Why do you ask?"

Silence hung between them. He did not repeat his question, but she did hear him sigh. Donovan knew that Alfredo could make an educated guess as to why she would ask. After several seconds, he stepped cautiously into her silence.

"Dear girl, have you left something somewhere that might show up here?" He sounded like an endlessly patient father.

She smiled. "Nothing of any consequence."

"Excellent. That's excellent. Consequences can be so awkward. So, there's nothing that you're reluctant to tell me?"

"Nothing, Doctor Ramos. Nothing at all."

"Mm-hmm."

"And I am truly sorry about Mrs. Chavez, Alfredo. It hit our boy Beau pretty hard too, I think, and I can't claim being completely objective. Are you okay?"

"Of course I'm okay, *mija*. My mother wanted me to be an optometrist. I chose this."

When the call ended, her radio resumed its normal volume. She jumped a little at the disembodied voice; she'd forgotten she had it on. The airwaves were burning with the news that yet another body had been found at Congressman Roy Barns's home. As she pulled into her parking space, news broke that Roy Barns was about to release a statement and that the statement would be read by his friend William Vandenberg. Donovan turned up the volume, listening to a story of loss upon loss. The Vandenbergs had been making arrangements for their daughter's funeral when they received word of this fresh atrocity. Bill Vandenberg rushed to his friend's aid to see if there was anything he could do to console a man while he was, himself, inconsolable.

As the commentator speculated about the crime and spoke gravely about Barns's fragility, Donovan's brain went into overdrive. If Vandenberg's statement to the press was one of consolation, she likely had some time to find Zunigas and take care of things. If the statement was confrontational or if Zunigas saw it that way, he might very well act again. If he said the wrong thing, he could be making his wife the next target of El Tortuga's caprice.

The reporter's voice modulated down to the hushed tones of a golf commentator as he painted for listeners the scene in front of the house. He made note of the fact that he was positioned at the curb precisely where Cynthia Vandenberg's body had been found. He then described the porch where a wan, disheveled William Vandenberg was about to speak.

In a broken, impassioned voice, the father of the slain girl found mere days earlier said he would be speaking for his friend Roy Barns, who was unable to meet with the press at present.

"First of all, Roy wants to thank the Chicago Police Department and all of the first responders for their diligence and professionalism throughout this … horrific ordeal. Law enforcement is still sorting through all of the logical questions and will be issuing their own statement shortly.

"In the meantime, Roy asked that I relay a message to the killer or killers responsible for the murders of Mrs. Selena Chavez, a woman who had worked for Roy and his family for over eighteen years, and … and my daughter Cynthia. Many may not know that Roy and his late wife Shirley were Cynthia's godparents." There was a pause and an audible sob from the man. "They were there at the hospital with Mary and me the day she was born."

Another pause halted the statement. When he resumed speaking, his voice was reedy and breathless with emotion. "Roy wants the people behind this to understand that he has always meant everything he has said regarding the prosecution of drug traffickers and his unwavering commitment to the legalization of street narcotics. He will not be dissuaded. They have his promise. And … and I want to add, on a personal note, my commitment and that of the CPD, that this killer or these killers will be found, tried, and punished to the full extent of the law. If these brutal murders were designed to stop this champion from waging war against drug violence, make no mistake, they will not. Thank you."

Damn.

Donovan turned off the radio and rubbed the back of her neck. She knew exactly in what spirit Zunigas would take that threat. What Roy had asked his friend to say was designed as a white flag, a truce, and that he had never wavered from his long-ago barter with the cartels. But William Vandenberg probably didn't know that. He had departed from Barns's script and sent a very clear message to Crazy Eddy that he was now Public Enemy Number One.

Another even more pressing thought occurred to Donovan. The video footage of her at the Chavez crime scene had, no doubt, been broadcast along with other clips of the coroner's van and yards of yellow tape. Zunigas would take her physical presence along with Vandenberg's incendiary statement as a dare aimed also at the threat in his note. Mrs. Vandenberg wasn't the only possible target of Eddy Zunigas's revenge.

No more playing nice. No more waiting for the department to figure things out. Angel's life was on the line, and Donovan knew that she had to find her before Eddy did.

Donovan grabbed her cell and called up Angel's number. If she picked up, Donovan would calmly convince her to stay put until she got there. Explaining such a visit would be tricky, but she would figure that out when they spoke. If Angel did not answer, she would call her sister to see if her friend had arrived or was in transit. If she was neither there nor on her way, Donovan would call the precinct and have an all-points bulletin sent to every cop in Chicago.

But Angel did answer.

"Hey."

"Hey, Ange." Donovan could feel her shoulders relax. "Glad I caught you. Say, are you on the road? I was hoping you hadn't already left for Xenia's."

"I'm here."

Donovan's relief was explosive. "Oh wow, you made good time. Bet those kids are so happy to see you."

"No, girl. I mean, I'm here at your casa. Check it out."

Donovan bowed her head toward the bay window in front of her house. She could see Angel through the drawn curtains standing with her cell phone pressed to her ear. Both women smiled and put away their phones.

Well, I guess it's no weirder that she showed up here unannounced than if I had shown up at her place.

Shortly after Donovan opened the front door, Angel had positioned herself on the couch. Wearing sweatpants and a Cubs T-shirt, her long hair hung in two ponytails moored high on her head. She sat cross-legged, smiling. A suitcase and canvas shopping bag rested on the hardwood floor at one end of the couch, her coat and purse nestled against the arm at the opposite end.

Setting her laptop and files on the dining table, Donovan turned in time to see Angel take a drag from the glass pot stick she kept in a Bolga basket by her favorite club chair.

"Hope you don't mind," Angel said, holding in the vapor. "I didn't bring mine."

"You know I don't," Donovan said, turning on the sound system.

"Please!" Angel bellowed over the techno music. Remembering her friend's disdain for the genre, she pressed another button, bringing in an "oldies" station that played pop music from the 80s and 90s. She adjusted the volume. The Spice Girls' "Wannabe" poured from the speakers. Donovan rolled her eyes and shook her head.

"Yes! *Gracias, mija. Perfecto.*"

Donovan sat down next to Angel and crossed her legs. "So, to what do I owe the pleasure of your company?"

The lighthearted vibe of the music was not strong enough to mask the genuine concern on Angel's face. Donovan watched her friend craft and edit what she was about to say, then throw those edits away before blurting out her intentions.

"I'm staying here tonight. I'll leave for my sister's in the morning. I'm not stupid, D. Maybe you're the country's preeminent profiler or whatever, but I've known you since you had braces, pimples, and a crush on Doug Terry. I know when I'm being shuttled away, and I know that if I am, there's a reason. A big, scary reason."

Relieved, Donovan nodded, but did not elucidate or act surprised. Angel did not push her to explain. It would have been a wasted effort. Briefly, the doctor did consider telling Angel about the threat on her life but quickly chose against it. There was no need to freak her out more than she already was, and she was here, so it was all good.

Glancing at the canvas bag, Donovan saw a Mystery Date board game peeking out of the top. "Is that what I think it is?"

Angel grinned. "That's the one. That's Xenia's old Mystery Date game we used to sneak out of her closet whenever she was out. Remember how mad she'd get?"

Donovan laughed. "Well, we never could borrow it without getting peanut butter or chocolate syrup on the plastic door. We just weren't very cunning."

"Right? I know. I mean the fun of that game is spinning the door-knob and seeing who your mystery date was gonna be."

"The bum? The hobo? The surfer? The dreamboat?"

The smile dropped from Angel's face. "Girl, there wasn't any hobo. Where did you get that?"

"You sure? There should've been. Why are you carrying it around with you?"

"I thought I'd return it."

"To your sister?"

"She's been very patient. Besides, maybe my baby niece will get a kick out of it in a few years. These original games go for big bucks on eBay. And this one is in pretty good shape, peanut butter notwithstanding."

Donovan gestured for Angel to hand her the pot stick. After a long pull, she got up and disappeared into her bedroom. Angel did not ask what she was doing because she knew. When Donovan returned, she too wore sweatpants and a Cubs T-shirt. When she'd joined Angel, sitting cross-legged on the couch, Angel put her hand on Donovan's knee.

"Listen, D, there's something you need to know."

Just then, there was a knock at the door. Hair rose on the back of Donovan's neck.

"I ordered a deep dish from Giordano's over on West Montrose."

Donovan uncoiled herself and got up to answer the door. It was probably just a pizza guy, but if it was anybody else, they would not appreciate the way she greeted them.

"And don't worry about tipping the guy," Angel added. "I already did. I put it on the business card."

Donovan checked the screen on the security station by the door. Pizza guy. She relaxed—a bit—and answered the door, returning to the living room with an extra-large pizza box, which she placed on the coffee table.

She gave a moment's thought to what she'd have done if Eddy Zunigas, the short, stubby man with wispy champagne-colored hair and diamond-shaped eyes, had been at the door instead of the high schooler with the chipper grin. Even now the specter of Zunigas on her front porch would not leave Donovan's thoughts. As she talked and laughed with Angel and ate exquisite pizza, he was there with them in the front room, sitting in a chair relaxed and smug, daring her to catch him.

What he had done and planned to do had her busy strategizing his capture and imminent demise. She could not afford to have him arrested. The system was too weak. Too many things could go wrong. She knew what she had to do. And as she made plans, she and Angel devoured most of the pizza and chased it with the Jiffy Pop and leftover ice cream Jordan had left behind. They ate, vaped, and played Mystery Date until well after two a.m.

Chapter Twenty-Two

Consciousness returned before Donovan was willing to open her eyes. Blinking away sleep, replaying the evening in her mind, she smiled and checked the bedside clock. It was after seven a.m. She always rose at six, even when she stayed up half of the night.

Carbs are not our friends, she mused, brushing the hair from her face and sliding into her satin slippers.

In the front room, she noticed that Angel's bags were absent. Assuming her friend had moved them into the spare room where she'd slept, Donovan went to the kitchen. She decided she'd insist that Angel stay with her for a couple more nights and go to her sister's the following weekend when the threat would have been eliminated.

She reached for the coffeepot, then hesitated. Funny, she didn't remember prepping it and setting the timer, but was glad that she had. She'd be all thumbs in her current state of sleep deprivation and would most likely screw something up. Pouring herself a cup, she leaned against the counter and took a long, satisfying sip. Her eyes caught on a sheet of her monogrammed stationary affixed to the refrigerator by a magnet shaped like a catcher's mitt. It was clearly a note. A note that had not been there yesterday.

She straightened and set down her coffee cup—almost missing the counter. Even before she could make out the words, she recognized

225

Angel's handwriting. She felt cold, as if the blood was draining from her body.

She snatched the note from the fridge and read what Angel had written.

Morning, D. I didn't want to wake you. We both had a night. :)) Just letting you know that I'm off to Xenia's. Thanks for the party, and though I don't know why you were concerned about me yesterday, it means a lot knowing that the most brilliant badass in the country always has my back. Love you!

She signed it the same way she'd been signing things since elementary school, with a pair of angel's wings drawn on either side of a heart.

As Donovan read the note, she could feel Eddy Zunigas's presence as vividly as if he was standing at her shoulder reading along. She hated that she actually pivoted, expecting him to be standing there smiling, slowly tapping his watch.

She shook herself free of the image and ran to the bay window. Angel's car was gone. She ran to the spare room. Her things were gone. A half-full cup of coffee sat on a side table. She wrapped her hand around it to see if it was still warm. It was.

She threw on a black, long-sleeved bodysuit and a pair of sleek leather pants, topped them with a hoodie, and jumped into her car. She called Hadley as she drove, instructing him to have Angel's cell phone traced and to put an alert for her car.

"I'll explain everything later," she told him. "But right now, Eddy, or Eddy's people, are looking for her. And Detective, if they find her before you or I do, she's dead."

"Son of a bitch," she heard him say to himself on the other end. "I'm on it."

"I need for you to do something else."

"Anything I can."

"I'm going to be making a surprise visit to Mr. Ortiz at MCC. I'm on my way there now. No one is expecting me, and I need to expedite the twenty-minute check-in and clearance as much as possible. Make that happen, okay?"

"I'll do my best. You want me there?"

"I want you to find Angel. And, Beau ..."

"... Donovan?"

"You don't need to clear this with anybody. Do you understand what I'm saying? Not one goddamn soul. No one but you and I need to know about the visit. We'll deal with protocol some other time. Just get it done."

"Will do."

"Do I have your word?"

"Of course you have my word."

That's what she wanted to hear. Ending the call, the doctor reflected on all of the good cops and bad cops she'd known over the years. Some started out one way and went another over time. But she knew that having Beau Hadley give you his word actually meant something because, at this crossroad in his career, his word still meant something to him.

While driving, she calculated whether or not a trip to MCC was the best use of her time. After reconsidering, Ruben Ortiz still seemed like the best shot she had at saving her friend's life.

And this time he better cough up some answers.

By sheer will, she made the fifty-minute drive from Lincoln Square to the Metropolitan Correctional Center in less than forty. Turning onto Van Buren, she saw the triangular twenty-eight-story concrete building that hopefully held the whereabouts of Eduardo Zunigas. Grabbing only her credentials and keys, she strode briskly toward the building.

When she reached the guard standing just beyond the entrance, he greeted her and placed his large hand on her shoulder, guiding her through the checkpoints.

"We were expecting you, Doctor Montgomery," he told her. "Officer Westmoreland took care of everything."

Without further discussion, he led her around the check-in point and detection machinery. Donovan could see Bernice Westmoreland behind her counter several feet ahead. She liked Officer Westmoreland, even when babbling affably about the Cubs or the weather. In Donovan's experience this officer always took care of business, and on this occasion she seemed to be doing just that.

The stout woman saw her, gave a warm, closed-lip smile, and rested her clasped hands on the countertop. When Donovan got close enough, she cocked her head toward the first transverse hallway, implying that the doctor should keep walking and not stop.

Donovan did but checked again to make sure she had read her correctly. "Unit 23 is all yours, Doctor," Bernice murmured as Donovan passed by her counter.

Hadley is turning out to be a rock star. And Bernice is getting a major box of chocolates when all of this is over.

Entering the white, sterile commons where she had last seen Ortiz, this time the place wasn't as empty as it had been at their first meeting, and the handful of inmates there ogled Donovan thoroughly but kept their thoughts to themselves.

She started to take a stool at one of the metal tables, but a guard intercepted her. His name patch was obscured and he did not share his name, nor did he meet her eyes directly. Peering over her head and scanning the room as he spoke, he said, "Ortiz has been moved to an interrogation room. You can see him there. Follow me."

Ruben Ortiz was seated at a table when she entered the small, spartan room, his wrists and ankles cuffed and chained to the chair. The guard who brought her to him remained standing at the door. Another was positioned outside the room on the other side.

Ortiz smiled. *"Hola, chica. ¿Qué pasa?"*

"I went to Chatham. Found the hotel you were talking about."

"Oh, yeah? You meet up with any of Eddy's crew?"

"I think you know the answer to that."

"How would I know? I'm in jail. So, what did you talk about? You get a meet-and-greet with Zunigas?"

Donovan slapped the metal table with both open palms, creating a loud bang that grabbed the attention of Ortiz and both guards. "Mr. Ortiz, I can see that you're in a playful mood. Unfortunately, I'm not. You knew that was a setup. Now, I don't know if *you* set me up or if you just alerted those thugs and somebody on that end took care of it, but that was an ambush."

"Setup? Ambush? No shit?" He laughed, leaning back in his chair. "Well maybe this Skinny that Crazy Eddy's so hot for is looking out for you too then, cuz here you are, *mami,* still among the living."

She leaned forward, forearms on the stainless steel table top. "Alas, two of Eddy's crew"—she tilted her head to one side—"not so lucky."

He hesitated a beat, then leaned forward as far as he could. "Yeah, I heard that."

Then Donovan moved in even closer, close enough that the guard could not hear. "You're going to set up a face-to-face for me with Mr. Zunigas."

"We did this dance already. It's not on me if they made other arrangements."

She bared her teeth in a feral smile. "Listen to me carefully, Mr. Ortiz. If you don't make this happen, if I don't leave here right now with a way to find Eddy Zunigas, you'll be dead before you even have a chance at WITSEC."

He chuckled. "Stop. You're scaring me."

Still whispering very near his face, she continued. "Did you hear all about what I left in Chatham? Did you hear how those gentlemen died? Must've taken some time and quite a bit of bleach to clean up a mess like that. Now, if you don't give me what I want, I'm going to take care of you much the same way. Personally. And on the off chance that you don't really give a shit about your own miserable life, I will lay you odds that your little brother will never see the light of day. So, how 'bout it, Mr. Ortiz? You have an address for me?"

All the while she spoke, Ruben Ortiz stared at Donovan with the flat expression of a mannequin. Then he laughed and leaned back in his chair again, glancing at the guard. The guard wore a deadpan expression. Donovan could see that a message had just passed between them, her instructions had been relayed.

Turning to the doctor, Ortiz said, "You might wanna take this down." Then, he rattled off an address in Englewood. As she rose from her chair, he added, "You're marked, bitch."

Donovan gave no indication she'd heard him, but as she left the room, she stared intensely at the guard before allowing him to walk her to a side exit. She knew that she was marked. She knew Angel was too.

Chapter Twenty-Three

Back in her car, Donovan programmed the Englewood address given to her by Ruben Ortiz into the GPS. Englewood had a hard-earned reputation as one of Chicago's most dangerous, depressed, and underserved neighborhoods. Donovan had remained happily unfamiliar with the area until today.

As she started the engine and turned on South Clark, another car in the prison lot did the same. She noted it only casually. But when the dull gray sedan followed her all the way to West Ida B Wells, Donovan reconsidered the expression exchanged between Ortiz and the guard, wondering if the instruction Ortiz had passed along had been somewhat different from what she'd demanded. He may have ordered her tailed … or worse. She didn't doubt he had the power to do so, even locked up, especially if he wanted to maintain a working affiliation with his fellow Empresarios lieutenant.

The gray sedan hung on behind the Prius all the way to I-290 West. It stayed so close to her bumper that the doctor had an opportunity to study the car and the people in it. The Chevy Impala was neither old enough nor new enough to be considered cool. The paint had oxidized the way a paint job does when exposed to years of Chicago harsh. Two men sat in the front seat staring straight ahead, no conversation

233

between them. Both were Hispanic, bald, and clean-shaven. Both wore open button-downs over T-shirts. If this was a tail, they were doing it very badly.

I could pick them out of a lineup. I could ID the car.

So, not just a tail then.

Her eyes shifted between the road ahead and the car in her rearview mirror as she determined her next move. She decided to make an effort to lose them. If she could do that, the maneuver would only cost her a couple of minutes. If they stayed with her, she would have to put an end to the situation … one way or another.

Donovan exited the freeway. So did the Impala. Quickly assessing her surroundings, she chose against turning right onto Sixty-Third, per the GPS directions, and instead turned left toward a row of seemingly abandoned buildings. She zigged and zagged a few more times, but the Impala clung like a burr.

Fine.

Donovan pulled into a short, broad alley tucked between two boarded-up warehouses, drove the Prius to the back end, and turned off the engine. Gang tags covered the brick walls on all three sides. Trash cans peeked out from beneath mounds of long-ignored refuse.

The Impala rolled to a stop several yards behind her, blocking the exit. She waited, thinking they would approach. They did not.

Seconds ticked by. Donovan knew that she had to locate Angel quickly if she planned on finding her alive. With her pursuers refusing to make the first move, Donovan decided she must indulge them. She got out of the car.

Her feet had barely touched the littered, crumbling tarmac than both men jumped out of their car, their hands empty of weapons. The two could have been twins, they looked so much alike.

Tweedledee and Tweedledum.

Donovan put one foot on her car's door sill and boosted herself onto the roof, where she perched casually.

Your move, boys.

After a moment of hesitation, during which they exchanged puzzled glances, the two men strode up the alley toward her—still, no weapons in sight. When they reached the car, they stopped about two feet away from the driver's side door and peered up at her. Tweedledee was smirking like the Cheshire Cat, clearly amused by her retreating to the roof of the car as if she'd seen a rat.

Tweedledum, however, fixed his round face in a scowl, opened his mouth, and grunted out, "Gi'down from there, you dumb bitch." Then he reached for her.

That was his first mistake. He compounded it by stepping in front of his twin when he did it, so that when Donovan lashed out with a heel-first kick to his face, he took Tweedledee down with him when he toppled backward.

Their surprise froze them for a moment, ridiculously lying there blinking up at her.

Donovan smiled. "Gentlemen, please. Is this any way to treat a guest? If you're Eddy's welcoming committee, you could use some pointers from Miss Manners."

The two men disentangled themselves from each other and regained their feet. Tweedledum seemed ready to fly at her again, but his twin put a beefy hand on his arm and smiled up at her.

"Eddy just wants to make sure you get where you're going safely. He's eager to meet you, but he's busy right now. We're your escorts, *mami*. Why you gotta make a detour?"

"Well," she said, "here's the thing. You gentlemen didn't make any attempt to hide the fact that you were following me. I made your car, your license plate, I saw your faces. You're not stupid. If you'd half tried, I'd never have realized you were tailing me. I took that to mean I was not going to have an opportunity to identify you … because you'd been sent to kill me."

Tweedledee put a hand over his heart. "Ah, you wound me to the soul, *mami*. To think that of us." He turned toward at his companion. "Doesn't that wound you, *hermano*? That she thinks so little of us?"

Tweedledum literally growled. "We ain't got time for this shit. You heard what the boss said." He glared at Donovan. "Get down, bitch."

She scowled at Tweedledee. "You gonna let him talk to me like that?"

The goon spread his hands in a what-can-I-do gesture. "I think you'd better come down."

"Or …?"

He pulled a gun out of the waistband at the small of his back and pointed it at her. "Down."

Okay. He hadn't just shoot her. That was good news. But if she was going to disarm him, she needed to get closer. She slid from the roof of the Prius, making her movements as slow and sinuous as she could, glad of the form-fitting clothing she wore. She kept a Mona Lisa smile on her lips and her eyes on the gunman.

She figured she'd turn on the charm when her feet touched down, try to get within arm's reach, but she didn't need to. The moment the soles of her boots hit the gritty tarmac, he was all over her, shoving her against the car and grinding himself against her. Apparently, their interaction had aroused his libido. She felt that clearly against her hip, felt his free hand go to her left breast. His breath smelled of alcohol and cigars.

"I think we got off to a bad start, *mami*," he crooned. "I think we just need to get to know each other better."

"You fucking kidding me?" snarled Tweedledum from behind his amorous twin. "I'll say it again. We don't got time for this."

Tweedledee kept his eyes on Donovan's face and his hand on her breast, massaging it through the thin, stretchy fabric of the bodysuit. It ignited a rage deep inside that she had to fight to control. Rage must wait. Rage made her impulsive.

"*Por qué no, hermano?*" pouted Tweedledee. "Why can't I have some fun? I'll share. You get some too. All Tortuga said was to make sure she's breathing when we hand her over and that we bring him the car." He winked at Donovan. "He likes your car."

When he laughed, she got a clear view of the pimp grill over his top front teeth—gold and rhinestones. The ludicrous bling made her own forced laughter easier to pull off.

"So," she said, "we gonna do a three-way? Or do you guys wanna take turns?"

Tweedledee stowed his gun, grasped her shoulders, and spun her around, shoving her backward toward Tweedledum. "Hold her."

"Shit," muttered the man behind her. But he obeyed, grabbing her arms, pulling her tight against his chest and half lifting her off the ground..

"Thank you," she said. "This is so much easier when my legs are free."

Donovan threw her weight against the man holding her, lifted both legs, and lashed out at her would-be assailant. The idiot was grinning and unzipping his pants when her booted feet connected. One caught him in the balls, the other took out his rhinestone grill. He dropped like a sack of rocks.

Tweedledum whipped Donovan around to face him. She rammed her forehead into his. He released her and staggered back a step. Donovan gave the guy on the ground a quick glance; he was still curled around his wounded dignity. From the corner of her eye, she saw Tweedledum haul back an arm to take a swing at her. She blocked him, then lunged forward, putting every ounce of weight and will into the attack. He toppled, off balance from the missed swing, and the two hit the ground together with her on top. She made damned sure his skull hit the tarmac.

In that moment of vulnerability, as he struggled to move, she broke his neck.

Less-skilled practitioners of Krav Maga might need two strong twists to deal death, but Donovan Montgomery had only ever used one, and always enjoyed the satisfying *crack* of parting vertebrae. She saw wild terror in her adversary's eyes, which were not trained on her but at something over her shoulder. She didn't bother to check; she already knew she would see nothing. But *he* saw it … and she might too, someday, and think, as she breathed her last, *Ah, yes. That was it. That was what they all saw.*

Donovan rose and turned back toward the Prius. Tweedledee stood, leaning against the side of the car. He had a knife in his hand now. She could only suppose that he'd lost the gun in the fight. Or maybe he'd decided her death needed to be more "hands on." He wasn't looking at her but staring at the corpse she had just made, its head tilted at an odd angle—a broken effigy of a human being. She waited for Tweedledee to process the fact that Tweedledum was dead.

When he finally turned to Donovan, his lips parted, revealing the damage her booted foot had done to his mouth. His lips were split and swollen, and the few rhinestones left in their golden settings were covered with bloody ooze.

"You know what, bitch?" he said thickly. "I don't care what El Tortuga says. Now you die."

He lunged. She dodged. With one swift karate chop, she flipped the knife from his grip. It flew only a couple feet before hitting the ground. He reflexively reached for it.

She saw the gun, then, still in the waistband of his pants. She took a step in and crushed his hand with her heel. As he shrieked in pain and rage, she snatched the gun from his waistband and yeeted it over the roof of the Prius into a pile of refuse.

Tweedledee cursed and grabbed her ankle with his free hand. Her knee connected with his head with enough force to knock him out. Kneeling next to his now limp body, Donovan could see a small trickle of blood oozing onto the concrete beneath his skull. She lifted his head and smashed it into the pavement until the blood pooled thick and she was certain he was dead.

Whispering into his deaf ear, she said, "I want my arrival to be a surprise." She got to her feet, brushing the hair from her face. "Besides, I like my car too."

She had to move her attackers' car to free her own from the alley. They'd left the keys in the ignition and the engine running, making that chore easy. Before she returned to her own car, she checked her clothing for blood. It wasn't her OCD—not really—but she'd just had the Prius detailed and really didn't want to mess up the pristine interior. She brushed any debris off her pants, folded her hoodie inside out on the driver's seat, and slid into the car.

She felt a visceral anger uncoiling inside her—dark, deep, and carnal—but knew she couldn't indulge it. She still had work to do. She tried calling Angel. No answer. She called Angel's sister. Xenia told her that Angel had not arrived and that she was getting worried.

That makes two of us, Donovan thought, but kept the conversation light.

"Don't worry, Xenia. I know her phone has been giving her trouble lately. Maybe it's on the fritz. I'm sure she'll be there in no time. And on the off chance she had car trouble, I'll check some places for her here in town."

Xenia agreed, adding that she hoped that the three of them could all hang out together sometime soon.

Again, Donovan thought turning the Prius out of the alley onto Sixty-Third, *that makes two of us.*

Chapter Twenty-Four

Donovan drove by the decayed remains of a train station, then an abandoned factory surrounded by broken fencing and tall weeds as gray as its walls. To her, the place more resembled a black-and-white photo than anything in the real, full-color world—a snapshot of something only serviceable to squatters and ghosts.

Metal bars covered the doors of every occupied shop that she passed: one liquor store, two selling used tires, another for work uniforms owned and operated by "The Church" according to its peeling wooden sign.

Farther up the street, a traffic light forced her to stop. At the exact moment the light went red, someone screamed. Donovan turned her head in time to locate the source of the cry; a shoeless skeleton of a woman hobbled out of a beauty supply store next to a bail bonds office, shrieking at no one Donovan could see. Her sharp cries morphed into a chorus of "Amazing Grace" before the light turned green.

Englewood makes Chatham seem like a vacation retreat.

Her cell phone rang. She glanced at the dash display. It was Hadley. Unwilling to be distracted, she let the call go to voice mail and then accessed the message: The cops had not found Angel but did locate her car on North Damen by Winnemac Park in Lincoln Square.

Her suitcase, canvas bag, keys, and purse were still inside, all seemingly untouched, including two hundred dollars in her wallet.

Donovan shook her head in disbelief; Angel had been kidnapped only blocks from her townhouse. Eddy's crew must have been tailing her. Possibly the same two who had tailed her. Possibly, they had even waited all night, then let her get a couple blocks away before somehow getting her out of the car. Well, good neighborhood or not, it couldn't have happened very long ago or someone would have tried the lock and grabbed her purse at the very least.

I've still got a shot at this, Ange. You hold on.

At the end of the message, Hadley asked that the doctor call him as soon as possible. She ignored the plea and pushed harder on the gas pedal.

A turn later, shops became less frequent. Another turn and she found herself driving past rows of small houses, most of them with plywood nailed over windows and gang tags scrawled across chipped stucco and brick. Two blocks farther, according to the navigation system, Donovan was nearing her destination, a two-story structure slightly larger than most of its neighbors. She assessed it as a generational house, enlarged and added onto as the family grew. It wore the vestiges of a once-nice paint job and boasted of a veranda that might have once been a pleasant place to sit and watch the neighborhood on a warm summer's eve.

This house's windows were boarded the same as many of its fellows—all but the two upstairs windows facing the street. Those had jagged panes still protruding from their frames. Black smoke stained the sills and surrounding wall, leaving clear evidence of a fire. The rotting façade had a vacant lot on one side and a large stretch of dead lawn on the other.

What a perfect place to cut out someone's heart.

Donovan knew that Zunigas and his men were expecting her, watching for her, but given that she had done away with the two escorts El Tortuga had sent, none of them knew when, and that's the way she wanted it. Her Prius, however, would give her away if she didn't take every precaution to keep it out of sight.

With that in mind, she took the next left, drove down two blocks, turned right, then right again so that she was approaching the house from the opposite side she had initially. Across the side street from the empty lot that flanked the house, screened by a surplus of shrubbery and tall weeds, were the remnants of a Phillips 66 station. Wishing it were night instead of a sunny afternoon, Donovan pulled off the street into the station's weed-riddled drive and rolled behind three rusted pumps. She was pleasantly surprised to find that her position allowed her to study the house without being seen.

A man in a bright yellow shirt sat on the top step of the porch flipping cards into an inverted hat on the sidewalk below. Rolling the car forward a few inches, she could make out someone on the back porch but could not yet deduce if the person was alone. Moving forward any further would destroy the camouflage that the pumps and distance provided. Donovan decided that was not a risk worth taking. Turning off the engine, she studied the house and the property around it.

The lack of fencing around the property allowed her to quickly confirm that only one man stood sentinel at the back, as at the front. She watched him as he lit a new cigarette from the one still in his mouth and sucked in the last gasp of the first smoke, which he dropped to the back porch and ground under his foot. Then he popped the new cigarette into his mouth and leaned against the flimsy porch rail three steps up from the weedy brown back yard. He seemed bored.

Good for him.

The doctor extracted surgical gloves from the Prius's console, along with a flip-top case designed for eyeglasses. After donning the gloves, she opened the brocade box, removing a small vial and hypodermic syringe. After filling the syringe from the vial, she tucked it into the left breast pocket of her jacket, then returned the case to the glove compartment.

Reaching into her purse, she took out the small plastic statue of Santa Muerte that had served as a totem for her in the days since the Vandenberg murder. Tucking her purse under the front seat, she got out, placing her keys and the tchotchke in the right-side pocket and zipping it closed.

Donovan surveyed the lay of the land, paying special attention to where the two guardians directed their gazes. Yellow Shirt was glancing down the street toward the original direction she'd driven. The smoking man really didn't seem to be watching at all. In fact, he was now doing something on his phone. Maybe he was trying to raise the Tweedle twins.

Good luck with that. They've moved to a new area code.

She determined that if she moved to roughly the center of the gas station's property and crossed the street where the weeds and volunteer shrubs were thickest in the abandoned lot next to the house, she could do it without either guard seeing her. After that, the sheer amount of foliage and crap in the empty lot should obscure her approach.

Smokey was still leaning against the porch railing with his back to her; Yellow Shirt was gazing down the street in the opposite direction. Donovan sprinted across the street and into the empty lot, then made her way as quietly as she could toward the rear of the house, keeping as low to the ground as possible.

She was almost to the side wall when a half dozen birds burst out of the tall grass and weeds right in front of her, their wings whistling through the air.

Adrenaline spiked and sent a shot of cold down her back to lodge in her stomach. She dropped to the ground and waited. When she sensed no movement from either of the guards and heard no sounds of interest or alarm, she took a deep breath and continued to the side of the house. She moved cautiously toward the back yard, tucking herself as close to the peeling side paneling as she could without touching it.

She paused at the corner of the building and peered cautiously around it toward the back porch. Beyond a row of sealed garbage bags and a rusted, padlocked cellar door, she saw that Smokey had bravely or foolishly boosted himself up onto the porch rail so that his butt hung over. Donovan decided to seize that opportunity.

She pulled out the syringe and crossed the space between the corner and the porch in three long strides, to plunge the needle through the guy's khakis into his ass. Grasping the waistband of his pants, Donovan half-emptied the syringe. As she pulled it free, she hauled on the waistband with all of her considerable strength, toppling him backward off the porch. He landed on his back among the trash bags.

He struggled to rise, his eyes finally finding Donovan looming over him. He opened his mouth to curse or shout a warning, but the drug was already beginning to have its effect and nothing came out but a garbled yowl.

"You look like you could use a nap," Donovan told him, then knelt and injected the rest of the serum into his neck. "Now, this is Diprivan, Smokey—can I call you Smokey?—and it's gonna keep you comfy until I figure out what's going on in there. Gotta make sure that I have the right house and that you are, as I suspect, one of the bad guys. I never kill anybody until I'm sure what side they're on. Night-night," she added, then rose, climbed the stairs, and carefully opened the back door.

Donovan found herself in a mud room that gave onto a dark, narrow hall. Death metal music blared from somewhere in the house. She recognized the distorted guitar, pounding drum, and growling vocal that brought to mind an indignant demon rather than an angry young man. It seemed perfectly appropriate here. The tonal assault pumped through the walls so aggressively that the light bulb hanging above her head jumped and swayed as if dancing to the rhythmic chaos.

She advanced up the hallway to a doorway on the left; it opened into a kitchen that held a plastic patio table and four mismatched chairs, but no people. Donovan entered and was drawn to the sink. A red-brown stain permeated the aged porcelain. The room smelled of ammonia with an under-tang of iron. Blood. The ammonia someone had used on the stain had not been enough to completely remove the residue or the smell.

Dilettantes.

Exiting the kitchen, she passed a bathroom and a small bedroom, both unoccupied. But across the hall on the right-hand side was another room. The door stood ajar. Donovan stealthily moved past the door so that she could peer in without opening it any farther.

This room was large. A five-inch-wide scar in the hardwood floor and an exposed beam told her that a wall had been crudely taken down to expand the space. In it, two men waited. One stood beside an open cupboard, its shelves stocked to capacity with lighted candles of various sizes and colors. His arms were crossed over his chest and he rocked back and forth as if bored or jittery … or both. The other man leaned against a large dining room table of dark wood. He, too, had his arms crossed; his head was tilted back as if he found the light fixture above him to be of great interest.

On the table, Donovan's oldest friend wriggled against her restraints. The nylon ropes around her wrists and ankles had been threaded through metal tie-down hooks sticking up from all four corners of the table. The only other thing on the table was a large pair of gardening shears. Angel wore the sweatpants and Cubs T-shirt she'd had on the night before, and her hair still hung in two fat ponytails. But now duct tape covered her mouth and a jarringly pink lace-trimmed sleep mask covered her eyes.

Donovan crushed her desire to simply storm the room and forced herself to a swift but cautious study of the end of the room she could see. There were candles literally everywhere, filling every inch of available space, all burning merrily. Incense smoldered from a smudge pot inside the room, sending billows of scented smoke out into the hall. Donovan wrinkled her nose at the heavy aroma.

Focus.

Against the wall at the far end of the long table stood a life-sized resin statue of Santa Muerte. It had to be over six feet tall. Robed in black, the icon held a scythe in her right hand and a globe in her left. A red resin owl roosted at her feet. The skeleton seemed to have a pleasant, satisfied look on her chalky face. The carnival glass necklace draped around her shoulders flickered like dying neon bulbs in the candlelight. The words "*Cuídanos*, Skinny" were spray-painted on the wall behind the effigy, while benches on either side of it held yet more candles as well as liquor bottles, packs of cigarettes, and an assortment of other things that Donovan could not make out from where she stood. Offerings, apparently. She wondered if Eddy or his crew ever nipped in to sample the goods. She supposed that depended on how deep their belief in the deity ran.

Donovan did a quick calculation. She'd seen four of Eddy Zunigas's goons, disabled one. She focused momentarily at what was reflected in the glass-paneled doors of the cabinet shrine. Bookshelves. No more people. She glanced down and across the hall at the staircase that ran from the foyer to the second floor. All the steps above the fourth one had been burned away. Unless there was an alternate way to reach the upper story, no one would be up there. But that left her with an urgent question: Where was Eddy Z?

She slipped silently toward the front of the house. Just past the foot of the staircase, she found a vacant living room to the right and a closed door to the left. The deafening music emanated from behind that door. She was aware that standing between the two rooms placed her precariously close to the front door and the man in the yellow shirt.

Donovan moved to the closed door and delicately turned the knob just enough to see if it was locked. It was not. Fully prepared to spring into action but preferring to buy a little more time, she managed to push open the door by an inch and peer in. The room was set up as an office or study. To her left, on an interior wall, a desk faced into the room, backed by a row of tall bookshelves. She could see at least one padded chair, its upholstery hideously stained.

At the center of the room, recognizable from his mugshot, Salvador Eduardo Ignacio Zunigas stood alone, seemingly enthralled by the aural cyclone swirling around him. Arrayed in a velour tracksuit and a clear plastic rain poncho, he spun and shimmied, waving a machete about as if it were a magic wand.

The audience for this performance seemed to be a smaller version of the grinning death saint that stood on a makeshift altar against the far wall. The strange imp danced seductively before her, pointing the machete this way and that—possibly at imaginary victims.

Atop Eddy's doughy head, puffs of champagne-colored hair wafted to and fro like wheat stalks in a farm field. His diamond-shaped eyes—which Donovan remembered clearly from the photograph—were closed. There was a good possibility he was high.

Donovan's throat tightened and her fingers clenched with the desire to take Eddy Zunigas out *now*. In his rapturous state, he'd not even see her coming. She could extinguish his worse-than-useless life before he'd even realize she was there.

She made a move to throw the door open, then hauled her emotions into check. The longer she left Angel where she was, the more anguish and trauma her friend would sustain. She needed to free Angel first and remove her guards from the equation. If she attacked Eddy now and they heard the assault, they might even harm Angel further.

Whether he was high or not, she could only hope that Eddy would be at his worship for a few more minutes.

Donovan carefully closed the door and hurried back to the dining room. She knew that Crazy Eddy had every intention of performing his next sacrifice before the wax burned down much more on those votive candles.

Peering once more into the murder room, Donovan saw that the man by the cupboard now sat in a folding chair thumbing his cell phone. The other man stroked Angel's ankle, staring at her intently, seeming to enjoy her futile attempts to free herself.

You first.

Donovan slipped into the room and, with a silence she had learned through much practice, glided up behind the guy and blew on his neck.

He whipped around, grabbing for the gun at the small of his back. She'd already removed it. She kneed him in the groin. He went down and she followed him to the floor, clutching his hair and smashing his skull against the wood. It only took two hard whacks before she heard it crack.

Momentarily stunned by what had taken place in front of him, the other man bounded toward her, switchblade in hand. He sneered and flipped open the knife as she rose from the floor. Donovan kicked it from his grip. They both dove for it.

She got there first.

With one man dead and one bleeding out, she turned to her friend. Donovan wished that she could remove the restraints, but there was every chance that the first thing Angel would likely do, once freed, would be to remove the sleep mask. Donovan was unwilling to risk Angel knowing that it was Donovan who had rescued her. Were she to know that, she would almost certainly put it together with what she knew about other conveniently unsolved murders. Donovan could not allow that to happen. She could never involve Angel in her particular form of justice. So for the moment, the restraints—and the sleep mask—would have to remain.

Angel had stopped thrashing and lay very still but breathing hard, her chest rising and falling with every breath. The doctor stepped to the end of the table near her friend's feet and lightly touched the hem of her sweatpants.

She spoke in a husky whisper—an affectation she had never used around Angel. "You're okay. I'm going to get you out of here. But I have to take care of something first."

Angel relaxed.

Donovan gave the Santa Muerte idol a glance (*not today, bitch*), retrieved the switchblade from her second victim, and slipped out of the room into the hall. She'd taken two steps toward Eddy's office when the front door opened and Yellow Shirt entered the foyer, his gaze intent on his phone.

Donovan froze and gave a moment's thought to ducking under the broken staircase, but as the guy took a step toward the office door, he glanced up and turned his head. The doctor and the man in the yellow shirt stared at one another for several seconds before he made a belated grab behind his back, no doubt for a gun.

This was a mistake that left his torso unguarded. Donovan leapt forward, thrusting the already bloody knife deep between his ribs, twisting it and yanking it free again. A back-handed swipe slit his throat. He crumpled silently and slowly enough that Donovan was able to toss the weapon beneath him on the threadbare carpet. His compadre's prints might still be on the hilt; let the police puzzle out what had gone down between them.

She gave the contorted face a vicious smile. "Never bring a gun to a knife fight," she said, stepping around the body.

Donovan turned to the closed door of the madman's office. "Okay, Eddy, showtime."

Chapter Twenty-Five

Donovan shoved the office door open hard enough that it slammed against the wall. The pudgy gyrating man in the tracksuit and rain poncho seemed not to have heard it above the pounding of his music. He continued dancing for a full fifteen seconds before realizing someone else was in the room. When he did, his eyes widened and a smile lit up his face as if he'd received a Christmas puppy.

Eddy slowly dropped his arms. "Doctor Montgomery," he mouthed over the pounding drums and screeching guitars.

She tapped an ear and shouted, "I can't hear you!"

He stepped to the stereo system and turned it off. The absence of sound was not silence; Donovan's ears hissed and rang and her body and brain felt woolly from the tonal assault.

Focus, Montgomery.

"Well, come in!" Eddy chirped. He bowed, gesturing for her to enter with the blade of the machete, but never took his eyes from her face. "*Mucho gusto! Bienvenido*! I am so very glad that my men were able to escort you here safely." He glanced past her. "And where are my good soldiers?"

She studied the masked unease barely readable on his comic book villain face. "They've joined the two goons in your dining room."

253

Donovan considered that to be an honest answer, though it implied the men were just down the hall having a pleasant chat.

Zunigas frowned, then shrugged as if it was too much bother to work out her meaning. He took his gaze from her at last, to study his reflection in the blade of his very shiny weapon. "Well, it does not matter if they have let you run loose in my house. You cannot harm me. I am invincible in her lovely arms." He nodded at the statue, brushing back a wisp of hair from his broad forehead with the back of his hand. "I am glad you are here, Doctor. I thought you might like to watch our little ritual."

Donovan remained in the doorway, effectively blocking it. No other exits existed but for the one she stood in, and the window had been boarded over from the inside. As if he realized this, Eddy moved toward the desk on the left side of the room. The cloaked skeleton that only moments before seemed to be making eye contact with the man now appeared to be staring at the pattern in the jarringly out-of-place Persian carpet on the floor.

The overstuffed room held an odd mixture of smells, from marijuana to motor oil with the faint but distinguishable aroma of enchilada sauce somewhere in the mix. Donovan was reminded suddenly and sharply of finding Mrs. Chavez's heart in a tatty piece of Tupperware. She shook off the recall and studied the clutter on the desk. There was a silver-plated skull with horns and a long jutting tongue, a boom box, and a goat-shaped paperweight with red glass eyes.

Following the profiler's gaze, Zunigas grinned and gestured at the motley assortment of items on his desk. "My treasures." He ran an index finger the length of the boom box. "Usually, I like to play my music from this wonderful old friend." He then allowed his gaze to drift over to the skeleton's empty sockets. "But when I prepare for my queen, when I ready myself to feed her, I use the system on the wall. Sorry if it was too loud. She likes it loud." He giggled, covering his mouth with his free hand. "*Por favor, Señorita* Montgomery, come in. Have a seat."

Donovan stepped into the room, keeping herself between Zunigas and the door. He dipped his pinky into a bowl of white powder atop the desk, inhaled the little mound of it, then extended the bowl toward her.

She shook her head. "No, thanks."

He set the bowl down. "I cannot convince you to sit?"

Donovan noticed the stains on both upholstered chairs and wondered who would take him up on such an offer. "I'm good," she responded, studying the wall shelf behind the desk. It held a row of mason jars with cheap plastic flowers braided around them. Some were empty, and others contained what Donovan deduced to be human hearts.

"Does one of those belong to Cynthia Vandenberg?"

"*Sí, hermosa medica*, the second one. The empty one next to that was for Mrs. Chavez, but I figured it would serve the White Lady better in your hands than in mine. And the one next to that—is for our Angel."

Donovan felt flames ignite in her core at the two words "our Angel." She wanted to tell him that Angel would never be his. Instead, she nodded toward the first jar in the row around which a black ribbon distinguished it from the rest. "And that one?"

He closed his eyes and shrugged. "Practice. My first."

In the brief moment that his eyes were closed, Donovan could see that the diamond shape of his eyes was an illusion created by thin scars that extended from the inner and outer corners of his eyelids to meet just below the center of his eyebrows. They had healed with a slight pucker. Enhancing this horror were small black dots at the center of each cheek, just below the eyes. Makeup, tattoos … scars?

Donovan took one step toward him. He stepped back, holding the machete closer to his chest.

"Yes, practice does make perfect," she said, studying his scars.

He nodded, his arms uncoiling, allowing the weapon to hang at his side. "You are too polite to ask. I can see that. Many people want to. No one ever does. But for you, I will share."

A wistful expression softened his elfin face. "*Mi madre* gave me these most precious reminders of my worth. I am an only child, and my father died before I was able to walk, so she and I were very close. She eliminated him to protect me. She loved me that much. And it was about that time, I understand, that her fear for my safety overcame her. She was unsure that I would be able to fend for myself in this brutal, wicked world, so she helped open my eyes."

He shook his head. "She was so right. This world is a difficult place." Gazing at the ribbon-wrapped jar, he added, "I am so grateful to have been with her when she took her last breath."

"And the other empty jars, who are those for?"

"I don't know yet." He shrugged. "They came twelve to a case."

"Funny," murmured Donovan.

Eddy's change of expression was lightning swift. He scowled, exuding sudden fury. "One is for Barns." He pressed the machete against his chest, again rocking back and forth as if hugging a favorite stuffed animal. "And one is for you, beautiful doctor. I will place fresh flowers around that one. Every day."

Donovan turned and addressed the first jar. "Why Mrs. Zunigas, look what you made. I bet your last breath was your proudest." She took another small step in Eddy's direction.

Again, he stepped back, but he was grinning like the Cheshire Cat. "Such lovely manners you have, Doctor."

"You don't like Roy Barnes. Did you orchestrate Cynthia Vandenberg's murder to send a message to him?"

Eddy nodded and grinned more exaggeratedly.

"In fact, you hate Roy Barns, don't you?"

Another tiny step. This time, Zunigas stayed put, but he glanced behind him at the desk.

Donovan drew his attention back to her. "I get it. I understand. You hate him for getting in the way of your livelihood. If he does get that legislation passed, well, just anybody will be able to buy dope and they won't need the cartel middlemen, right? Those junkies and wannabe junkies won't need you."

He nodded, his expression somber again.

A man of many moods is our Eddy.

Donovan altered her course slightly to aim at the end of the desk opposite where Eddy stood. "Well, Mr. Zunigas, you are not going to like this, but …" She reached the desk, pushed aside some of the clutter, and perched her left hip on the corner. "You want the bad news first, or the good news?"

He raised his chin. "What news could you bring me that I don't know?"

"Good or bad, Eddy. C'mon. Play the game."

"Bad news."

"Congressman Barns is being paid off by the very cartel you work for. Isn't that hilarious?" Zunigas frowned and cocked his head. "Being paid to advocate for legislation that would legalize street narcotics. Los Empresarios has had him in their pocket for years. Now, imagine the congressman's confusion as people he loves keep getting murdered at his house when he's been doing exactly what your higher-ups paid him to do. And all because *you didn't get the memo.* How the hell did you miss the damn memo, Eddy?"

She rose and went around behind the desk to observe the jars more closely, but still watching Zunigas out of the tail of her right eye. "What's your capo's name again? Oh, I remember, Octavio Luis Jimenez. Now, I know he's been underground and unavailable for the past three years, and I understand how his disappearing act placed even more responsibility on the shoulders of his lieutenants, such as yourself and Mr. Ortiz. You've all had to step up and make some of the hard decisions on your own, and deal with things the way you've seen fit. I get it. But—don't you guys ever talk?"

She turned her head to look at him directly.

His eyes scanned the air as if he were trying to read "the memo." When he met her eyes again, Donovan knew he was considering the possibility that she might be right. She came back around to the front of the desk, a move that forced him to back away toward the wall lest he be trapped in the corner between the desk and the boarded-up window. She kept talking, kept moving, while he continued to clutch the machete to his breast.

"See, there is a belief that legalizing dope will actually help your side. You follow? If it's legal, surely more people will use. The more people who use, the greater the demand. They have to get it from somewhere, so legal or not, the cartel wins. Of course, your misdirected anger has allowed you to pursue this little hobby of yours. That must be so rewarding."

She smiled into his eyes. He stared back as if mesmerized by hers. She inched even closer, bringing them face-to-face. "I didn't have to tell you any of that. I just wanted you to know before you go to meet your goddess."

She saw the sudden dawn of uncertainty in his widened eyes. Saw the way his gaze sought the doorway. "Bernardo!" he roared, his breath hot on her cheeks. "*¿Dónde coño estás? ¡Entra aquí ahora!*"

"Bernardo's not going to answer you, Eddy." Donovan nodded at the statue. "Have her call him. Your whole crew and my two escorts are a lot closer to Madam Muerte than they are to you."

Now, finally, Eddy tried to wield his machete, but Donovan was too close and he had backed himself to the wall. What he did next took Donovan by surprise. He drove the blade into the top of the desk. Did he expect her to make a grab for it, giving him a chance to pull a second weapon from concealment? That wasn't going to happen.

"Anyway, Eddy, they don't matter now. That's all blood under the bridge, and there are a few things I want clarification on. Who killed Cynthia Vandenberg? I'm guessing you didn't do that all by yourself."

Zunigas's expression seemed one of fondness as he lightly balanced the tip of his index finger on the hilt of the machete still stuck in the desk. Turning his loving gaze to the weapon, he said, "I performed the ceremony, as I always do, with the assistance of *mis soldados. Mis maravillosos soldados.*"

"Your crew here? May they rest in peace."

He smiled. "No. Three friends of hers." He tilted his head toward the statue. "It was better that way." The smile disappeared and a madman stared up into Donovan's eyes. "Now one of them is dead. Found behind his favorite taqueria. Someone cut out his eye." He stroked one of his damaged lids. "That makes me very sad."

One of them? Did he not know about the one found near the train tracks? Was he not the one responsible for them?

"Who killed him?" she asked.

"I don't know," he said mournfully. "No one can tell me, it seems."

"So, not the same crew that killed Mrs. Chavez?"

"No, Bernardo took care of that. All by himself." He shook his head, seeming perplexed. "Why would Bernardo do such a thing? And without telling me? No. Though I will ask him."

"Bernardo's dead. Somewhere. Maybe he's bleeding out in the room where you have Angel. Or in the hall. Or on the back porch. I don't know who Bernardo is. Maybe I left him in an alley with his twin. Point is, he's dead."

Zunigas nodded acceptingly. "That, too, makes me sad."

"No doubt. Good help is hard to find. Know what makes me sad? My best friend is tied to your dining room table."

Eduardo wiped an invisible tear from his eye and chuckled. Then he seemed to disengage from her, his gaze wandering over her shoulder toward the door.

She wanted his attention back on her. "Hey, Eddy, you wanna know something really funny? You thought you were going to cut out her heart and feed it to a plaster statue of your mom."

"You want to know something even funnier?" he asked, the hot crazy pouring out of his eyes. "Bernardo has come back from the dead."

A shiver up her back and a tiny sound behind her alerted Donovan to the danger she was in. She dropped and rolled toward the center of the room. Coming up behind the blood-stained overstuffed chair, she saw what Eddy had seen over his shoulder; the man she'd left paralyzed on the back porch had overcome his debility and was standing in the doorway, leaning heavily against the frame. He held a handgun, none too steadily, but even a wild shot could be deadly.

Donovan kicked herself for not taking care of Bernardo permanently, or at least not throwing his gun out into the weed-infested yard or onto the roof.

Eddy was grinning again as he yanked the machete from the desktop. "You will pay, Doctor, for your slur against my goddess. She is like no human mother."

"Sorry," Donovan said, "but it's so easy to confuse the two, don't you think?" Maybe it was crazy to antagonize him further, but she had only instinct to guide her, and instinct told her that the more off balance he was, the better her odds.

"You know what?" said Eddy. "Santa Muerte is weary of your insults. My enjoyment is not important. Bernardo, shoot her."

Bernardo said something that may have begun in his mind as words, but came to his lips as inarticulate gurgling. He raised the gun, though, aiming it in Donovan's general direction. She hit the floor and rolled again, this time in a direction that took her farther away from Eddy and closer to Bernardo, but not in the direction he was facing. He fired the gun, the report deafening in the relatively small room. The bullet flew close enough to Donovan's head that she heard the bee-buzz whine a fraction of a second before the side table next to the overstuffed chair exploded, shooting wooden shrapnel everywhere. Something stung her neck; she put a hand up, reflexively, and found a splinter the size of a thumb driven just below her right ear. Her fingertips came back smeared with blood.

No time for that now.

Donovan rolled again, this time straight at Bernardo. She came out of her tuck into a half crouch and used her momentum to bull him against the wall. His head, still fogged by the drug she'd given him, hit the door frame hard. The gun tumbled from his hand into the hallway.

Roaring inarticulately, Bernardo reached clumsily for Donovan's throat with both hands … and Eddy launched himself across the room, machete raised above his head.

Donovan caught the movement from the corner of her eye. She swung Bernardo around in a drunken dance and dropped to a half-crouch.

Eddy Zunigas swung his machete. It bit into Bernardo's unprotected back. The roar became a shriek of agony. Donovan shoved the dying man away from her; he toppled backward, taking Eddy down with him.

Bernardo was a big man—tall and broad of shoulder. His much smaller boss struggled beneath the dead weight of the body. By the time he managed to roll the corpse aside and pull the machete from its back, Donovan had pulled a handful of zip ties from her jacket pocket. She was still angry at herself for Bernardo. Because of her error in judgment, Angel was having to spend far more time in this literal hell hole than Donovan had intended. She'd meant to be away by now, with Hadley and his cohort on their way at flank speed.

Someday, I will learn not to fucking play with my food, she thought, resisting the urge to yank the damn splinter out of her neck. It hurt like hell, but she ignored it stoically.

"Get up, Eddy. We have a ritual to perform."

"My queen will send someone else to aid me."

"There is no one else, Ed. I killed them all. I should've killed Bernardo too. Oversight on my part. Thanks for doing it for me. So, now that it's just you and me, get up."

Eddy didn't move. He lay on the floor, supported on one elbow, the machete loosely held in one hand. He might've been loafing on a beach somewhere. He raised the blade and pointed it at her. "You think I am alone. I am not. I am never alone. My queen will guide me. *Bendita señora de las sombras, escucha mis oraciones para que tu ayuda venga a mí, te pido tu protección en esta difícil situación que estoy atravesando.*"

Donovan translated in her head: *Blessed lady of the shadows, listen to my prayers so that your help comes to me, I ask for your protection in this difficult situation that I am going through.*

Difficult situation. Right.

"You know, Ed, I've met some very colorful people in my life, and admittedly, I, myself, have done some very colorful things. But you are, hands down, the creepiest piece of human trash I have ever had the pleasure of taking out."

He laughed. A seemingly delighted guffaw. Donovan caught him under the chin with the side of her boot, snapping his jaw shut. As his head hit the floor with a satisfying thump, she gave him a swift boot toe to the groin. He uttered a squeal that sounded like a rush of air escaping a balloon. Donovan kicked him a third time, her heel connecting with his forehead, knocking him unconscious. He sprawled, limp, on the floor, his eyes rolling back in his head.

She stripped the strange elf of his rain poncho, then used the zip ties to secure his wrists and ankles. She then dragged him across the room so that he lay in front of his makeshift altar, placed so that the statue, once again, appeared to be gazing directly at him.

She donned the poncho herself, picked up the machete, and proceeded to efficiently remove his clothes with the blade. As she worked the steel up each velour pant leg, she grimaced.

"I do hope it's easier to cut out your heart."

Eddy's naked body told its own shocking tales. Scars covered it from head to foot. Self-inflicted? More evidence of childhood abuse? She would never know, and told herself it didn't matter. There came a time in everyone's life when they had to assume responsibility for their behavior and could no longer blame someone else. Donovan was, herself, far past that point.

She looked down at the naked man and sighed. "Go home to your mama, Eddy. She's waiting for you."

One slash was all it took to slice open his chest. Blood was suddenly everywhere. Eddy Zunigas jerked only once before surrendering to death. Donovan then folded back his skin, cracked open his rib cage, and studied the barely pulsing heart. Cutting the organ free with the blade, she lifted it out and placed it at the statue's feet.

Donovan got up and went to the mason jars with their grisly contents, separating the one containing Cynthia's heart and placing it on the desk for high visibility. Taking off the bloody plastic poncho, she laid it on one of the soiled chairs, musing that this may well have been the way the stains got there in the first place. Disposable raincoats were definitely going on her shopping list.

Returning to the mangled corpse, she took the small statue of Santa Muerte she'd tucked into her pocket and considered her next move. On the altar with the heart? In a flash of inspiration, she knelt beside the remains of Salvador Eduardo Ignacio Zunigas and dropped the plastic skeleton into the center of his chest where his heart had been.

"Eddy," she said, "I believe this belongs to you."

Chapter Twenty-Six

Stepping over the corpse in the hall, Donovan returned to the dining room to check on Angel. She was trembling and whimpering quietly. She'd heard the demise of her tormentors—probably smelled it as well. And despite Donovan's earlier assurances, she must have heard the gunfire down the hall. For all she knew, her rescuer had been dealt with and her own death was nearer than ever.

Donovan weighed the circumstances for only a moment. Angel's peace of mind was paramount and her recognition of Donovan's voice was a risk she simply had to take. She stood in the doorway of the room, lowered her voice to a growl, and said, in Spanish, "You're safe now. The police will soon come."

Angel inhaled a sharp breath and made a muffled sound through the duct tape over her mouth.

"*Prometo*. I promise," Donovan added, then got out of El Tortuga's house of death as swiftly as she could.

The Prius had not been vandalized in her absence. A small miracle, she thought, peeling off the bloodied latex gloves, turning them inside out before climbing into her car. Retrieving her purse from underneath the driver's seat, Donovan removed a burner phone and, using a voice-altering app, called Hadley.

When he answered, she simply said, "Los Empresarios are not happy with Eddy Zunigas. He's costing us more than he's bringing in. So we have left a present for you, Detective. Come and get it." She gave him the address. "Oh, and we found that missing item you've been looking for. It's in the dining room."

"Is she safe?" Hadley asked. "The woman he kidnapped?"

"She's alive," Donovan said and was surprised at how close her voice came to breaking.

She hung up with Hadley and moved her car around behind the gas station's decaying garage, drawing up between a rusting Honda Accord and a dumpster. Turning off the engine, she reached for the medicine kit in her center console. She spent the next several minutes focused intently on removing the splinter from her neck. The pain was both sharp and deep, but it kept her from succumbing to the insistent, rising clamor of the carnal urges that rolled through her in waves.

She'd never known what to make of this directionless desire. Movies made idiotic noises about "life-affirming sex"—whatever the hell that meant. She'd begun to think of it as similar to the way a capacitor works in an electrical system—building up a charge and then dispersing it in a tiny, though sometimes noisy, explosion.

She pulled down the driver's side visor, opened the vanity mirror, and went to work. Yanking out the shard of wood, disinfecting the two-inch-long wound, then patching it with some gauze and medical tape, she methodically cleaned up the mess it had made of her neck. She regretted the possible loss of the shirt she wore and dug a winter scarf out of her glove box, using it to conceal the wound. That done, she gathered up the gloves and wipes she'd used and stuffed them into a plastic bag. That she would dispose of elsewhere.

She got out of the car and squeezed between the dumpster and the cinderblock building, working her way along until she could see the house—or at least most of it—while she remained hidden in the shadows. She'd been stationed there for mere minutes when the first three patrol cars arrived in the company of Hadley's unmarked vehicle. Officers in flak jackets scattered, positioning themselves around the property with their guns drawn. Hadley pulled up behind the house, leapt from his car, and went directly to the back porch, his weapon also in hand.

Good cowboy. You listened.

As Hadley disappeared into the house with a pair of uniformed officers, an ambulance pulled up beside his car. They had a gurney and a backboard out of the ambulance with a speed that spoke of much practice, and were on their way to the house with the backboard, when Detective Hadley appeared again, a disheveled Angel clinging to him like a limpet. He turned her over to the paramedics, who wasted no time getting her into the ambulance. They left immediately, siren screaming, passing a second emergency unit on its way in.

If they need that, Donovan thought, *I didn't do my job right.*

She watched Beau Hadley return to the house, appreciative of the fact that he'd put Angel's well-being ahead of everything else, including a perfectly preserved crime scene.

"Cowboy, I'm going to kiss you for that," she murmured. Her libido rose up, hot and feral, and insisted she'd do more than just kiss him.

Yeah, she could do that, but it didn't fit into the time frame and might severely impact their ability to work together. She made her way back to her car and got in, listening to that insistent voice telling her she could surely find Jordan. He'd be in his office next to the DA's, where they would have privacy. She was damn sure Jordan wouldn't object. He'd made it clear that he wanted her. She could drive to his office. She could get in to see him. She could tell him to lock the door.

But then what? Then he'd expect something of her, even if it was only more of the same. He would hardly be willing to wait until the next time she had blood on her hands.

Suddenly, she was remembering the scene in her foyer—Jordan looking at her expectantly, hands full of silly little presents, Tristan stepping out of her bedroom "naked as a jay" her gran would've said.

Tristan.

Suddenly, she wanted Tristan with an urgency that had less to do with capacitors and adrenaline charges than with an emotion Donovan Montgomery was reluctant to put words to. The thought of fucking Jordan seemed suddenly unappetizing; the thought of doing it with Hadley made her feel shame—something she hadn't experienced for a very long time.

She shook herself and started the car as the buzz of desire—this time extremely directional—waned. She would go home and wait for the call telling her that Angel had been found. She would not have to feign relief or anger or grief for the way her dearest friend had been drawn into the darkest corner of her existence. All that was in there, waiting to come out. She was eager to let it.

Driving back to Lincoln Square, she turned on the radio, allowing it to distract her. Among the headlines was the report of a body discovered behind a taqueria. The young man's left eye had been removed. At first, Donovan assumed it to be the most recent Los Empresarios foot soldier found in Little Village, but when the broadcaster noted that this taqueria was in Pilsen, she knew that he was talking about a different one-eyed corpse, this one identified as Lupe Belmonte.

What was it Crazy Eddy had said—that three friends of Santa Muerte were his helpers? These were three corpses that Eddy did not make. He thought all but one were still in play right up until the moment he died.

If not Eddy Zunigas, then who?

Donovan flashed on the news footage of the Vandenbergs leaving Alfredo's office the morning that their daughter's body was found—the footage that she and Detective Hadley were watching when officers recognized the Vandenbergs' driver as Jerry Dillard, a retired dirty cop with a penchant for killing people he didn't like and somehow walking away clean.

He'd helped Mrs. Vandenberg into the back seat of a limo and they'd exchanged a glance as Mrs. Vandenberg wiped tears from her eye—her left eye.

An icy jolt of electric energy seared its way down Donovan Montgomery's spine. What if it hadn't been a tear? What if it had been a signal?

"An eye for an eye," she murmured.

She got home and poured herself a finger of Woodford Reserve before jumping into the shower. Ten minutes later with one towel around her body and another around her hair, she checked the phone. No call.

Throwing on jeans and a Cubs sweatshirt that neatly covered the bandage on her neck, the psychiatrist walked to her bay window where, looking out onto the well-manicured street, she reflected on all the kills she had made preceding Eduardo Zunigas. She had to admit, of them all, this one took the prize. Eddy's motivations may have seemed mundane, but they were only mundane on the surface.

Eddy Zunigas was trying to exorcise the demons given him by a murderous mother. The irony was that everything he did to exorcise them only made them stronger and more plentiful. What was that line from the Gospels where Christ asks the demon of a possessed man his name?

Legion.

"My name is Legion," the demon had said, "for we are many."

Donovan felt no animosity toward the strange, scarred imp. He had brought her to something buried, a territory darker than she had previously explored. He had robbed many people of their lives and might have added Angel to that list—possibly even Donovan herself—but Donovan understood demons. Understood how they could rob you of the people you loved.

Eddy had known that sometimes your demons *were* the people you loved. At least she had never had to face that.

She realized she was pacing her living room and made herself stop, go to the kitchen, make a cup of tea. She wanted to call Tristan, ask him when he'd be back in Chicago. But that was foolish on two counts. She might miss Hadley's call, and she would have drawn Tristan a step further into her life. If she did that, she would have learned nothing from what had happened to Angel.

She stood at the kitchen island, staring at the refrigerator. There might be some of that Americone Dream left. She was reaching for the freezer door when her cell phone rang. She let out a breath of relief and frustration and answered.

Hadley was quick to tell her that Angel had been found and that she was all right. His voice shook as he went on to tell her about the macabre scene at the Englewood house.

"I got a tip call from someone in Los Empresarios. Zunigas was our man. You were right. And odds are good that one of these ... one of these hearts belonged to Cynthia Vandenberg. DNA will clear that up. Anyway, the fellow won't be hurting anybody else."

Donovan let out a gust of air. "Thank you, Detective. I am more relieved than you can imagine. Where's Angel now?"

"They took her to St. Bernard off of Sixty-Third for tests and assessments, but she truly does seem to be okay, Doctor. I mean as okay as a person could be, given the circumstances. Strangest thing—she swears that the person who murdered all those guys was very ... kind to her, was the word she used. She said he took out the two guarding her, then when he was done with the rest of them, he made a point of coming back and telling her she was going to be okay."

He. "That's ... extraordinary, Detective."

There was a moment of silence. "Can I ... can I get you to call me Beau? It is my name."

"Only if you call me Donovan."

"Donovan. I'd like that." He laughed, sounding a little shaky. "You know, I do believe I need a drink."

The little demon just south of her navel reared its horny head; Donovan almost told him to drop by and she'd make him his drink of choice ... seeing as how they were now on a first-name basis. She bopped the demon with a cartoon hammer and took a sip from her glass.

"I'll bet you do," she said. "Thank you for calling me, Beau. Stellar work. I'll leave for the hospital right now."

"Before you go, I should tell you they just found another one-eyed man. This one's in Pilsen."

"Really? Well, you fill me in when you sort it out. I plan on spending the night next to my pal at the hospital."

"You do that. And I think before I go see one more mutilated body, I'm going to take a shower."

The dying sunset cast sharp-edged shadows across the freeway as Donovan drove to the South Side hospital. On her way, she called the precinct and spoke with Officer Stevenson, the desk sergeant who had gathered information from Roy Barns and William Vandenberg.

"Officer Stevenson, hello. This is Donovan Montgomery. Glad you answered. You know about Englewood?"

"Yes, ma'am. Just heard. What a mess."

"Even for Chicago."

"I'm so glad that your friend is all right, Doctor Montgomery."

"Me too. I'm on my way to the hospital now. If the DNA on the hearts proves that one of them belonged to Cynthia Vandenberg, I think her parents are going to be fairly shaken by the discovery. I'd like to drop in on them tomorrow, just to see if there's anything that I or the department can do. Would you text me their address?"

"Sure thing. That's so nice of you."

Goodbyes exchanged, she ended the call and turned into the hospital parking lot, finding a space near the emergency room entrance. Her phone pinged as she passed through St. Bernard's double glass doors; Stevenson had texted her the Vandenbergs' address.

An ER nurse informed Donovan that Angel had just been moved to a private room.

"Wow, that was fast."

"Well, she's stable, and we wanted to get her situated and comfortable before the press infiltrates." The nurse smiled. "You know how it goes. The specifics that brought her here are about to make Ms. Torres a very popular woman. We need to do what we can to shield her from all of that while we evaluate her condition."

Angel's sister Xenia was already at her bedside when Donovan located the room. The patient slept while an IV pumped fluids into her arm and the pulse oximeter clipped to her finger monitored her vitals. Xenia had drawn a chair up as close to the head of the bed as she could and rested a hand on Angel's shoulder.

"Donovan! Oh my God!" Xenia cried, leaping from her chair and rushing into familiar arms. Donovan held her as she wept and stammered. "What happened? They said they found her in Englewood? Why was she …? Why? Why would someone kidnap *Angel*?"

Why, indeed?

Because she's my friend. Because I didn't tell her enough to protect her. Or maybe I told her too much.

Donovan thought about giving a pat answer (she was a woman alone in the wrong place at the wrong time, could've happened to anyone, et cetera), but none of the pat answers fit. She led Xenia back to her chair, making consoling noises, saying nothing.

But when Xenia was seated again, she looked up into Donovan's face and asked, "Why would someone target Angel? Why would they take her to Englewood of all places?"

"It's related to a case I was profiling," Donovan told her. "And they targeted Angel because that's the way they send messages in their world."

Xenia sniffled, her brow furrowing. "Sounds like *The Godfather.*"

Donovan smiled. "Yeah. It *is* a bit like *The Godfather.*" She turned a physician's eye to the monitors assessing Angel's vitals. "They give her a sedative?"

"Yeah. I think so … A case, you said. You mean the Santa Muerte Murders?"

Donovan resisted the urge to roll her eyes. "Yeah. That one."

"God, Donovan, our grandmother used to *pray* to that thing."

Donovan perched on the edge of the bed and took Xenia's hands in hers. "I know. Ange told me. Lots of people pray to Santa Muerte, Xeny. She's not the bad guy. The man who had Angel kidnapped and several other people murdered was the bad guy, and he's dead. Detective Hadley told me."

Xenia's face contorted as she squeezed her eyes shut. She pulled her hands from Donovan's and reached for Angel's unfettered hand, murmuring an *Ave Maria* in Spanish.

Donovan's attention caught on the last line of the prayer: "*Santa María, madre de Dios, ruega por nosotros los pecadores ahora y en la hora de nuestra muerte.*"

Saint Mary, mother of God, pray for us sinners now and at the hour of our death.

The irony of this was not lost on Donovan. In Xenia and Angel's form of Catholicism, Saint Mary served as the Protector of Souls.

A nurse entered the room, smiling, and approached the bed. Donovan rose and moved out of her way while Xenia continued quietly reciting Hail Marys, rocking slightly and petting her baby sister's hand.

The nurse—her badge said "Brewer"—moved to the monitor, tapping notations into a handheld device. She glanced at Donovan as she checked the IV stents and the oximeter. "Doctor Montgomery. I recognize you from your book jackets. Ms. Torres asked after you. We told her you were on your way. Glad you actually were. I'm Pat Brewer. I'll be checking in on her throughout the night."

"Nice to meet you. What did they give her?"

"Diazepam. I'm hoping that will keep her calm for the next few hours, but we're focused on keeping her anxiety level in check, so we'll be closely monitoring that while she's here."

"Good. I'm sure her doctor will send her home with a script for some sort of benzodiazepine. Medically induced mood dysregulation is going to be necessary until she regroups from that nightmare. It's going to take her some time. How is she physically?"

"Except for some abrasions on her wrists and ankles from struggling against the nylon rope, there doesn't appear to be any other physical damage. Doctor Karnowsky will determine what tests he wants to run in the morning after she gets hydrated and has a good night's sleep." The nurse turned to face Donovan. "And, as I said, we'll be checking on her throughout the night. You can count on that. We'll do everything in our power to keep the press away from her. I haven't passed a TV screen lately, but I'll bet that creepy old house and some high school yearbook headshot of Ms. Torres are occupying every station by now."

"I gather she's been questioned briefly."

"Yes, in the ER. A detective was with her when she came in. Young guy, blond, cowboy boots." The corners of her mouth twitched. "He left when we gave her the sedative, which was just before we moved her here."

The nurse and doctor simultaneously glanced over at Angel's sister still murmuring prayers. She seemed to be more traumatized than Angel.

"Can't you give her something?"

"You know I can't. But, hey, you're a doctor. If you want to prescribe her something, just let me know." Nurse Brewer slipped her handheld into her pocket and left the room.

Donovan crouched next to Xenia, resting her hand on her leg. "Xeny … Xeny, look at me."

Xenia turned toward Donovan as if confused by the request.

"Is Paciano with the kids?"

She nodded.

"You know, they're probably pretty upset. All they know is that their mom wigged out and left in a hurry. I'll bet Paciano would like to have you there too."

Xenia shook her head. "I … I should stay."

Donovan stood, offering her hand. "I'm going to be here, right here, all night. Maybe you should go home and take care of your family, get a little rest so you can be fresh in the morning. You'll want to talk to the doctor. You'll want to talk to Angel."

Xenia took Donovan's hand but did not rise. Donovan coaxed her out of the chair. "God forbid Paciano has turned on the TV. This is going to be all over the news … in Swiss cheese form because the police are not going to spill all the beans. You don't want Mona and Peeps to see any of that, right?"

"Oh," said Xenia, realizing what Donovan was warning of. She was on her feet in a fraction of a second, a determined expression on her face and a finger pointed at the profiler's nose. "You promise me. You promise me, *mija*. You'll stay right here in this room until I get back in the morning. Yes?"

Feeling like a chastised child prone to step out of line, Donovan smiled. "Cross my heart," she said, cringing a little as the words came out of her mouth.

Xenia didn't seem to notice. She snatched up her coat, put it on, slung her purse over one shoulder, and kissed Donovan on the cheek. "Call me if—"

"Nothing is going to happen to her. I swear I'll eat anyone who walks through that door with ill intent. Listen, Xeny, d'you have any sedatives or sleep aids at home or need me to prescribe something?"

"I have some valerian," she said. "Is that what you mean?"

She'd hoped for something stronger, but she knew Xenia's family was into herbals. "That'll be fine."

Xenia kissed her little sister on the cheek and left.

Once alone, Donovan took out her cell and called Hadley. "Beau."

"Donovan. How's our girl?"

"Sleeping like she's been drugged. You still with our new one-eyed friend?"

"Yep. You staying there tonight?"

"Yep. When do you plan on getting back here for further questioning?"

"I'll be back before she wakes up, which hopefully won't be for several hours."

"Listen, we both know that the press is going to be ridiculous about this. Can you put someone on the door?"

"Done. Take a gander in the hall."

Donovan stepped to the door and poked her head out. A man stood about fifteen feet away, near the nurses' station, leaning against a wall, reading something on his phone. He looked up and nodded before returning to whatever he was reading. She checked the other way. Another plainclothes guy stood at the opposite end of the corridor near the second bank of elevators. He, too, nodded in her direction.

"You're that good," she told Hadley.

"Yep."

For the next hour, Donovan sat in the chair Angel's sister had left by the bed, staring at her friend and remembering the wild bike rides, birthday parties, sleepovers, crushes, school dances, apartments, and minimum wage jobs they had shared. Through all of those regular experiences that inform so many young lives, Donovan always knew that she was somehow different. That her reactions to things were unconventional, even out of scale. But Angel had kept her grounded, normalizing her, anchoring the humanity that might have withered once her vengeful nature had asserted itself.

How is it that she never knew?

Maybe she did.

She set aside that disturbing thought and checked in with the office voice mail. There were two appointments to schedule, one cancellation, and a call from Cameron Nessel, the former med student and current junkie whom she had met in Chatham four days earlier. Pleasantly surprised that he had not only kept her card but used it, she returned his call. He'd taken her advice and was staying at a friend's apartment. He asked her, timidly, if she could help him get clean.

"Cameron, I assure you I will do everything in my power to help you. You should be proud of yourself for taking that first step. It's often the hardest. I'll line up some resources and fit you into my schedule and call you back tomorrow or the next day. In the meantime if you need me, you have my number. Once we get you safely over that first abyss, I'll see what I can do to help you get your medical education back on track."

"Dr. Montgomery, I … I feel so … tentative. So weak."

"Nonsense, Cameron. Calling me took great courage. It tells me that you are as smart as I surmised you were when we met. You'll find that I'm a very good ally. And rest assured, I never let the bad guys win. Now you make your friend keep their eyes on you. Eat well. Sleep well, and I'll call you tomorrow."

Donovan said her goodbyes, tucked away her cell phone, and scanned the room. She felt … peaceful. The day had played out, if not exactly as she would have liked, close enough. The feeling was foreign to her. Especially given the several errors in judgment she had made in her desire to get Angel out alive and whole. She realized that in all the years she had been pursuing extrajudicial justice, this was the first time since her first kill that the stakes had been so personal. Had that made her careless? Sloppy? Unobservant?

Or had it, instead, added an edge that she usually lacked? She remembered the blur of moves she'd made when Bernardo had interrupted her confrontation with Eddy Zunigas. Had the high stakes—the very personal stakes—clouded her instincts or heightened them?

She did not want to even side-eye the elephant in the room—that her much-vaunted isolationism was sheer hypocrisy. She preached "no attachments" like a hellfire and damnation minister, but even the choir wasn't listening.

Her eyes wandering the dimly lit hospital room, she realized that there was a sweater on the floor near the window. Xenia's no doubt. She'd forgotten it in her rush to leave. The doctor stared at the crumpled heap of yarn and realized, with a sense of muted awe, that she had no impulse to pick it up and fold it or arrange it over the back of a chair.

Maybe, she thought, *maybe sometimes people heal.*

Chapter Twenty-Seven

"Hey. Hey, D, wake up."

Donovan opened her eyes; the hospital room rose from a gray blur to pastel clarity. She focused on the head of the bed. Angel peered back at her, blearily.

Donovan moved from her chair to the edge of Angel's bed. "Morning, Ange. How are you doing?"

"I'm ... I think I'm okay," she answered barely about a whisper. "Why'm I still in the hospital?"

"They just want to make sure they didn't miss some unseen trauma. No worries. You're doing well."

"Where's Xeny?"

"I convinced her to go check on Paciano and the kids last night." Donovan put air quotes around the words "check on," then glanced at her watch. "It's almost six a.m. She'll be back soon, I suspect."

Angel's face contorted and she laid a hand on Donovan's arm. "Donovan ... that place ... those monsters. There was this guy like ... I can't even describe this guy. And Santa Muerte shit all over the place."

Donovan's skin crawled. When she'd gotten to Angel, she'd been wearing a sleep mask. "They let you see—?"

"When they took me into the house, I ... I fought back. The smells ..." She shivered. "The mask got pulled down around my neck. I wish it hadn't."

Donovan put her hand over Angel's and squeezed it. "Hey. Don't. Try to clear your mind, Angel. You're going to have to talk about every detail in a little while when Detective Hadley gets back here."

"Detective Hadley." Angel relaxed. "Ya cowboy saved my ass."

Donovan laughed.

"Seriously, D. Like some storybook hero. Literally carried me out of that dungeon."

"I know. Hadley told me. When the media gets hold of it—"

"Oh, no. No way. You think I have to put out a statement? Stare into a camera and talk about that shit? Really rather not."

Donovan leaned in. "Calm down, Ange. Look at me. You don't have to say a goddamn thing. Let them go wild trying to decide whether the guy is Batman or if Daredevil's moved to Chicago."

Angel gave her a wan smile, nestling her head against the pillow. "Good. I'm gonna wait for the book deal." She closed her eyes. In moments, she had drifted back to sleep.

When Xenia returned at around seven o'clock, Donovan left. She went home and showered, trading in her jeans and sweatshirt for a red power suit. Back in her car, she headed for the Vandenbergs' house in Bridgeport near the Loop.

Mr. Vandenberg answered the door. His posture and pallor made him appear frail despite his height and broad shoulders. He seemed shocked when he saw her, though Donovan deduced that it was because of something that happened before opening the door, judging by the way he kept glancing over his shoulder.

"Good morning, Mr. Vandenberg. I'm Doctor Montgomery. We met at the precinct ...?"

He stared at her blankly. "I remember. We didn't even know it was Cynthia then, just some poor kid murdered and left at Roy's curb. Is this about what they—what they found in Englewood? We got the call earlier this morning."

Donovan could see that he was in shock but was relieved to know that the couple had already been contacted by the CPD. It meant she would not have to be the one to tell them that their daughter's heart had been found. Even without being the bearer of unbearable news, she would have to step cautiously if she was to accomplish what she had come there to do.

"Not directly. I just want to extend my sincere condolences and speak with Mrs. Vandenberg about a group I chair that might help her. I can't imagine what she's going through—what you're both going through. May I come in?"

He glanced over his shoulder and then back at the doctor. "She's not doing very well. Can this wait?"

Donovan had no intention of waiting. "I'm not sure she can wait, Mr. Vandenberg. Your wife is vulnerable right now. Meeting with other mothers who have lost children to violence would provide her with support and a sense of community. It could mean the difference between your wife harming herself, shutting down completely, or slowly pinning her life back together. It will only take a moment, sir. I know this is an inconvenient time, but … it is the most crucial time. However, if you wish to wait …" She extended a business card for her private practice. "You can call me anytime if either of you need to talk."

He took the card without looking at it. Again, he glanced over his shoulder. "Let me see." He was gone for only a moment before he returned to usher Donovan into the house.

Mrs. Vandenberg was sitting on the couch in a well-maintained, smartly decorated front room. Her hands were clasped in her lap, but they were not still; they worried the hem of the oversized sweater she wore over a pair of black leggings. She wore fuzzy slippers resembling twin sheep.

What caught Donovan's immediate attention was the fact that, across the room, in front of the fireplace, a flat-screen television lay on the hearth, shards of black plastic covering the area around it. A hammer lay beside it on the sage green carpet; Donovan suspected it had played a part in the TV's demise.

Had this pale, spiritless woman done that?

Bill Vandenberg noticed Donovan assessing the wreckage. "Mary turned it on as soon as we got the call this morning. Every station, talking about our daughter, our Cynthia, all those dead bodies, mason jars filled with …" He gestured to the TV. "I … lost control. For a moment, it seemed the only way I could make it stop."

He knelt next to his wife, who was peering at Donovan as if she was struggling to place her. "Honey, this is Doctor Montgomery. She's a psychiatrist who works with the Chicago Police. Roy and I met her the other night. She would like to talk to you for a minute. I think she might have something that could help us get through this. That okay, sweetheart?"

Mary Vandenberg, her gaze still on Donovan, nodded listlessly, prompting Donovan to sit down next to her on the sofa. William Vandenberg disappeared into the kitchen to get them coffee, he said, but Donovan knew it was a move to give her a moment alone with his wife. She planned on taking full advantage.

Leaning in close to the grieving mother, she cut directly to the chase. "Mrs. Vandenberg," she murmured, "Mary, I know what you had Mr. Dillard do for you."

The older woman's gaze was suddenly focused on Donovan's face, reading it.

Donovan pushed harder. "I know what he did to those three young men—'an eye for an eye'—or, in this case, three eyes for a heart?"

All the blood seemed to drain from Mary's face. Her hands stopped working the hem of her sweater, and Donovan grasped them in her own.

"Who are you?" Mary asked. "How do you know anything about … anything?"

"Right now, I'm your best friend," Donovan told her. "I've studied the video of you and your husband leaving the medical examiner's office. You weren't wiping away a tear when you were waiting for Dillard to help you into the car. You were signaling Dillard—and everyone involved in your daughter's death—that you were going to find them and exact revenge. Then you had those men killed—two in Little Village, one in Pilsen—because somehow you, or maybe Mr. Dillard, concluded that those were the three responsible."

There was a hard gleam in Mary Vandenberg's blue eyes. "And you're threatening to go to the police, is that it? What do you want?"

"I don't want anything except to know how you made the connection between your daughter's death and those three men. Right now, all of this is our little secret. No one needs to know. But in return for my silence, you need to tell me how and why you set it up."

"Why? Why would you stay silent? Why wouldn't you tell the police everything you think you know?"

"Let's just say I have a keen appreciation of the urge for revenge. I empathize with you, Mary. You are not alone here."

A stew of emotions roiling in her eyes, Mary Vandenberg began to cry. Just then, her husband reentered the room carrying a tray holding a pot, cups, and coffee fixings. He placed the tray on the coffee table. "Is ... everything all right? Do I need to ask Dr. Montgomery to leave?"

His wife took a deep breath, patted at her cheeks with a sleeve, and straightened herself slightly. "No, not at all, honey. The doctor and I are having a ... a good chat. She thinks she can help me." She turned her head to meet his gaze. "Bill, would you mind running over to the pharmacy? They just texted me that I have a prescription ready—the sleep medication. I need it."

He got it; Donovan could see the comprehension in his eyes. He knew they were having a breakthrough but had to wonder if he knew what it was about.

He smiled briefly, a spot of sunlight on a cold, gray day. "Sure, honey. You two talk. I'll be right back. It's just down the road."

"No hurry, sweetie." Mary smiled.

Bill nodded and left.

Donovan leaned back into the sofa. "Well done, Mary. Please, tell me what happened."

Mary was toying with the hem of her sweater again. "What if I said nothing happened? You have no proof."

Donovan poured coffee for them both, setting Mary Vandenberg's cup on the table. "Assume that I do. And I suspect that, pretty soon, that young hotshot detective is going to pin it all together too. He knows as much about Mr. Dillard's past as I do and the type of work he takes on—possibly more. But right now we have an opportunity to sort things out and make some intelligent decisions. You don't want to be charged with three counts of murder, Mrs. Vandenberg. You're going through quite enough right now."

When the other woman remained silent, Donovan pressed more firmly. "Mary, your options are limited and you're scared. I get that you're calculating right now whether or not I might genuinely be able to help. Trust me when I say I can."

Mary Vandenberg pressed her lips together as if weighing the risk of opening them again.

Donovan considered her next words carefully. "I know what you're feeling, Mary. I lost my sister to drugs my first year in college. As I said, I understand the thirst for revenge. I can't judge you for acting on those strong emotions."

Mary Vandenberg peered up into Donovan's face, her self-protective barriers crumbling as their eyes met. She deflated visibly. "I'm not a cold-blooded killer."

"I'm certain that you are no more of a killer than I am. So let's stay focused. We only have a few minutes to cover a great deal of ground. Unless, that is, your husband knows—"

She shook her head emphatically. "No. Bill knows nothing about … any of it." She paused, took a deep breath, and said, "All right. This last time we got Cynthia out of rehab, I knew she was going to stay clean. I could *feel* it. See it in her eyes."

"Your daughter was in rehab more than once?"

Mary nodded. "The day of her release the time before, Bill was working, so I picked her up from the rehabilitation center. When we walked out, three hoods were leaning against my car. I was … deeply disturbed—scared, actually. But Cynthia seemed to know them. She threw her arms around one of them, squealing, 'Chi-Chi! Chi-Chi!' I couldn't speak, I was so shocked. Then she turned to me and said, 'Don't worry, Mom' and introduced them to me as Georgie, Lupe, and Chevy—the Chi-Chi she'd been so happy to see. None of them seemed happy to be called out like that. In fact, Chi-Chi gave her a little shove away from him."

Donovan nodded. Chevy Velasco and Jorge Perez had been found in Little Village, Lupe Belmonte in Pilsen. "Go on."

"Cynthia shoved him back, giggling like a little girl. She said, 'Mom these are my friends. I'm staying with them for a while.' I argued, but she insisted. They weren't her friends—they were her enablers. Before we knew it, she turned up here, sick and miserable and with bruises all over. This last time she got clean, she did everything she could to distance herself from those devils. She was even in the process of having those horrid tattoos removed. I asked if those three were the problem. She said yes, but that they were part of a bigger problem, and she wasn't going to have anything to do with it. That's all she would say. But I watched her take more than one call that made her uncomfortable. Maybe they thought she knew too much. Maybe that's why they …" Her voice gave out.

"That was probably part of it. But the way it's being reported would suggest that someone wanted to leave a message for Congressman Barns. The fact that Cynthia had been involved with the cartels, denounced them, and was the daughter of the congressman's closest friend must have made her the perfect victim."

"Cartels? Dear Jesus. I thought these men were just small-time dealers."

"Oh, no. Not at all small time. That man I'm sure you heard about on the TV this morning—before it stopped working—the man who owned the house in Englewood, where they found his ... trophies—I'm certain they worked for him. They didn't kill your daughter, Mary, but they brought her right to her murderer."

"They said on the news he was dead. That man."

"That's what I heard as well." Donovan grimaced, a part of her wishing she could tell Mary Vandenberg that she had made certain "that man" was dead. So dead there wasn't a saint in heaven or a demon in hell that could bring him back to life. "How did you reconnect to her three 'friends' if they were out of her life?"

"When she got clean the last time, she moved in here with us. One day she left her phone out on her desk and I ... I went through her calls, voice messages, and texts. Between that and her contact list, I found all three numbers. It wasn't hard. I didn't know what I was going to do with them then. I don't even know why I did that, but I did. When I saw her in that cold, sterile lab, lying on that table, her light extinguished ..." She started to shake, but her voice remained level. "Something in me changed, I could feel it. Something ... broke. And I knew exactly what I was going to do."

Donovan frowned. The timeline didn't make sense. "But you must've already contacted Jerry Dillard. He drove you to the ME's office."

"Jerry was a family friend. I was close with his ex-wife. He offered to drive us to the examiner's office the moment he found out there was a good chance ... this was Cynthia. He knew neither of us was in any shape to drive." Mary Vandenberg picked up her coffee cup and took a drink, wrapping both palms around the ceramic mug. "He ... indicated to me that if it was our daughter, he'd track down whoever did this and 'take them out.' He said all these drug dealers were illegal aliens who didn't belong here anyway."

"Family friend, bad cop, racist, open to violence. The perfect guy for the job."

Anger flushed across Mary Vandenberg's face. "He's not the bad guy, Doctor. Those so-called 'friends' of Cynthia's were the bad guys. I wanted the men who killed my baby to pay for it."

"So you just called him and told him you had work for him, or ...?"

"He was at the house when we got the call that Roy had recognized Cynthia. He saw the effect it had on us. That's when he offered to drive us and ... that's when he took me aside and ... and told me what he was willing to do. If I needed him to do it. If Cynth was really ..."

"Did he ask for money?"

Mary frowned. "No. In fact, I offered, but he said he had a good paying job as a corrections officer at the Metropolitan Correctional Center."

"Corrections officer? I understood that Mr. Dillard worked as a cop-for-hire since his retirement from the force."

"He just started. I guess lots of retired police officers do it."

The sound of a car pulling into the driveway made both women turn toward the front window. Donovan took out another business card and placed it on the coffee table.

"I conduct a group for mothers who've lost a child to violence. You really should consider sitting in. It might help you process all this. Meanwhile, all you need to take away from the other part of our chat is that it didn't happen. Jerry Dillard is a friend who offered to drive you to the ME's office. Period. If you tell anyone else about it—even your husband—I can't protect you. Do we understand one another?"

The older woman nodded slowly.

"And since you've cleaned the streets of everyone involved in your daughter's murder, you will not be having anybody else killed— ever—no matter how horrible they are. You're not cut out for it, Mary. You'll slip. This is your one free pass."

"I ... of course not. I'd have no reason—"

"Now. *Now* you have no reason, just as you had no reason before your daughter was murdered. The unexpected in life changes us, Mary. It ... unmakes us in one form and remakes us in another. Don't let it unmake you again. Trust that God or karma operates in the world."

With a little help.

Again, Mary nodded, this time vigorously. "What now? What are you going to do?"

Donovan lifted her chin. "We all have secrets, Mrs. Vandenberg. Don't ever make me sorry that I protected yours."

William Vandenberg entered, jingling his keys loudly. Donovan stood. After a moment to steady herself, Mary Vandenberg did too. She even managed a smile for her husband. Donovan knew how hard the loss of a child—especially an only child—could unhinge a marriage. She could tell the Vandenbergs were still much in love with each other and hoped they weathered this storm. She approached the bereaved father and shook his hand, reminding him to call if he felt he would like to talk. Then she turned and hugged his wife.

"Goodbye, Mary. I am truly, truly sorry for your loss."

While Donovan had no intention of outing Mary Vandenberg, she could not allow Jerry Dillard to walk away from three murders without consequence. He'd gotten the blood of innocents on his hands when he worked for the force, and he'd never paid for those crimes. Turning him over to the police was not an option—the first thing the DA would do was work to determine if someone had paid him for his services or if he had done it for reasons of his own.

No, she would have to find another way to take care of it.

Chapter Twenty-Eight

"Surprise, surprise. I've seen more of you this week than I've seen any of my grandkids for the last six months," Officer Bernice Westmoreland noted wryly as she watched Donovan sign in at her counter.

"What can I say—Ruben Ortiz is a charismatic guy," Donovan said with all the sly sarcasm she could put into one sentence.

Bernice laughed and directed her to the guard who'd take her to Ortiz's unit, where the inmate had a similarly surprised reaction.

Ortiz sat, already chained in place, when Donovan entered the common area of the prison. He nodded to the guard standing nearest the table, and the man ambled away. Ortiz no longer made much of an effort to hide his authority on the inside, at least with certain guards, those who had been bought or worked both sides. She also knew that with his chance at the witness protection program still being negotiated, the powerful cartel lieutenant would continue to play the impotent captive for as long as it took. WITSEC was a lever that Donovan was willing to pull.

Ortiz grinned up at her. "Third visit in a week. I'm starting to think you have a crush on me, Doctor. People are starting to talk."

She positioned herself on one of the built-in stools and folded her hands on the stainless steel table. "Hello, Mr. Ortiz. Have you heard about the sad mess they found in Englewood yesterday?"

"No, mami, I don't hear shit. I'm in jail. How 'bout you tell me."

"Oh, it was quite the scene. The police, responding to an anonymous tip, found your colleague Eduardo Zunigas lying in front of a Santa Muerte statue with his chest ripped open and his heart cut out. They found four dead soldiers strewn about the place too. Brutal stuff. And, icing on the cake, the woman Eddy had strapped to a table—his next sacrifice—Detective Hadley carried her out alive. One more unfortunate humiliation for your … fraternal organization."

Ortiz's eyes widened, then narrowed. His jaw tightened, making his grin twitch at the corners, but it didn't drop. "Detective Hadley. That vato has turned into quite a Golden Boy."

"Mm-hmm. I hear it was a real mess. And just on the down low, between you and me, I heard that they found two other soldiers in an alley a few blocks away, equally dead."

"Yeah?"

She smiled and met his gaze. "Well, no. They haven't found them yet, but somebody will find 'em. If not the cops, maybe an Empresarios cleanup crew."

She watched for a response. His grin remained in place, but something changed behind his eyes. "Well, if I had heard anything like that, I don't know if I'd be pissed or happy." He laughed. "El Tortuga! What the hell was that guy? Some kind of fucking clown freak. But, wow, that must have been gnarly. Must have taken an army of badasses to pull off something like that."

"You're sweet." She inched as close to him as possible. "Here's why I'm here. I want to give you a present."

"Yeah? I love presents. Where is it, *mamacita*? You got it between your legs?"

He nudged the tip of her shoe with his. Donovan retracted her foot but stayed close enough for whispered communication.

"Those three dead one-eyed soldiers of yours were killed by a man named Jerry Dillard, dirty ex-cop, hates everybody unless they're White. And get this—he's working here as a corrections officer."

The smile slid from Ortiz's face. "Is that a fact?"

"It is. He believed those three men were responsible for the death of that young girl found at the congressman's curb. Turns out he knew her, was a friend of her parents. Small world. Guess he took it upon himself to do them a solid by avenging that girl's murder ... maybe have a little fun at the same time. What're three more dead Mexicans, right? So ... do you like your present?"

Ortiz rolled his head as if to loosen the muscles in his neck. His smile returned. "I do. Why would you give me such a nice gift?"

Donovan got up and started for the exit.

"Because I'm a busy woman. But while we're doing Q and A, why didn't you give Hadley that Englewood address when he came here?"

"Because Eddy didn't want him. He wanted you."

"It's nice to want things."

"You know, there are people even higher up in Los Empresarios than the clown freak, even more powerful than me."

She nodded and moved toward the door.

"Hey, Doctor Badass, you ever want to switch teams, I'll hook you up."

On her way out, Donovan thought about what the cartel lieutenant had implied. She did not like the implication. It was clear that she and the cowboy were going to have to watch their backs—something she did as a matter of course.

It doesn't matter how many cockroaches you kill, there are always more under the floorboards.

Chapter Twenty-Nine

"My Aunt Helena had back surgery two years ago. Seventy-five years old and they released her the next day. Me, they keep for four."

Angel Torres sat curled comfortably in her sister's most comfy chair, sipping tea, and surrounded by Donovan, Jordan, Alfredo and his husband Mark, and her brother-in-law Paciano. Across the room, near the hearth, her niece and nephew sat cross-legged on the carpet pretending to read to one another, neither old enough to do so, while Xenia refilled drinks for her sister's guests. All had gathered in Angel's small Albany Park home to celebrate her homecoming and clean bill of health. She was still on some mild antianxiety meds but had left the stronger tranquilizers behind at the hospital. Nevertheless, Paciano and Xenia had insisted she stay with them at least until she was completely off the medication.

Donovan moved from the couch to the arm of Angel's recliner. "Well, part of that time was over the weekend, and besides, the longer you were in there the easier it was to keep the press from hounding you."

"You telling me you did that?" she asked Donovan.

"Not me. I have to give Detective Hadley the credit for that."

Alfredo rose from the couch to go to the dining room table, which held an impressive spread of food. He placed another two empanadas on his plate.

"Seriously?" Mark commented. "Isn't that thirds for you, Alfie?"

"What? They're good. Okay, here's one for you." He picked up a third and carried it back to his husband. "Fortunately, the press had their attention diverted yesterday with the Dillard murder. Otherwise, they would probably be lined up outside the house like vampires waiting for you to open the door and hoping you were naive enough to invite them in."

"Jeez, Alfie." Mark chuckled, taking a bite out of the little meat pie. "How uplifting."

"Sorry, luv," Alfredo said to Angel. "But it's true. We all know it is."

Angel's brother-in-law Paciano stood between Jordan and the table sipping a beer. "What a menace that guy was. All day yesterday the news kept talking about all the racist stuff they found in his house and a bunch of hate propaganda on his laptop. Guess he was hooked up with some pretty radical online groups."

Donovan listened, delighted that Dillard had so blatantly incriminated himself. It tied up the whole package with a neat little bow.

"How was he killed again?" Mark asked.

"Shot in his driveway while he was vacuuming out his truck," Jordan chimed in. "Distance shots—one in the head, one in the chest. Clean and professional. Must've been a crack shot. Ex-military maybe. Could've been a literal blast from his past."

Mark made a face over the bad word play. "Well, judging from what I read, the guy wasn't lacking for enemies. I wonder if they have any leads yet."

"Chief Newsome gave a press conference this morning. Nothing yet." Jordan continued, "Hadley was there, standing at her shoulder. She gave him a big, fat shout-out, as well she should. That fella pinned together all of that crazy Santa Muerte business nice and neat." He looked over at Angel. "And carried our girl to safety."

Everyone cheered. Angel smiled. "My hero," she added, and yawned. She hadn't been sleeping all that well, and Donovan had already enlisted Xenia to push valerian, a natural soporific and muscle relaxant.

"I hear Dillard knew the Vandenbergs and their girl," Ramos interjected. "Wonder how they're taking it. Not well, I imagine. First their daughter, now this. I mean, the man was a friend of the family."

Mark reached across Alfredo for another chip. "Not someone I'd want as a friend. Hard to imagine a couple as involved in social activism as the Vandenbergs befriending a guy with his record."

"Well, people change," Donovan said. "It was an old friendship. Maybe he wasn't always quite so dangerous or so racist."

Jordan shook his head. "That's not what I hear. I think he just hid it well."

Xenia placed a casserole dish on the dining room table, adding to the excess. Mark jumped up. "May I help?"

"Thank you, *mijo*. You could grab that other dish and set it on this hot plate."

She and Paciano shared a passing kiss as she moved behind her sister's chair and patted her shoulder. "One of the many unbelievable things about my Angel's recent adventure is that she got all of her stuff back! Not one dollar missing. *Increíble*."

"Thank God," added Angel. "Now Mona will have the pleasure of playing Mystery Date on her mom's old board game."

"Why would she want that old thing? The box is ripped, one of you wrote 'I love Doug Terry' on the board, and you took a brown crayon and colored in the faces of every 'date' behind the little door. I suppose you both wanted your imaginary men to be more ethnically diverse."

Everyone laughed and started splintering off for one-on-one conversations. Xenia put together two small plates for Ramona and Pepe.

Donovan sat on the arm of Angel's chair. "Xeny thinks we colored in those faces when we were kids."

"Yeah, let's not tell her we did it last week."

"Here. I'll get you some more tea."

Donovan lifted the mug from Angel's hand. As she did, Angel grabbed her wrist and pulled her back. Her placid, pleasant expression turned to something darker.

"I seem okay to you?"

"Yes. Why?"

"Look, I don't want to freak out Xenia any more than she already is. But D, I'm not okay. I can't stop thinking about that place. I can't get that skeleton out of my head. I don't know how to shake it. Sometimes she's this looming Santa Muerte and sometimes she morphs into that crazy guy I saw when my mask slipped. How do I get it to stop?"

Donovan squatted next to the chair and took Angel's hands in her own. "You give yourself time, Angel. It was only four days ago. It's a process." She scanned the room. "You want me and Xenia to gracefully get the other guys out of here?"

Angel shook her head. "No. No, I think I'm better when people are around. Things seem more—normal."

"That's good to hear." Donovan started to get up, but Angel pulled her closer.

"It's all kind of mixed up in my head, but there was a moment when I was in that place that I thought ..."

"Thought what, sweetie?"

"That you were in the room with me, telling me things were going to be okay. Isn't that crazy?"

Donovan blinked, assessing this unexpected turn. "You were in distress, Ange. Makes perfect sense that your mind would conjure up a friend."

"I *had* a friend—the guy who swooped in and rescued me. But D, I could smell your perfume. I swear to God I could. It ... it made me feel calmer. Like I was going to get through this."

The doctor had not anticipated this particularly impressive recall. Though she loved the Tiffany perfume that had long been her signature scent, she was forced to consider the consequences of wearing it, given her extracurricular activities. She hadn't put any on that morning, but allowed that it probably left residual scent on her clothes and skin.

Time to divert and deflect.

The psychiatrist knelt again, giving Angel a fond smile. "All I can say is, I'm honored that you find my presence calming. And that need to be calmed is no doubt why your mind called up a memory of something that made you feel less afraid. When we're under that much stress, it triggers strong emotional reactions. Sometimes the smells are real and present, sometimes they're conjured to trigger a comforting sensation. It doesn't mean you were losing your mind, if that's what you're thinking."

"No, I just thought it was ... odd."

Donovan shook her head. "Not at all odd. It's a coping mechanism, that's all."

Angel appeared relieved. "You'd think I'd know this stuff cold by now, working with you for so many years. Well, this is good news. It means I don't have to tell my doctor I was hallucinating."

"No," said Donovan, "you don't have to tell your doctor anything of the kind."

Everything she'd just told Angel had the benefit of being true. If she told her doctor any of this, he'd likely say the same thing. But Angel Torres knew her friend better than anyone, and Donovan knew it. Was she even now reading between the lines?

"Fantastic. Hey, D, if you could get me one of those valerian capsules and some tea to wash it down with, I'd appreciate it." She squeezed Donovan's wrist before releasing it.

Donovan smiled reassuringly and got up. But on her way to the kitchen, she reflected on the conversation and wondered if Angel would truly be able to overcome the trauma she had suffered. Shocks like this could lead to acute stress disorders of the type that kept people from ever moving on with their life as they'd known it. She'd hate for that to happen to Angel just because she had the bad luck to be friends with Donovan Montgomery, killer shrink.

I'll watch her. I'll catch her. I swear I will.

The duality of Donovan's life was both fulfilling andburdensome. She knew that her ability to compartmentalize that duality had been the only thing allowing her to be whomever she chose to be—and do whatever she chose to do—without suffering any moral or ethical pangs. Though Angel experienced a completely different scenario, the doctor knew that if she could teach her how to flip that light switch in her head, her friend might be able to adjust.

If it weren't for you, said an intrusive voice in her head, *she'd have nothing to adjust to.*

She pushed the unwelcome voice away, but it refused to be silenced.

You drew her close enough to you to make her vulnerable, told her just enough to almost get her killed, but not enough to make her be careful. Now, there's no going back.

There was a profound ring of truth to that. She needed to make sure that Angel realized proximity to Dr. Donovan Montgomery, profiler, came with risk and required care and a healthy dose of paranoia.

Donovan was searching through a cupboard for the valerian when Jordan approached. "Hey, Doc, how are you doing? This has been quite an ordeal for everybody concerned."

He seemed legitimately concerned, his gaze warm. They hadn't spoken since his absurd. testosterone-charged intrusion into her relationship with Tristan. "I'm good, Jordan. Thank you."

His concern melted into something more playful. "If you really want to thank me, maybe you'll let me take you out for that dinner. We got a little sidetracked last time."

"*We* got sidetracked? As I recall, it was Tristan and I that got sidetracked … by you."

He laughed and put up his hands in surrender. "*Mea culpa*, Doc. But then it means I owe you."

"I ate the last of the ice cream. I think we're even."

"No. I ruined your evening with the other guy. Where would you like to go? And when?"

She found his determination not to take no for an answer equal parts annoying and endearing. Before she had a chance to answer, there was a knock at the door.

Xenia was at the dining room table, wiping bits of dinner from her son's mouth. She frowned and started to put down the paper towel she was wielding.

"Stay put, Xenia. I'll get it," Donovan said.

Detective Hadley stood on the welcome mat holding a grocery store bouquet of spring flowers.

"Beau! You are the only missing piece to this little soiree. We figured you got waylaid with police business. Come in." She opened the door wider and stepped to one side, but he declined.

"Angel's seen more of me in the last four days than anybody should ever have to, including my momma. I did bring her these." He extended the flowers, already in a vase.

Donovan placed them on a small table just inside the front door before stepping back to the threshold. "She'll love them. How are things going with the Dillard murder?"

"I'd say between that, the three one-eyed gentlemen, Eduardo Zunigas, and the mess in Englewood, I've done well to fit in a shower or two. But there's been a new development. In addition to the hate porn that he had on his phone, he had contact information for those three dead men. In combination with motive, opportunity, and abiding affection for killing folks he didn't take a fancy to … it's beginning to appear as if he's the likely suspect in their murders. The fact that he was taken out by a sniper kind of suggests tit for tat."

"Yes, it does, doesn't it. Nice work. Sure you won't come in? Take a bow?"

The sun was disappearing, twilight crowded around the porch making the creases on the detective's brow and the dark circles under his blue eyes more prominent. He shook his head. "I don't feel like I have much to take a bow for. I feel like I'm missing something. I mean, if it weren't for whoever took out Tortuga's gang and called in the tip, I'm pretty sure I wouldn't have carried Angel out of there alive."

"Nonsense, cowboy. Right now Chicago's attention is on you, on every station and in every headline. And you deserve it, Beau, every drop of it."

He shook his head in an "aw shucks" kind of way, pushing back his Stetson. "You say that like it's a good thing. It's been nuts, Donovan. Everybody acting like I just landed a plane on the Hudson. I'm just doing my job, and I caught a couple of *very* lucky breaks."

"Yeah. Like God is your copilot." Donovan leaned against the door frame, crossing her arms. "I think that's what every hero says."

He lowered his chin and cocked his head. "Now we both know I had some very serious help. We did this together."

She placed her index finger lightly against his chest. "But you're the face they associate with all of it. Chicago wanted that girl's murder wrapped up and for their favorite gubernatorial candidate to find some closure. Right now, Roy Barns is this city's cause célèbre, and they see you as the champion that got things back on track for him."

All the humor drained out of his face. "Yeah, um, look, there's something else. Another … development. I'm just not sure if now is the time …"

Donovan straightened. "Tell me."

"I got a call driving over here. Roy Barns died in a car accident about an hour ago. Hit and run, DOA."

Donovan let out an explosive breath. Of all the things she might have expected ... "You said car accident. Do you think it *was* an accident?"

"Well, they might find some sedative and/or opioid and/or liquor in his system, no doubt. Be easy to blame it on that and his current state of mind. But, no. Of course it wasn't an accident."

"He was of no further service to the cartel."

"And he might start talking. Decide to come clean."

"Safer to just get rid of him."

"Yep."

Something wet hit Donovan's face. She wiped the splatter from her cheek, then checked her fingers. They were red. Then she noticed the hole in Hadley's forehead, his eyes open but blank, focused on her, his lips parted as if they were still talking.

When the second bullet penetrated his back, he fell forward into her arms. Stunned, she laid him down across the welcome mat and leapt over his body, reaching the street in time to see the back end of a car with no plate fishtailing away into the dusk.

Donovan rushed back to the detective and dropped to her knees beside him. She heard Jordan calling 911 as Paciano and Mark stepped past her into the street. She saw Alfredo's hand reach around Beau's neck and feel for a pulse. But her eyes stayed on his, still at half-mast, mannequin-like, the same as she had seen on dozens of other dead bodies.

She could not make sense of what had just happened. It would be harder to hit only Hadley than to shoot them both at the same time. Ortiz knew about her involvement, her culpability. Why would she be spared? The answer came to her as Alfredo brushed his palm over Beau's lids, closing them completely. She had just been given a "thank you" for her present; Beau had died, but she was still alive ... for now.

Donovan picked up Beau Hadley's hand and kissed it. "Thank you, Beau, for getting Angel out of that place." Another drop of something wet hit her cheek. She knew it was a tear before she wiped it away with her fingertips.

This is not over, cowboy. It's never over.

Epilogue

Entering the Hancock Building on North Michigan, Donovan made her way to the elevators and pressed the button for the ninety-fifth floor. Jordan had chosen the Signature Room at the Ninety-Fifth, but she felt more like staying in and eating pizza … alone. While being lifted from the lobby to the restaurant, she mused about how stubborn he'd been about this "date" and how she'd let him wear her down.

"Just a friendly, collegial dinner," he'd said, though they both knew he was lying.

Was I lying when I told myself I was taking a cab tonight because I knew there would be drinks with dinner?

She wondered if Jordan would have been as insistent if he'd known she'd called Tristan and told him how her case had gone and how gutted it had made her feel.

Surgery went brilliantly. The patient survived, but we lost one of the surgeons.

They'd had Zoom sex. She wondered if there was VR for that. Maybe it would feel more real, more comforting.

Since when do you *need comfort?*

She stepped out of the elevator and surveyed the room, spotting Jordan at a table next to the floor-to-ceiling window with a panoramic view of the lake and the city curled around it like a watchful cat. Seeing

311

her, he stood and smiled. When she approached, he kissed her cheek and pulled out her chair. A bottle of Krug rested in a silver wine bucket next to the white linen cloth.

"You look amazing," he said, admiring the warm tan Kamperett sheath dress she'd chosen for the occasion.

Approving of the man's tailored black suit, white button-down, and glistening gold cuff links, she responded in kind. The solitary rose dressing the table and spectacular view of Chicago at night had a strange effect on her. She was in awe of the view, but the juxtaposition of Lake Michigan's stygian darkness and the twinkle and shimmer of city lights reminded her of her own inner contradictions. The lake and city were emblematic of her soul—half alive and lit, half in darkness so impenetrable that it devoured whatever light touched its surface.

"I was half convinced you'd cancel on me," Jordan was saying, pulling her out of the dark waters. "You must be beat. How was the flight from—where was it—Cheyenne?"

"Gillette. About an hour from there to Newcastle. Flight was fine. Jordan, you've outdone yourself. I can't think of anyplace I'd rather be."

A lie. She'd rather be wherever Tristan was. And that was a problem.

"May I ask how things went? I do hope the service was befitting the man."

Donovan accepted the glass of champagne Jordan handed her and took a sip. "It was nice. Newcastle seems like a charming place—what I saw of it, anyway. Touristy because it's so close to the Black Hills. His family was devastated, of course, but warm and more stoic than a lot of folks would have been." She appreciated that. "I suppose every parent with a child in law enforcement tries to prepare for the worst-case scenario. But preparing for it and living through it are two very different things."

Jordan lowered his head, staring at the glass in his hand. "I wish I'd gotten to know him."

Donovan felt the sincerity of the comment. The glib deputy DA persona was tucked away. Was this the real Jordan Payne? "I wish you had too. I believe you two would have liked each other quite a bit."

A plate of oysters arrived. "I ordered for us. Hope that's all right."

She could feel her brow beginning to furrow. Was there a message in his choice of appetizer, or did he just like oysters? She was in no mood for subtext or food signaling.

"Oh my God. Relax. Sometimes an oyster is just an appetizer." Eating one of the oysters, he added, "I got a deep dish. You'll love it. Trust me."

Donovan laughed and took an oyster, trying to trust that he was not scheming to end up in bed with her tonight.

And what if he is?

"Did Newsome check in with you while you were in Wyoming? Did she call his parents?"

"She was there. We flew together."

His brows rose. "No kidding? Excellent."

"Yes, it was. It was also appropriate. But as understaffed and overworked as the department is currently, I was surprised she decided to come. Surprised, but pleased. I think it meant a great deal to Beau's family."

Reflecting on his loss, Donovan replayed in her mind that moment on Angel's porch less than two weeks prior. She blinked to "flip the switch," shut it down for the night. It nearly always worked. Not this time. The image of Beau dying right in front of her, his mouth open to speak, remained stuck in her head.

As if reading her, Jordan smiled broadly, refilling their flutes and making an effort to redirect the conversation. "Look at that view. Isn't it extraordinary?"

Avoiding the hungry dark of the lake, Donovan scanned the shimmer of electric jewels—topazes, diamonds, rubies—and found it beautiful, though she knew that beneath that blanket of light, the world-renowned music, the classical and contemporary art, the Michelin-starred restaurants, and pure glamour lay another city swaddled in pain, addiction, poverty, perversion, and pure evil. An underworld no less real than the sunken city that lay beneath the foundations of this one.

That is my Chicago.

In that moment, she was unable to take the electric bling seriously. She'd try, anyway. IF that failed, she'd pretend.

"Yes," she said. "It is extraordinary." That was not a lie.

Dinner arrived. Over lobster, she tried to iron out Jordan's understanding of Santa Muerte.

"So," he said finally, "some people pray to Santa Muerte to deliver them from addiction, and others pray to her to protect them so that they can sell drugs without getting arrested. That's crazy ironic. Or maybe hypocritical is the word I'm looking for."

"Well, people pray to her for all sorts of things, but yeah, she is a multipurpose deity."

"Man, the press is still feeding on the death of Roy Barns and Detective Hadley, but they cannot get enough of that ritual sacrifice business. I can tell you that I've had more than enough."

"I agree, Counselor. As far as the press is concerned, the uglier a story is, the better. Can't blame it all on them, though. It's the audience they're trying to please. These are the same people who've read their kids fairy tales about ogres and monsters and baking children into pies for millennia. I've come to the conclusion that this society wants their criminals and candidates, their heroes and villains to play out every detail of their lives with all the irrational drama of a reality show, the bloodier and more salacious the better. At least we knew fairy tales were fairy tales. Reality TV?" She shook her head. "There's an oxymoron for you."

Jordan placed his hands on his lap and scooted closer to the table. "Tell me, what's next for Doctor Montgomery?"

She rested her fork on her plate. "I do believe that I'm going to have to rework my book. The publishing house will have to recalculate a release date what with everything we found out about Barns and his association with Los Empresarios. Of course, just because he'd been bought doesn't negate the possible societal incentive to decriminalize street narcotics."

"You think it's a good idea?"

"Legalizing drugs would mean fewer convictions, better treatment options, and more rehab programs that went somewhere besides back to jail because the ex-user can't get a job or a find a place to live. On the other hand, legalizing some of these drugs sends the message that they're no longer dangerous. Though I think the FDA could be a check on quality."

"True. But only if politics allow. And anyone investing in the infrastructure around the drug business would profit big time off of the system." He dabbed his mouth with the linen napkin. "It would not be altogether altruistic. Legalizing drugs would mean a boon for the entire medical community."

"Would it? It could. I'm not sure it would. I guess I'm hopeful it might. We've kept alcohol and smoking legal while lessening their impact somewhat, but some of the drugs we're talking about aren't safe in any situation or any amount."

A vanilla bean crème brûlée and two cappuccinos were placed on the table between them. Donovan watched him consider her question as he reached across the table and laid his hand over hers. Her eyes veered back to the cityscape, avoiding his gaze.

"You're right," he said. "There's a lot to think about."

Yes, there was—for both of them. What had happened to Angel and Beau had awakened Donovan to a glaring inconsistency in her life. She'd held Tristan at arm's length because she feared attachment and grief and because she was falling—no, because she *had* fallen—in love with him. She'd told herself it wasn't fear, it was just a rational avoidance of complications.

She'd held Jordan at arm's length because she knew she wouldn't fall in love with him. He was a shadow of Tristan—handsome and entertaining and smart, but not Tris. She'd toyed with the idea of shutting Tristan out and turning, instead, to Jordan. With Jordan, she could have a casual, low-risk sexual relationship. He'd be a safety zone for her and possibly even a willing recipient of the rapacious sexuality her activities triggered … while he walked around with a target on his back because the next Eddy Zunigas wouldn't care what zone he occupied in Donovan Montgomery's complicated life.

That was reason enough not to let Jordan Payne get any closer to her, wasn't it?

She stared out at the sin-covering blanket of Chicago finery and knew the problem she faced was deeper than deciding who was in or out. People like Angel and Alfie and Mark had already penetrated her bubble. They were on the inside of the danger zone and there was no feasible way to push them out again.

Because I love them.

Which meant they needed her to guard and protect them, and not make the mistake *again* of failing to warn them of danger even if she couldn't explain exactly why that danger existed.

She glanced up at Jordan, who was telling her about making friends with the Cubs' dugout manager. For just a moment—for a split second—she saw Tristan sitting across from her. Tristan, about whom she knew so little because she'd conned herself into believing that, if she didn't know the details of his life, she wouldn't *care* about him.

As to the man sitting across from her, wondering why she was so quiet, so unlike herself, she would let herself live in this moment and save the agonizing for tomorrow.

He invited her to his place for a nightcap. It was very nice—a 1,500-square-foot condo in Irving Park.

At first, everything was civilized enough. They sat on the mid-century modern sofa before a gas fire, sipping black cherry brandy from oversized snifters while jazz played softly in the background. Donovan had just decided she'd be mellow and let Jordan lead, when he said he wanted to "slip into something more comfortable." They both laughed over the cheesy line and he disappeared for several minutes. When he returned, he was wearing a pair of black silk lounging pants and a matching thigh-length kimono, which hung open to reveal his torso.

Donovan gave him an arch look. "Really, Counselor? Your jammies? Isn't that a little obvious?"

"I'm an obvious guy, Doc. What you see is what you get. No hidden agendas or depths, no complicated backstory. I'm just a dude who happens to think you're one of the sexiest women he's ever met, and is letting you know in his uncomplicated way that he's open to all possibilities." He settled himself on the sofa and picked up his brandy.

Donovan leaned toward him to give him her best "Dr. Montgomery, profiler" face. "Tell me, Counselor, do you think that might be because you've thought of me as unattainable? You know what they say about wanting and having."

"Oh, I'm pretty sure I'd find the having every bit as delicious as the wanting."

"Let's find out."

She set her glass on the coffee table, then stood and unzipped her dress, letting it fall around her feet. She stood before the man wearing only a red lace thong and a freshwater pearl choker. Her hair was pinned loosely atop her head, one strand drifting down to curl above her right breast. She pulled out the long, faux tortoiseshell hair pins and let her locks fall around her shoulders.

The mixture of lust and admiration in Jordan's eyes ignited a little heat between her legs. It wasn't the same *look* that Tris gave her, but that was a good thing, because she was fairly certain that Tristan's lust and admiration was woven into a much deeper fabric. Unfortunately, her reaction to Jordan was a pale wraith of her urgent desire for Tristan. Maybe that could change.

She arched a brow at him. "Your turn, Counselor."

Jordan set down his brandy, stood, and slid the kimono off, flinging it over the arm of the sofa. "I think I'll need your help with the pants," he said, glancing down to where the silk had tented over his growing erection. "They seem to have gotten caught on something."

Donovan smiled crookedly and moved to stand face-to-face with him. She caressed his shoulders, ran her hands gently down over his chest, followed the "treasure trail" of springing black hair down to just below his navel, then tugged teasingly at the waistband of his pants, staring up into his eyes. He smiled back at her, wetting his lips in anticipation, clearly expecting her to kiss him.

She didn't. She dropped to her knees and pulled the pants from his hips in one swift move, letting them drop to the floor. His cock, released from its wrapping, sprang fully erect. For a second, she found herself comparing him to Tristan—his face, his body, his penis. She pulled herself up short with a will.

I will not compare them. I won't.

Donovan focused her attention on the thick shaft growing out of its thicket of ebony hair. It was long, elegant, beautiful, and she wanted to want it. This close, Jordan smelled of Viktor&Rolf Spicebomb—one of her favorite colognes. She wondered if she'd ever mentioned that in his presence.

She leaned in close and blew a gentle current of breath onto Jordan's balls. He drew in a hissing breath. She felt her inner heat increase. Good.

She put out the tip of her tongue and licked his cock from base to head. He let the breath out on a long "aa-aah." She felt more heat, felt the wet flow of desire. Better.

She took his penis in hand, lowered it slightly, and took the head gently between her lips for a lingering kiss. Jordan said, "Oo-oh." When she flicked the tip with her tongue, he stiffened, and when she took the head fully into her mouth, he quivered and gasped.

Her body responded eagerly to his willingness to give her control over his. And the more she worked him, the more she wanted him ... but still not as much as she *wanted* to want him.

I need a fire starter.

She knew thinking of Tris, of the many times they'd done this dance of foreplay, would only distract. So she thought, again, of Beau Hadley dying in her arms, of her certainty that that was not the end of it, of the people in her danger zone. People who were still under threat from the men who had killed Hadley.

She thought of how badly she wanted those men dead—all of them. Dead, like Crazy Eddie. She remembered that kill ... remembered every second of it.

In mere moments, her pulse was racing, her adrenaline spiking crazily. Her mouth still working on Jordan's cock, she growled low in her throat like a wild animal.

"Girl!" he groaned, sounding breathless. "I'm about to—"

Donovan lifted her head and gave Jordan a shove. He fell back on the sofa, eyes wide, his smile more tentative now.

She let the rage burn through her—the rage she'd unleashed on Zunigas, the rage of losing Hadley, of almost losing Angel. And with that fierce flame stoking her desire, Donovan climbed onto Jordan's thighs and straddled him. Before he could do more than blink, she pulled aside her thong, grasped his cock, and drove herself onto it, hard and fast, all the way to the root. She felt it filling her, took the measure of its shape and size, and tried not to notice the ways it felt different from Tristan's. Closing her eyes, she drew Jordan's hands to her breasts and held them there while she worked him, writhing, squeezing, pulling, devouring.

When Donovan opened her eyes and stared down at him, she could see in Jordan's face that he had not expected anything like this. Not from her. Not from cool, collected Dr. Donovan Montgomery. His stunned expression struck her as funny and surprised her into laughter. She threw back her head and howled. She could only imagine how she must look to him, laughing her head off with her hair a chaotic cloud around her shoulders, riding him as if he were a bull in a rodeo.

"Oh, damn!" Jordan gasped, and with this crazy, wild woman in possession of his cock, Jordan Payne came—explosively. "Damn!" he said again, then followed it with a series of sharp grunts.

Donovan came too, as he bucked, spasming within her. She turned her mind away from any comparisons to the quakes Tristan provoked, and simply let the tremors of pleasure ripple through her.

When they were both spent, she pulled herself from Jordan's lap to go clean up in his bathroom. His cum had run down the inside of both legs, so she pinned her hair back up and took a quick shower to wash it away, staying under the hot water a moment longer than was strictly necessary, wondering why the sex hadn't relaxed her. Hadn't released her.

Wondering if she'd just started something she shouldn't have.

When she came out of the bathroom no more than ten minutes later, once again clothed, Jordan had pulled his pants back up and fallen asleep, slouched against the back of the sofa.

Donovan sat down next to him and sipped her brandy, studying him. He was a damn handsome man. Young, vital, funny, likely a skilled lover. Not that she'd given him a chance to show any such skills. Maybe next time. If there was a next time.

It was good, she decided, that Jordan was so unlike Tristan. Possibly it was also good that she was so unlike herself with him. Their encounter was more like her sacking of the hapless Rick than it was the give-and-take she'd found with Tris.

Donovan finished her brandy, called a cab, and went outside to wait for it, leaving Jordan to sleep. He'd gotten what he wanted; it was up to him to decide if he still wanted it, or if having had it once was enough.

Donovan came to a decision as she stood on Jordan Payne's doorstep in the bracing chill that rolled up off Lake Michigan: She would hold Jordan at arm's length, but she could never allow Tristan into her danger zone.

There were already too many people in it.

INTERVIEW WITH AUTHOR WILLIE MAE JACKSON

Q: Could you tell us about your professional background?

A: I'm a forensic psychiatrist currently working with the Circuit Court of Cook County Forensic Clinical Services in Chicago. In addition to this, I've worked in various social service agencies, including the Department of Children and Family Services and the Orthogenic School at the University of Chicago.

Q: Can you share some details about your early life and education?

A: Of course. I was born and raised on the West Side of Chicago. I was brought up by my single mother and our community that followed the old-school mantra "it takes a village." For my education, I attended William H. King Elementary School and Hugh Manley High School, both part of the Chicago Public Schools system. I then went on to the University of Illinois at Chicago, where I majored in psychology and minored in theater while also fulfilling all of my pre-medicine requirements.

Q: Did you have any additional educational pursuits after your undergraduate degree?

A: Yes, I pursued a master's degree in clinical psychology from Roosevelt University while working. Later, I studied at Ross University School of Medicine, co-authoring two academic articles with world-renowned community psychiatrist Dr. Carl Bell during this time.

Q: Your work often revolves around mental health in underserved populations. Could you tell us more about that?

A: As a product of an underserved environment, I have a personal understanding of the issues faced by these communities. I strive to spread hope, reduce the stigma associated with mental illness, and improve access to mental health services, not only in underserved communities but also on college campuses in the Chicago area. I believe that education about mental health can empower people.

Q: We understand that you also mentor medical students?

A: Yes, I mentor Ross University medical students, aiming to serve as an example of what can be achieved if people believe in themselves and their dreams, regardless of the odds.

Q: Could you tell us about your social media engagement and its purpose?

A: Sure, I maintain active profiles on Instagram (@dr_willie_mae) and Facebook (Drwilliemae). My goal is to use these platforms to promote good mental health and to reach out to more people about the critical importance of mental health education.

Q: Can you share some personal insights or philosophy that has helped you through your journey?

A: My motto is "living by your own rules and maintaining one's moral compass." It has served me well through various adversities, helping me to become a Chicagoan truly living her dream.

Q: What can you tell us about your second career as an author?

A: This has been a very exciting turn in my life. I've recently completed the manuscript for my second novel in the Donovan Montgomery suspense thriller series, *Dark Protection*. The first book, *Make It Right*, has been a huge success. I'm very excited about this new foray as a published author!

Q: Tell us more about that success!

A: *Make It Right* has over 230 reader reviews on Amazon, a 4.5 star rating [as of this interview]. *Publishers Weekly/Book Life Book Review* wrote: "Jackson's debut novel blends elements of suspense and legal drama to create an action-packed, fast-paced crime thriller." Imagine that! This has been a learning experience for me, working with beta readers, the marketing, creating the book cover—yes, that's me on the cover!—the interaction with fans.

Q: What are some of the other things in life that give you this kind of pleasure?

A: That's easy: Being the best mom possible to my very special son!

Q: What inspired you to write your books? Were there any particular events or experiences that influenced your writing?

A: I drew my inspiration from a plethora of sources. Personal experiences, current events, recent historical events, and even tales from other books have all contributed to my inspiration. For instance, my adult experiences, as well as my hometown of Chicago play significant roles in shaping the characters and obviously the setting of my books.

Q: Can you tell us about your writing process? How do you approach developing characters, crafting dialogue, and building the story?

A: My writing process is unique to me. I start thinking about lots of ideas and will probably kick them around with friends and colleagues. Then I begin with a detailed plot outline and character profiles. The revision and editing process is also rigorous, often taking multiple rounds before I am satisfied with the final outcome. In fact, on those editing rounds, I often will dive back into the story and let the characters and plot evolve as I write.

Q: What themes or messages did you hope to convey through this book? Are there any particular lessons or takeaways that you hope readers will gain?

A: Look, primarily I write entertainment. But I do want to deal with major themes such as terrorism, white nationalism, drug abuse, the challenges of our justice system, the state of psychiatry in society, mental health issues, the American prison system, bigotry. Through my books, I've explored a variety of themes, but some of it boils down to limitations, such as the limits of justice and injustice, the limits of anger, the limits of retribution, of love, loss, resilience. My hope is that readers gain a fresh perspective on these themes and learn something new after reading my book.

Q: Were there any challenges that you faced while writing this book? How did you overcome them?

A: Writing a book is no small feat and I faced my share of challenges. These included writer's block, time management, and occasional difficulties with plot points and character development. However, through determination, feedback from peers, and continuous editing, I managed to overcome these hurdles.

Q: Can you discuss any research that you did for this book? How did you incorporate this research into the story?

A: That's easy. I set the book in Chicago, because I love, love, love this city. And I happen to be born here, too. My lead character is a psychiatrist, so I use my experience as a reference. And as to the police, corrections officers, attorneys, judges, and other professionals? Well, those are the very same people I work with in my job on a day-to-day basis—I'm familiar with their jobs and how they work together in the system. But when it came to the crimes, I had to conduct extensive research. This involved reading related literature, conducting interviews with experts, and even visiting specific locations.

Q: What are your favorite scenes or chapters to write, and why?

A: My favorite scenes are those that allow me to delve deep into my characters' emotions and reveal something crucial about them. I found immense joy in envisioning and penning down those particular scenes.

Q: How do you see your book fitting into the larger literary landscape? Are there any particular authors or books that influenced your writing?

A: I see my book as a unique addition to my genre and believe it fills a gap in existing literature. There are many authors who write in the same genre or explore similar themes that have significantly influenced my writing. As to other authors? Yes, there are many in my genre including (obviously) *Darkly Dreaming Dexter* by Jeff Lindsay, *Heartsick* by Chelsea Cain, *My Sister, the Serial Killer* by Oyinkan Braithwaite, *American Psycho* by Bret Easton Ellis, *Zombie* by Joyce Carol Oates, *I Am Not a Serial Killer* by Dan Wells, *The Silence of the Lambs* by Thomas Harris, *Killer on the Road* by James Ellroy, *The Killer Inside*

Me by Jim Thompson, *My Lovely Wife* by Samantha Downing, *The Wasp Factory* by Iain M. Banks. I am also inspired by so many female mystery and thriller authors of color.

Q: Can you talk about any upcoming projects that you're working on? What can readers expect from you in the future?

A: I am always bubbling with new ideas and am planning my next book, especially in the "Donovan Montgomery" series. I've already got tons of notes and ideas. Whether it is writing a sequel to my current works, exploring a new genre, or tackling a different theme, I always aim to keep my readers intrigued.

Q: Are there any specific messages or ideas that you hope readers will take away from your work as a whole?

A: I aspire for my readers to gain a deeper understanding of my themes, to feel a connection with my characters, and above all, to enjoy a good story.

Q: Do you have any advice for aspiring writers? What would you tell someone who is just starting out on their writing journey?

A: My advice would be to read widely—including newspapers, online news media; write regularly; seek feedback; join writer workshops; and stay persistent even when facing rejection or criticism. Finding your unique voice is also crucial. Always write about what you're passionate about and enjoy the process.

BOOK CLUB
DISCUSSION TOPICS

Themes: *Dark Protection* intertwines various themes such as justice, morality, and race. Which theme struck you the most and why? How does Donovan Montgomery's dual existence as a psychiatrist and a serial killer influence your interpretation of these themes?

Exploration of Themes: The book deals with profound themes like vigilante justice, racial identity, and psychological manipulation. How do you think these themes were woven into the story and characters?

Impact of Themes on Reader: Which themes resonated with you the most? Were there any themes that made you uncomfortable or challenged your beliefs?

Donovan's Actions and Themes: Do Donovan's actions throughout the book, especially her choices of victims, shed light on any specific themes? If so, how?

Plot Twists: *Dark Protection* boasts a unique premise with potentially several shocking turns. Can you pinpoint any plot twists that caught you off guard? How did these surprising moments affect your overall engagement with the story and your perceptions of the characters, particularly Donovan Montgomery?

Author's Message: What messages or lessons do you think the author wanted to convey through *Dark Protection*? How do Donovan's actions and motivations reflect these intended messages?

Setting's Role: The story takes place in Chicago, within the judicial and prison system. How does this setting contribute to the plot of *Dark Protection*? Could the story have occurred elsewhere, or do you believe the setting was crucial to Donovan's actions and the unfolding of events?

Challenging Aspects: Were there elements of *Dark Protection* you found particularly challenging or thought-provoking? How do these aspects affect your overall understanding and appreciation of the book?

Quality of Writing: Did you find *Dark Protection* to be well-written? How do the author's style and narrative techniques contribute to your reading experience?

Book's Structure: How did the structure of *Dark Protection* (such as its chapters, pacing, or use of alternating viewpoints) influence your reading journey? Did it enhance the suspense and your understanding of Donovan's dual life?

Change in Perspective: Has *Dark Protection* altered your perspective on any issues or topics, such as the justice system, morality, or vigilante actions? If so, how?

Recommendation: Would you recommend *Dark Protection* to others? Please share your reasons. How would you describe this book to someone who hasn't read it?

Donovan's Victims: Donovan targets individuals she believes have escaped justice. Did you agree with her judgments and actions? Why or why not? How do you think the book navigates the moral complexities of her decisions?

Donovan's Role in Society: As an African American female psychiatrist in the judicial and prison system, Donovan is a rare figure. How does her professional role intersect with her secret life? Does her societal position influence or justify her actions as a serial killer in any way?

Psychological Insights: Given Donovan's profession, the book provides a lot of psychological insights. How did these insights enhance your understanding of her character and her motivations? Did any of these insights challenge your preconceptions or provoke deeper thought?

Climax and Resolution: What did you think of the book's climax and resolution? Was it satisfying, surprising, or thought-provoking? How would you have preferred the story to end, if differently?

Future Expectations: If there was a sequel to *Dark Protection*, what would you expect or hope to see in Donovan Montgomery's future?

About The Author

Willie Mae Jackson was born and raised on the West side of Chicago, IL. She attended William H. King Elementary School and Hugh Manley High School, both Chicago Public Schools. She was raised by a single mother but as she grew up, she very much experienced the old African proverb, 'it's takes a village to raise a child.'

Dr. Jackson attended college at the University of Illinois at Chicago where she majored in psychology and minored in theater while simultaneously fulfilling all of her pre-medicine requirements. After college, she worked in several social service agencies, including the Department of Children and Family series and the Orthogenic School at the University of Chicago. While working at these jobs, she attended Roosevelt University and earned a Master's Degree in Clinical Psychology. Upon completion, she focused on continuing to work in the non-profit sector until she began her studies at Ross University School of Medicine.

As a medical student and, later, as a resident physician at the University of Louisville School of Medicine, Dr. Jackson recognized the importance of understanding behavioral sciences and medicine in the African-American community. She has published articles focusing on mental health in underserved populations in the City of Chicago. Dr. Jackson had the privilege of being mentored by and co-authoring two academic articles with world-renowned community psychiatrist (the late) Dr. Carl Bell. She continues to promote and advocate for good mental health through her various social media sites (i.e., Instagram @ dr_willie_mae & Facebook Drwilliemae).

Currently, Dr. Jackson works as a board certified adult and forensic psychiatrist in private practice. She has also served, in the past, as medical officer/forensic psychiatrist for the criminal courts at Cook County Forensic Clinical Services.

Dr. Jackson has embarked on a second career as a fiction writer, creating the popular Donovan Montgomery mystery-thriller series. So far she has written two critically acclaimed books in the series: *Make It Right* and *Dark Protection*. Both novels are available on Amazon.com

Dr. Jackson, who emerged from an underserved environment herself, is deeply committed to enhancing access to mental health services and diminishing the stigma surrounding mental illness. Her work spans not only underserved communities but also college campuses, where she focuses on empowering people through education about the vital importance of maintaining good mental health. By mentoring Ross University medical students and actively working to spread hope to individuals from similar backgrounds, Dr. Jackson stands as a testament to the power of self-belief and perseverance against daunting odds, striving to give back to the communities similar to the one she came from.

Having overcome a variety of adversities, Dr. Jackson is an example of a Chicagoan truly living her dream. Her motto of "living by your own rules and maintaining one's moral compass" has served her well.

Dexter, Hannibal Lecter, Villanelle, Carrie– Now Meet Donovan Montgomery, the Smartest, Deadliest of Them All

WHAT CRITICS ARE SAYING

"Donovan Montgomery is a badass forensic psychiatrist with a versatile arsenal of weapons, both mental and physical. She's going to need all of them, because her testimony in the trial of a White Supremacist has put a target on her back. A gripping tale with more than one mystery at its core."
— **New York Times Bestselling Author Maya Kaathryn Bohnhoff**

"A malevolent, intricate tale of murder and madness."
— **USA Today Bestselling Author David Niall Wilson**

Jackson's debut novel blends elements of suspense and legal drama to create an action-packed, fast-paced crime thriller. Crime junkies and thrill seekers will enjoy the twists and turns. Readers will be guessing until the end. **Takeaway:** Fans of true crime and courtroom legal dramas will delight in this tale of vigilante justice.
—**Publishers Weekly/ Booklife**

www.ingramcontent.com/pod-product-compliance
Lightning Source LLC
Chambersburg PA
CBHW070532260626
47161CB00002B/348